Missing Pieces

Missing
Pieces

James Pendleton

Ivy House
Publishing Group
United States of America

This is an autobiographical work, and every effort has been made to insure accuracy, but the names of several people have been changed to protect the privacy of their families.

PUBLISHED BY IVY HOUSE PUBLISHING GROUP
5122 Bur Oak Circle, Raleigh, NC 27612
United States of America
919-782-0281

ISBN: 1-57197-322-2
Library of Congress Control Number: 2002101710

Printed in the United States of America

For Rosemary DeAngelis,
who inspired the writing of this book

And for Catharine, Lelia, Eve and Caroline,
who lived with the reults of the story that it tells

Prologue

The last time John and Alfred and I were together was at the Raleigh railway station in early September 1948. That morning, Alfred and I had accompanied John to the clinic for his naval pre-induction physical examination, and he had walked out of it almost shouting, "I made it! I made it! They didn't find out about my bad knee." And the three of us had scrambled into his father's white Kaiser sedan, with Alfred driving, and hurled ourselves into the Carolina afternoon toward Raleigh to take John to his embarkation point. We embraced him at the gate and watched him board the train and then waved to him through the window as the big steam engine spun its wheels once and slowly shouldered its way out of the station.

John was eighteen, Alfred was twenty-one, and I was seventeen. The following week, as John would enter navy basic training, Alfred and I would enter college. And though the tracks of our separate lives would not be so visible as the steel rails that carried John to California, they would carry us, none-the-less, along routes that would never again meet in the same station at the same time. It was the end of childhood and, for us, the beginning of the second half of the twentieth century.

Chapter One

Of all my friends, Alfred was the most problematical. He was four years older than I and much larger than the other students in our junior high school. But since at age twelve, in 1943, I had already reached what would be my full adult height, I was almost as tall as he, and our age difference was not immediately obvious. I knew that he had been away at a military school and that at some point he had endured a long illness that held him behind his regular class. But he bore no trace of his illness, other than a fever line across his lower front teeth, and I remember that he was incredibly strong. I remember also that he had absolutely no fear of pain—or of anything else that I ever discovered. In a wrestling match or a fight, he was implacable. His goal was to win, and if he or his opponent got hurt, it was just part of the acceptable cost. Public approval meant nothing to him. If a teacher reprimanded him in school, he wouldn't hesitate to tell her exactly where she could "cram it" or to tell her, as I was once alarmed to hear him tell Miss Pruit in the science lab, to "blow it out her ass." This sort of thing, of course, got him propelled frequently to the principal's office and subsequently resulted in a number of suspensions and the creation of general consternation. The principal, Miss Gray, became so concerned when she discovered our friendship that she even called my mother and warned her that I was associating with a bad companion.

But, like Alfred, I was an only child and we both lived outside the town. His family had only recently moved to Fayetteville, where they operated the Buckingham Court Motel and Restaurant, and mine had always lived in the country. So although I knew many people in town through church and school, I had always felt like an outsider, and Alfred's proximity had made me feel for the first time that I had a close friend. I didn't approve of his behavior, but I wasn't about to let it interfere with our friendship. He visited in my home regularly and I visited the apartment at the motel where he lived with his parents. We talked almost daily about anything and everything—except, of course, his behavior. We rode bicycles together, often riding the three miles to school when he bothered to go. We ran laps together around the football field. He taught me calisthenics and ways to build upper body strength. And we hunted together.

Now understand, this was early 1943 in the American South. Violence and guns were a normal part of everyday life. We lived within earshot of the firing range at Fort Bragg, which was the largest military post in the world and where military training of all kinds was constantly in progress as the United States prepared counter-offensives against both the Japanese and the Germans. Every day we could hear the distant boom of cannon fire and feel the earth tremble from the explosions of 105- and 155-millimeter shells in the target area of the artillery range. Overhead, low flying formations of B-17 bombers, C-47 troop transports, and P-39 Bell Airacobra fighter planes with their menacing 37-millimeter cannon were daily in our skies from Pope Field. Nearly everyone I knew had an older brother or a father in the armed services. My own father had just returned home on leave from a tour of duty on the personal staff of General Hap Arnold in Washington, and he was now being assigned to North Africa where he would be in charge of an Air Force Ferry Command installation in Liberia, transporting bombers to the combat zone. My older cousin and all my uncles were serving in either the Army or the Marine Corps, and they were all using or learning to use every weapon known to man in performance of their daily duties. So weaponry and skill in arms were part of the given.

But more profound for us even than the war was the long Southern tradition that every boy should have a gun and should hunt and should have easy access to the forest. My father had given me a .410-gauge shotgun when I was ten and a .22 rifle when I was eleven. For protection, he had given my mother a .45 revolver which she kept in easy reach beside her bed when he was not at home. He had taught us both how to use these weapons safely. Men hunted and brought home meat for the table as routinely as they planted victory gardens, raised chickens, or went to church on Sunday. And in those days, I never heard anyone question it. My mother only stipulated that I had to dress whatever game I brought home. But she showed me how to do it, and during fall and winter, I kept the house regularly supplied with squirrel, rabbit, dove, duck and quail. And she was always glad when Alfred and I brought in fresh meat.

So my mother was surprised when she received Miss Gray's call complaining about Alfred's behavior and expressing her fears for my welfare. "That's very strange," my mother told Miss Gray. "He's always been well behaved around here." And in truth, that was the case. Around my parents, Alfred was the personification of good—even courtly—manners. He always stood respectfully whenever an adult entered the room. He said, "Yes, sir," and "Yes, ma'am." If he ate dinner with us, his table manners were impeccable. In a way, I think he idolized the silver pilot's wings on my father's uniform—as did most of my classmates whenever my father came to my school with the wings on his chest and the fifty-mission crush in his hat. Alfred engaged my father in intelligent conversation to the point that my father had even referred to him once as "charming," a word my father did not often use. So after Miss Gray's call, my mother did not seem especially concerned. She asked me what was going on and I said I didn't know. "But I'll find out," I told her. And I picked up my Remington .22 and walked up to Alfred's house to go squirrel hunting.

Now I had long before realized that Alfred's behavior was, to say the least, inconsistent. I had been shocked not only at the way he talked to his teachers, but also at the rude way he talked back to his own parents. He would shout at them and they at him for reasons I never fully understood. Sometimes these outbursts appeared to be about his getting up on time in the morning or about his going to school or helping with the work around the motel. But they always seemed to be about something else as well, something that neither he nor his parents ever actually gave voice to. And during these tirades, he would curse at his parents and say things that I could never imagine myself uttering to any adult, much less to my parents. And then, on the day following one of these rages, I had seen him come in and embrace his mother and kiss her all over her face and then start kissing his father until his father would have to laugh and push him away. He would even go into the kitchen and kiss Phrobe and Jack—both of whom were black and long-term employees of the motel. Then he would come back and lead me behind the counter of the restaurant and scoop large quantities of ice cream, nuts, fruit, and chocolate syrup into sundae glasses and we would gorge ourselves. It was all very mysterious and, in a way, frightening. I had never seen anyone in my family shout in anger. I had tried it once at about age six when my mother had angered me in some way. "I don't love you even as much as a germ!" I had shouted at her. And she had simply grabbed me, turned me across her knee, and spanked me in a way I would never forget. I don't know that she taught me to love her more, but she did teach me not to express my rages out loud. So to me, it was always an enormous relief to see Alfred reconciled with his parents without anybody getting hurt.

But on that day, I went to see Alfred with a mission, and I think probably that it was the first time in my life that I was playing a kind of parental role. My buddy was in serious trouble and I wanted him to straighten up. But I wasn't sure how he would take it. He was older and had always been the one to teach *me* things. Far from leading me into delinquency, as Miss Gray feared, he had always been the one who had kept me in line, herding me the way an older sheep dog or an old hunting dog herds a puppy. He saw that I always obeyed my mother and got home on time, encouraging me, sometimes even helping me to do my chores around the house, counseling me always to do my homework the way I was supposed to. In short, he tried to corral me into doing all the things which he himself never did.

Now it was *my* turn. And I remember being enormously nervous. I simply did not know how I would handle it if he should ever turn and unleash his fury against me. I wanted to persuade him to apologize and cooperate with his teachers and save himself from being expelled. But I wanted to do it without setting off the bomb that I instinctively knew was primed and ready to explode somewhere just beneath his surface.

Watching Alfred walk through dense forest was like watching a ballet dancer or, maybe more accurately, a modern dancer, low to the ground, poised, lithe, and graceful in the extreme. In the street or on flat ground, he walked with his hips back and his legs out in front like a country boy plowing a furrow behind a mule. But when he got into the woods, he was transformed. He could go through the tangled briars of North Carolina thickets with the speed and facility of Bre'r Rabbit himself. "When I lived in Virginia, an old Indian taught me how to go through the woods," he told me once. And indeed that old Indian had apparently taught him a lot more. Alfred knew the names of the mosses and lichens that grew along the creek banks. He knew where to find crayfish and salamanders, and in the spring, he taught me how to make a seine and catch the silver minnows in the small streams so we could use them for bait when we went fishing later in the river.

On that day, I remember that we headed for the woods directly behind the new Veterans' Hospital, which had recently been built near our homes. The hospital sat on a large tract that included hundreds of acres of game-rich forestland and which extended all the way to the Cape Fear River. I never understood why the government needed so much land in order to build the hospital on a small fraction of it. But I was already beginning to see that the ways of the federal government did not necessarily conform to reason, and I was further confirmed in this view when government agents nailed "No Trespassing" signs around the borders of the reservation. For both Alfred and me, this was an affront of the highest order. Keeping boys out of the forest was nothing less than a crime against nature. And never in all those years did we hesitate to violate the law and enter that beautiful forbidden territory.

But we were careful. Between our homes lay the twisting earthen defenses that nearly a century earlier had been dug by the Confederate Army of General Joseph E. Johnson to defend the town of Fayetteville against the expected attack of Federal Forces under General William Tecumseh Sherman. These breastworks, now covered with pine needles and lined with trees of various sizes, snaked for miles through the woods and across the posted government land. And we—good Southern scouts that we were—used them regularly to cover our own incursions into federal territory.

We would enter these trenches near the highway and slip silently along on the soft carpet of pine needles until we were well beyond earshot of the hospital guards. Then we would go anywhere we wanted. If we found game, we would fire our guns, gather our quarry, and escape silently beyond the borders of government land before the guards could ever reach us. But on that day, I remember that nothing was stirring. It was a warm day and the distant rumble and thump of the artillery shells at Fort Bragg seemed closer than ever, so I suppose the game animals had been spooked and returned to their dens long before we got there. But it was probably just as well because I was so busy thinking about what I was going to say to Alfred that I wouldn't have been able to shoot straight anyway. So we continued along through the woods until we came to the banks of a small and very clear stream that we had often visited. It was one of my favorite places. I remember so well how the force of the water had cleared the creek bed of leaves and surface earth, leaving a channel of white sand that led to a kind of limestone basin where small shiners darted back and forth just beneath the surface.

For a long time, with our guns across our laps, we just sat there on a log and listened to the gurgle of the water as we watched the fish. And then, still looking down at the minnows, I said, "Miss Gray called my mother."

For a moment, Alfred didn't say anything, but without glancing up from the fish, I knew he was looking at me. "What did she say?" he asked finally.

"She told Mom all the things you've been doing at school . . . how you talked back to the teachers . . . how you skipped school. How you were suspended."

"What did your mom say?"

"She said she had never seen you do anything wrong. But Miss Gray doesn't think we should be friends. She says you're too old . . . that you're a delinquent."

"What did you tell her?"

"I didn't tell her anything," I said. "I just came up to tell you what Miss Gray said." And then I looked him straight in the eye. "Why do you do it?"

He looked away, gazing for a moment somewhere above the opposite bank. "I don't know," he said. "I just hate the Goddamned place." He stood then and began to pace in the narrow clearing beside the stream. "All those old maid school teachers thinkin' they're God's gift to the world," he said. "Poo-poo this and poo-poo that. Butter wouldn't melt in their mouths. Old Maids walkin' around like they had corn cobs crammed up their butts tellin' everybody else what to do!" He was clutching his shotgun in one fist and he shook it defiantly as he turned back toward me. "I hate the fuckin' place!"

My own pulse was pounding then until I thought my ears were going to explode. I don't know where I found the calm to continue. But I remained sitting on the log and I said, "Alfred, they're going to expel you."

"So what?" he said. "Would be good riddance on both sides. Good riddance!"

"Listen," I said, "you're already three or four years behind your class. If they expel you, it's gonna mess up your whole life. Why do you want to let 'em beat you?"

The change in him was sudden and completely surprising. He looked at me for a moment as though the idea of being beaten by the system was the most nauseating thing he could imagine, and then he came back to sit on the log. His words were the very last thing I expected, "What do you think I should do?"

"Well," I said, trying to look at the fish and remain as calm as possible, "I think you should go back and apologize to your teachers and promise to do your work for the rest of the year."

"Apologize?" His face screwed up as though I'd asked him to swallow a spoonful of horse manure.

"Alfred," I said, "they can't help being old maid school teachers." And we both began to laugh at the idea.

But the thing was that he did it. The following week, he went to Miss Gray and the other teachers—even to Miss Pruit, the science teacher whom we all despised—and he persuaded them to take him back. He would finish that year and the following year before his parents would again send him away to a private school.

Afterward, it was as though the problem had never existed. We never talked about it again. But I remember that one Saturday morning about a week after our conversation in the woods, I went to his house to rouse him, and we were standing in the kitchen of the motel while Phrobe cooked his breakfast. He was on the opposite side of the room, playing with a heavy chef's knife and joking with Phrobe as he usually did, when suddenly he turned toward me and with one continuous motion, hurled the knife in my direction as hard as he could. It stuck, embedded about two inches deep in the solid doorpost barely eight inches in front of my face. When I looked back at him, he was laughing and dancing around the room in high glee at my shocked expression, but for a moment, I was totally unable to speak. Then all I could say was, "Suppose you had missed?"

But he only laughed more and shrugged. "Then I guess you'd be pushin' up daisies," he said. "Let's have some breakfast."

Chapter Two

The incident with the kitchen knife was not to be my last "near death" experience with Alfred. But it, like the conversation in the woods, was a thing we never mentioned again. And surely at that period in our lives, so many other things were happening that we hardly had time to think of the past at all. For one thing, my father had just received orders to report to his embarkation point—Morrison Field in West Palm Beach, Florida—for travel to his overseas assignment, and for a time, his departure was the thing that most concerned my family. It is only now, after half a century that I can truly begin to say what it meant to me.

My father had always been my strongest supporter, and even at age twelve, I continued to think of him as my champion and my ideal of what a man should be. In the 1930s, in that small Southern community where people knew little about aviation and where the town had no airport until he managed to build one, my father stood out as a kind of dare devil or superman figure. He was "that feller who flew airplanes"—the man who did frightening stunts and who had conducted an air show with Amelia Earhart in her Beechnut sponsored autogyro in 1935. And with it all—at least in those days—he did everything with such a courtly and graceful manner that everybody he met liked him. Of course, all his singularity had changed by World War II when the world was suddenly glutted with airplanes and pilots. But at twelve, I was still basking in the halo effect of his former importance.

Both my parents were children of the rural 19th century American South, and the distances they traveled early in their lives were immense. Born in 1890 and '91—barely twenty-five years after the end of the Civil War—they came into a world in which the Reconstruction was still very much in progress and the horse and buggy were the main methods of transportation. Their world was a world without electric lines, telephone lines, or movie houses. And then, by 1916—when my parents were married at age twenty-six—my father was flying airplanes for the U.S. Army and dreaming of a time when the bulk of all future travel would be conducted through the air. Everything had changed.

During the 1920s, the United States greatly reduced the size of its armed forces and my father's commission was transferred to the Air Corps Reserve, and he was returned to civilian life. The problem was that although his own father had been a lawyer and a newspaper editor, my father himself had received very little formal education and, consequently, had no civilian career to return to. In the immediate postwar years, he worked in the various fields of lumber, electrical power, and telephone communications, but I think that nothing ever matched for him the fulfillment of military command and the thrill of flying military aircraft. During World War I, at Kelly and Randolph Fields in Texas, he had trained the fighter pilots who would distinguish themselves above the fields of France. Flying the Curtiss JN-4 biplane, the true workhorse of the first twenty-five years of aviation, he had been part of an aerial demonstration team. It was a kind of Blue Angels of World War I, which conducted air shows at towns throughout the United States and then landed at whatever open field was available to sell Liberty Bonds and promote the Allied war effort in Europe. And more than once, as a result of engine failure, he had slammed into the trees at the end of one of those unimproved runways and been lucky enough to walk away from a Curtiss Jenny that would fly no more. Compared with these activities, office routine and work in pursuit of mere money offered him nothing but consummate boredom. So I think he rather lived for those tours of duty with the Air Corps Reserve, which he seemed able to obtain at regular intervals. He was on one of these extended tours of duty, stationed at Fort Bragg, North Carolina, when I was born on December 12, 1930. My mother was thirty-nine and my father was forty. They had been married for nearly fifteen years.

Now, giving birth for the first time at age thirty-nine may not seem unusual at the end of the 20th century, but in 1930, it was exceptional indeed. So my impending arrival was the cause for both great excitement and great anxiety. Although my parents apparently had always wanted children, it hadn't seemed possible. My mother was troubled by some kind of physical problem that had previously caused her to suffer several miscarriages. And—as she later seemed to delight in telling me with meticulous detail—she had been so close to miscarrying with me that her army doctors had simply confined her to the hospital for the last two months of her pregnancy. My mother was a thorough Calvinist Presbyterian and liked to think of the ordeal of my birth in Biblical imagery. It was all "miraculous." My arrival was like the Old Testament story of the long awaited "birth of Isaac to Abraham and Sarah in their old age," she would later tell me. And then, since I was in fact finally delivered by Caesarian section, the comparison of me with Julius Caesar was not lost on her, either. It remained for my father to deliver the final poetic touch.

From the late 1920s until the Hindenburg disaster of 1935, the world's industrial nations had been experimenting with the use of dirigibles and blimps for both international transportation and military purposes. And Pope Army Air Field at Fort Bragg was scheduled to receive a new blimp, which my father was scheduled to fly. The due date for both the blimp and me fell on the same day. My father later told me that he didn't want to be too far away from my mother on that day, but that flying the blimp meant both new opportunity and new experience for him. So after stopping by the hospital in the morning to see that my mother was all right, he went on the scheduled flight. When he returned to base after dark that day, he found that he was indeed a new father. After visiting briefly with my mother and being told that everything was all right, he went to the officers' club where he celebrated for a time with fellow officers and then decided that a larger portion of the world should be involved in the festivities. From the club, he went back to the blimp hanger, where he apparently stole an observation flare from the supply room, commandeered a motorcycle from the MP on guard duty at the gate, and headed for the City of Fayetteville.

In those days, the highest point in town was the water tank that stood on top of Haymount Hill. From there, one could see the entire town and a good portion of the Cape Fear River valley, and my father headed straight for this tower. I remember later seeing that the access ladder to the water tank did not extend all the way to the ground, so he must have had to devise some way to reach it. But reach it he did and he climbed all the way to the top where he hung the flare over the side and ignited it.

Those who have seen a flare in use know that for a brief time it burns with the brilliance of a miniature super nova, sending light into the shadows for thousands of yards. Most of the time, flares are attached to tiny parachutes that allow them only a few seconds to blaze high in the air before falling to the ground. But this one was hung to a fixed tower, and to say that it alarmed the city would be an understatement. At least three fire companies responded to panicked callers who told them that the entire western part of the town was on fire. My father watched from the shadows as hundreds of people flocked from their homes and gazed into the night sky to see "this thing, which had come to pass." "Of course," he would tell me later, "nobody knew the meaning of what they were seeing, but then most people never know that anyway."

In any case, where my mother had thought of me as one part Old Testament prophet and one part Roman emperor, my father, by hanging my star in that dark December sky, clearly had thought of me as the embodiment of the new Messiah. They were ideals doomed to failure, of course, but I think that during those hard years of the 1930s they served all three of us in beneficial ways.

At the end of his tour of duty in 1932, my father was again released from the Air Corps and sent back to civilian life, again with no job or career and now just in time to face the full brunt of the Depression and President Roosevelt's closing of the banks.

Surely, he must have been appalled at his financial prospects. But he was only in his early forties and I think he was still young enough to be able to think even of himself as a kind of superman. After all, if he could walk safely away from airplane crashes, why should he not be able to walk away from financial crashes as well? And he had not been idle. During his tour at Fort Bragg, he had gotten to know the political leaders in the City of Fayetteville and he had been able to convince them that air transportation was the thing of the future and that Fayetteville needed a municipal airport. He, of course, an Air Corps Reserve captain with extensive flight experience, was to be the man to run it. He had also found that part of President Roosevelt's national recovery program included the development of commercial aviation. The federal government was offering incentive grants in the amount of forty thousand dollars to any city that would match the grant and build a modern commercial airfield capable of serving the Ford Tri-motor, the Boeing 247, and the soon-to-appear Douglas DC-3 transport planes.

The author's father, J.D. Pendleton, with his Curtiss JN-4, "Jenny."

For my father, it was the chance of a lifetime. He went to Washington and persuaded the FAA and the commerce department to commit money to the airport project if Fayetteville would match their grant. And then he was able to obtain a *verbal* agreement of support from members of the Fayetteville Board of Aldermen. The only catch was that he would first have to build and operate a viable airport for small aircraft before the city would take it over and invest in the larger project. It was the best he could get. Significant government support along with money, permanence, and position lay in the future. In the meantime, he—an unemployed veteran—would have the job of obtaining the land, building a hanger, buying an airplane, preparing a safe runway, hiring an aircraft mechanic, equipping a maintenance shop, and attracting customers, all in the midst of the most severe depression the country had ever known.

The miracle was that over the next three years, he did it. Or I should say he and my mother did it. The city advanced him a small amount of money to help with buying the land, but the bulk of the initial investment had to come from private sources. And the main source was my mother.

At about that time, she inherited five thousand dollars from the estate of her aunt, Dr. Annie Alexander, who had reared her, and she offered the entire amount to my father for his airport. It doesn't seem like much now, but then it was a fortune. She told me later that at first he had refused it out of hand. "He wasn't going to touch a penny of my money," she said. But she persuaded him. And although she personally hated flying and its dangers and had once asked my father to give it up permanently, she also recognized the future promise of aviation and the airport, and she pressed him to take the money and continue.

I think that those next few years of developing that airport were really the happiest years of my father's life, and this is where it affected me directly, the time when I came to think of him as my dearest friend and champion. I was only two or three or four years old and he worked long hours putting together his airfield, but he always had time for me. He would come home in the evenings and play with me on the floor of the log cottage that my parents had rented in the country only a few miles from the site of the airport. The house had been built during the affluent '20s, near what was still known as the Country Club Lake, as the vacation home of one of the wealthier mercantile families of North Carolina. But by 1932, when my parents took over the house, the owners were no longer wealthy at all and seemed to be quite happy to receive the fifteen dollars per month that my parents paid as rent. (Remember, this was a time when bread cost eight cents per loaf, gasoline cost twenty-two cents per gallon, and you could buy a new Ford or Chevrolet for about six hundred dollars.)

Anyway, I came to think of that log cottage with its open fireplace as a kind of paradise with my father as my main play-mate. He would wrestle with me, he would box with me, he would race with me around the yard, and he would read to me. My mother would read to me, too, but my father would augment his reading by making up stories of his own, stories of his boyhood adventures with his brothers along the James River in Virginia, stories of hunting, stories of flying airplanes. He would tell me stories about Davy Crockett, Daniel Boone, and Meriweather Lewis, and of course he told me stories of the exploits of his own heroes—Robert E. Lee, Stonewall Jackson, and Jeb Stuart.

I said that he had little formal education. The small school he had attended in rural Virginia had offered classes only through the seventh grade. But he grew up in a home with a large library and he could quote from memory the verse of Shakespeare, Byron, and Kipling. (I remember that my moth-er strongly disapproved of some of Kipling's raunchier bar-racks ballads.) He knew the Roman Empire through Gibbon; he knew Macauley; he knew the horrifying story of the Conquest of Peru through Prescott. And always beneath his stories there lay the message to me in the subtext, "Get learning, my son, get learning. It's the most valuable thing you can possess."

And then when I was about three, he began to take me places with him. By that time, he had obtained a beautiful English setter named Belle, and he took me quail hunting. He would carry his double barrel 16-gauge shotgun and I would carry my popgun, and we would go off through the woods and fields behind Belle. When I got tired or when we came to water or woods too thick for me to navigate, he would simply hoist me onto his shoulders and go on. He took me with him into town when he needed to talk to the men in local politics. Often the meeting place would be Sauders' Drug Store with it's marble top tables and slowly rotating ceiling fans where the local lawyers and political kingpins seemed to congregate with their cigars and cigarettes as they sipped their cokes on summer afternoons. He would introduce me to these men as though I were one of them and then, to entertain me, he would give me an ice cream cone (I remember my favorite flavor was strawberry) while he conferred with whoever was there.

And then, he took me flying. One of my earliest memories is of seeing the earth beneath my head and the wheels of his Rearwin airplane pointed toward the sky as he did a roll with me strapped in the seat beside him. And I remember that once, when we were preparing to go for a flight, that I nearly destroyed his entire operation. He had strapped me into the seat and started the engine and then for some reason he had gotten out of the plane—probably to remove a chock from in front of a wheel. And while he was outside, I, in my three-year-old exuberance, pushed the throttle forward. It's the only time I ever saw my father in a state of total panic. The plane leaped toward the pines on the opposite side of the field and I remember seeing the trees draw near and hearing my father's shout as he ran after the plane in the cloud of dust from the propeller blast until he finally caught up and saved us all from disaster. I don't remember that he ever reprimanded me for my action, but I don't believe he ever again left me alone in a running vehicle of any kind.

It was about this time that I remember first seeing my parents in disagreement, and their fight was over me—or rather I should say, over my hair. My mother, in spite of seeing me as the reincarnation of an ancient patriarch, also saw me as the personification of a living doll requiring constant attention, pampering, and dressing. Her aunt, a medical doctor, whose medical offices were in her home, had brought her up, and consequently my mother was hypersensitive to every physical symptom I might show. If I sweated too much or breathed too hard or sneezed, she more often than not would consider it the sign of immanent disaster. She would take my temperature—rectally, of course—and then she would begin to treat me with a variety of home remedies such as soothing eucalyptus vapors and "hot water tea" and cod liver oil. I loved the cod liver oil and the hot water tea—made sometimes with sassafras root or sweetened lemon juice. But then periodically (It was probably once a month, but it seemed like once a week.), she would dose me with castor oil chased by orange juice, which I felt to be, but lacked the vocabulary to describe, as one of the tortures of the damned. I felt constantly under siege, and I remember just wanting her to leave me alone. It took me well into my adult life to regain my enjoyment of orange juice. And then there was the question of my hair.

By the time I was three years old, my hair was thick and golden. And looking at photographs from that period, I must admit that indeed I was "plumb precious," as the old Southern expression goes. But my mother was not content to cut my hair neatly and let me be. She wanted to preserve it in all its shining beauty, and she began to curl it. I remember that every morning after my father left for work, she would set me in my high chair and, using the barrel of a pen or the hard rubber case of the thermometer, she would curl my hair into long golden ringlets, which hung down to my shoulders. At home, the main thing I objected to was the fact that she frequently pulled my hair in the process. Otherwise, since the reflection in the mirror showed the only picture of me I'd ever known, I had no objections. Until I went with my parents into the town.

Adults are not kind to children. And more than once I remember a clerk in a store or even a friend of my parents looking down at me and saying, "Are you a boy or a girl?"

"I'm a boy."

And then they would begin to tease me, "No you're not. I can tell."

"Yes I am."

"No. You're a girl."

"I am not!"

"Then why do you have that long hair? You're a girl."

If my parents heard this sort of thing, they would become indignant and come to my aid. But the business of having to defend myself in this way rankled enormously. It wasn't that I evaluated boys or girls differently. Surely, in all my childhood I never heard the slightest tone of disparagement toward women. It was quite the opposite. My father was a thorough 19th century romantic who viewed women as superior creatures sent to this earth to reform unregenerate males and lead them toward the good, the true, and the beautiful. But I was one thing and not another, and I clearly didn't like being called what I was not. My father all along had clearly shown that he didn't like my hairstyle and saw no need for any of my mother's pampering and decorative folderol. However, since he habitually deferred to my mother in most domestic matters, he did nothing to change the situation until after an especially rancorous exchange with a clerk in the shoe department of the Capitol Department Store one afternoon when he saw my discomfort and ordered a trip to the barbershop.

My mother, of course, was horrified at the thought. Her baby boy was about to be mutilated! Her lamb to be shorn! It was too early. "He's only a baby!" she said. But my father was adamant. The time had come. As for me, I remember being

somewhat divided. Certainly, I wanted to be more like my
father. It was only fitting that I should have short hair like his.
And surely I wanted to stop the ridicule and challenge that I
had to endure each time I appeared in public. But the thought
of being physically changed and of losing something I possessed was somewhat daunting, and more daunting still were
my mother's tears. In any case, I wasn't consulted before my
father ushered me firmly into the car and took me to the barber. I just remember that my mother went with us and that,
with tears streaming down her cheeks, she stood beside the
barber chair with a handful of ribbons and caught each gold-
en curl as it fell from my head. (For years afterward, even after
she died in 1980, I would find these remnants of my childhood in unexpected places among her possessions—
corkscrews of blond curls still tied in their red and blue ribbons in the back of a dictionary along with pressed flowers, in
the middle of the family Bible, or in a jar of potpourri at the
back of a closet.) *Sic transit gloria.*

But I was delighted with the result of the haircut. I liked
the unquestioned boy I saw in the mirror. I certainly looked
more like my father. And best of all, no one ever challenged
my maleness again—at least not until many years later when
an angry woman expressed doubts about it after I had
declined her sexual advances. But in 1934, I felt enormously
grateful to my father for having engineered the whole thing,
and more than ever, I felt that he was my champion.

However, this transition of the haircut, important as it was
for me at the time, proved to be only a gentle finger exercise
compared with the more radical changes that were soon to
come upon my family and me. The greatest of these was, quite
simply, that my father lost everything.

Now understand, he had met his commitments. In the
three years of his allotted time, he had built the airfield and
attracted a clientele for it. By 1935, the national interest in
aviation was growing rapidly. More and more, transient aircraft were flying along the East Coast needing fuel and ser-

vices. An increasing number of students were coming to my father for lessons in flying. The future looked promising, but my family was still living on what little remained of my mother's inheritance. And then, as a stellar climax to celebrate his three-year accomplishments, my father blew the rest of that inheritance on one of the most spectacular air shows ever presented in North Carolina. He invited famous pilots from World War I and the itinerant barnstormers who regularly gave Sunday exhibitions across the South. And then, as reigning queen of the whole extravaganza, he invited Amelia Earhart. I remember that she arrived early on the day of the show, and I was still playing in the yard of the cottage waiting to go to the airport when she buzzed the house, zooming in barely one hundred feet above the trees in her autogiro. It was the first time I had ever seen such an aircraft, and later when I met her, it was the first time I had ever met a woman pilot. It was all very exciting, and with the crowd that attended and the public interest that resulted, the show was clearly a great success.

I remember that my father flew one of the aerobatic exhibitions. He programmed himself to be last, waiting to put on the finishing touches until all the other pilots had finished before he catapulted himself into the skies using, as I remember it, a borrowed Waco biplane. Looking back on it now from the advantage of years, I think he must have been trying to prove a point that day, that in front of those well-known pilots from World War I and with Amelia Earhart and his political supporters watching from the stands, he set out to prove that, even at age forty-five, he was indeed the world's best pilot. And this proof involved some truly frightening and dangerous maneuvers—diving, turning, spinning, flying by the stands inverted and rolling the airplane upright so close to the ground that there was barely enough room for the wings to clear the runway, then pulling up into a loop and rolling again inverted as he zoomed past his audience—pushing the airplane to its limits, or maybe beyond the limits of its structural design. I didn't understand it all then, of course. I only remember that my mother covered her eyes with her hands and that my heart was about to pound out of my body as I watched him. It was only much later, from a conversation I overheard between him and another pilot, that I learned he'd nearly killed himself. Flying the Waco that day, he had somehow gotten himself into an inverted spin from which he almost did not recover. The audience had thought it an exciting part of the show, but the other pilot had a different view, "I tell you, Penny," he said, "the day you spun the Waco, that was the day I wouldn't have bet a nickel on your life."

But my father had salvaged that maneuver and come safely back to earth, maybe having truly convinced himself that he *was* some kind of superman. In any case, he returned full of hope and expectation that the city council and the Federal Government would honor their commitments and come forward with their contributions for further development of the field and the future of aviation and, of course, for the future of his career.

The problem was that during the three years my father had devoted to the initial project, and without his even being conscious of its importance, the world had changed in two significant ways. Three new members had been elected to the seven-member city Board of Aldermen and the Prohibition Act had been repealed.

Now, although the relationship between Prohibition and aviation may not be immediately obvious, recall that Prohibition was one of the great failures of American law making. It never really prohibited anything except the *legal* sale of alcohol while at the same time it inhibited the government's ability to collect its alcohol taxes. With repeal, however, in 1933, the Congress, while ending Federal prohibition, left it up to the individual states to decide whether or not to permit the legal sale of alcohol. North Carolina elected to remain *legally* dry. Of course, the *illegal* distilleries of North Carolina were notorious nationwide. The history of

The author's father (far right) with Amelia Earheart (center), Fayetteville Air Show, 1935.

Cumberland County around Fayetteville and its nearby neighbors of Robeson and Johnston Counties could hardly be told honestly without incorporating the exploits of their famous (alleged and sometimes convicted) bootleggers, such as Percy Flowers, Doc Bennet, the Lowry Gang and, according to rumor, even Ulysses S. Page, who was also a Federal marshal. Prohibition or not, their backwoods stills turned out thousands of gallons of crystal clear 150 proof "white lightning" corn whiskey every year for a large and thirsty clientele. But there were also more refined palates waiting eagerly after the repeal of Prohibition, waiting for good bourbon, Scotch, rye, or cognac. And those delicacies had to be brought from somewhere else—usually from a state in which legal sale was permitted.

Within a day after my father's gala air show, he received a call from his main contact on the Board of Aldermen. The air show had been wonderful, he was told. He was doing the right thing. The men on the Board were pleased. "Let's get together and talk," the man said.

I never learned the councilman's name. Years later when I asked my father, he simply turned to me and said, "That's a thing you'll never need to know." But piecing together what I overheard him tell my mother and what each of them told me separately, I know that my father met the councilman as usual at Sauder's Drug Store. Of course, everyone in the place knew him. News of the air show had appeared in every paper in the state. His picture, with Amelia Earhart at his side, had appeared on the front page and everybody came forward to greet him: "Great show!" "Nice work." "Aviation is really the road to the future!" And then he saw his friend from the Board of Aldermen coming forward to shake his hand. "Penny, my friend. It's wonderful. You've done more than we ever thought possible!"

They sat at one of the marble top tables, smoked their cigarettes, drank their cokes, and talked about the effects of the Depression and how Roosevelt's policies seemed to be making a change for the better. And then, it was my father who raised the question. He could circle like a dog for a little while, but he was usually the one who first went for the bone. "When do you think the Board can certify funds so I can get our money from Washington?" he asked.

"Oh, soon, soon. Just as soon as we make sure our new Board members are with us."

"We still hold a majority, don't we?"

"Oh yes. But I'd hate to make our new members feel we were forcing anything. It's better to get consensus, if we can."

"Is there any danger it might not be approved?"

"Nooo. Nooo. It's just going to take a little time."

"The thing is, and I hate to bring this up," my father said, "but I've invested a lot of money in the airport. There are debts . . ."

"Oh, Penny, Penny, we haven't forgotten you . . . not for a moment. We take good care of our friends. And I think we've finally found a way to put you on the payroll. We want to hire you as a courier pilot."

"Courier pilot?"

"Several members of the Board have formed a kind of mercantile corporation. We'll pay you a thousand dollars a month to work with us."

I'm sure the sound of the amount ran like lightning through my father's veins. It was many times more than he had ever earned or ever would earn in his entire life. "A thousand dollars a month! What would I have to do?"

"Just set up a schedule to fly to Washington, New York, or South Carolina, other states—wherever we have business."

"What would I be carrying?"

"Different things. Sometimes a passenger, business papers, or merchandise."

"What's the merchandise?"

"That depends on the orders we get. But it's not a thing you'll ever be concerned with."

"I have to be," my father said. "There are questions of weight, balance, and load limits."

"Don't worry. We're not going to overload your airplane. But aside from the weight, you'll never have to be concerned with our products."

And then this elected public leader went on to explain that all my father would have to do was fly the airplane and land it—say, in Washington—where he would leave a small envelope in the passenger seat and then go into the terminal for lunch. When he returned to the plane, he would find it loaded with merchandise and he would fly it back to Fayetteville where he would leave the plane again unattended while it was unloaded by men he would never even have to see.

"It's illegal liquor, isn't it?" my father said.

"Penny, it's merchandise. You don't have to know the nature of the merchandise."

"But . . ."

"Do you think every truck driver on the highway knows the contents of every parcel in his truck?"

"But I *would* know," my father said. "And if I were asked, I would have to tell the truth."

"But you don't object to drinking. I've seen you take more than one drink in my house and enjoy it a lot."

"I enjoy a good drink as much as any man," my father said. "And I think prohibition laws are stupid from the start. But I will never become a criminal for you, for the city, for the airport, or for any amount of money you can name."

"I can't believe you're turning this down."

"You heard my answer."

"After all we've done for you. You're making things very difficult."

"No. *You're* making things difficult."

My father later told me that for a moment he was undecided whether to punch his contact in the jaw or just to walk out in silent contempt. In the end, he decided simply to stand

and walk away. The other man, with his law degrees and political prominence was not a worthy foe on which even to soil his hands. Still, it was the other man who had the final word. "Think it over," he said. "It's going to be very hard to find those additional airport funds for a man who won't cooperate."

My father would live for another twenty-two years, but on that day, a certain grayness began to settle around him, and I think he began to die. How had he done it? Surely, he had been naive, but he had grown up in a world in which "a man's word was his bond," certainly the word of one who appeared to be a Southern gentleman. At least, it was *supposed* to be that way, and he had believed it. I think now that he had *had* to believe it. He had grown up also on stories of how his widowed grandmother had been cheated by her husband's business associates and on stories of how his own father, a newspaper editor, had run afoul of powerful but corrupt politicians—"gentlemen" all. And I think that somehow he wanted to transcend that corrupt world. It's probably what made flying so attractive to him—the idea of getting above it. Airplanes, after all, fly according to the laws of physics, which, like God, are infinite, eternal, and unchangeable. The laws that drive the actions of men are a different matter.

Pilots, of necessity, are somewhat schizophrenic; there are just certain facts and possibilities that it's better not to dwell on. Being borne aloft by invisible forces is an unnatural human act. Manmade machinery is fallible. Human skill is limited. The environment of air is always changing and disaster is always possible. All pilots are trained in the possible dangers and are taught how to avoid at least ten thousand ways of killing themselves. And then, knowing the dangers, they have to *behave* as though the dangers didn't exist. If a pilot dwelt too much on the possibilities for disaster, he would never find the courage to climb into the airplane at all—certainly not in the early days of aviation. And as I myself would later learn in army flight school at the time of the Korean War, any pilot who pulls onto a runway and pushes the throttle forward for takeoff does so as an act of faith. He knows the possibilities. But he forces all doubt and fear out of his mind and goes forward in full belief that one more time the engine will perform as it *should* and will not drop him into the trees at the end of the runway. If he has flown as long as my father had, and if he has been lucky enough to walk away from the same number of disasters, he's likely to begin to feel that the "charm" is really with him and that, in fact, he is a kind of superman who can handle anything that comes along.

So it was, I think, that my father approached the political arena and the airport. He knew the possibilities, but he chose to believe that the world really was the kind of place it was *supposed* to be—a place where a man did not promise what he could not deliver and where a promise and a handshake were as good as money in the bank. It was a world in which an honored name and an honorable reputation—obtained because one was, in fact, honorable—were the most valuable thing one could possess. But now in his naiveté, my father had allowed himself to be tricked by criminals, had consumed his wife's inheritance, and had led his family into bankruptcy. When a student attempting to make a crosswind landing destroyed his airplane the following week, my father's civil aviation career came fully to an end. But I think the seeds of bitterness and anger that later seemed to consume him were planted on that day in Sauder's Drug Store.

Chapter Three

He survived and we survived the rest of the Depression on
odd jobs, occasional tours of active duty, family handouts, and
the simple kindness and understanding of creditors. My father
tried selling insurance, and I cannot imagine anything for
which he was less suited. My mother occasionally found work
for a day or two as a substitute teacher, but opportunity was
rare. The army developed a program so that reserve officers
could receive alternate six month tours of active duty, and my
father became part of that program: six months on and six
months off. Sometimes he would be assigned to an air corps
unit and put on flying status. Sometimes he would be assigned
to command a company of the Civilian Conservation Corps,
the CCC, which President Roosevelt had created to help preserve our forests and parks and national water resources, as
well as to provide employment for the down and out. Of
course, the bulk of the income from these alternate tours of
duty only went to pay the debts that had accrued during the
previous six months of unemployment. And even then,
unpaid bills mounted in grocery stores and clothing stores. I

know that for months at a time we were unable to pay the rent. The landlords, though—the Kinleys—were the most understanding and forbearing of people. They themselves were having a hard time paying their own mortgage, and they had no heart to take action against someone similarly stressed.

All these creditors, however, in addition to being unbelievably patient and kind, did have one other thing in common: my father's promise, "These debts will be paid." And his word actually was "as good as money in the bank." When things finally changed, the debts were paid—and with interest where it was called for. But in the meantime, life teetered on the edge. I remember once sitting with my mother in the car as she waited to buy gasoline. We had to have the car since we lived in the country and had no other form of transportation. She held up a dollar bill and said, "I want you to look at this and remember it. It's the last dollar we have to our name, and I don't know where the next one's coming from." And then, I remember that the very next day in the mail, she received a gift of five dollars from her sister Norma who still had a part-time job as a reporter for the *Charlotte Observer* and had thought we "might need something."

So we lived from day to day, but I remember also that there were periods of hard manual labor for my parents. They planted a large garden, and I remember that my father borrowed a mule and a plow from a neighbor, an elderly black man with white hair who was known throughout the community as "Uncle" Sandy and who was the only person I ever met who had actually been born in "slavery times." I remember Uncle Sandy helping my father with a hoe and I remember watching the two of them with the heavy mule as it swung around at the end of a furrow with the steel plow turning the earth and transforming smooth green lawn into rows that, over the summer, would produce corn, beans, peas, lettuce, carrots, tomatoes, turnips, and potatoes. My mother even planted blue morning glories to flower among the corn stalks.

We also had a peach tree, and at the end of summer, my mother would begin canning everything we didn't need for daily use. I was still no more than six years old, but she pressed me into service to help her mount shelves in the attic. It seemed to me that ever afterward those shelves were filled with sealed Mason jars containing the fruit of her summer's labors—canned peaches, beans, tomatoes, pickled beets, chow-chow, watermelon pickle.

Also in those days, especially in spring, I remember entering the post office and hearing the soprano chirp of mail order baby chickens behind the service window, and of course, I wanted some biddies of my own. So my parents ordered me a dozen mail order chicks as my special project. I kept them in a cage on the back porch at first, and then as they grew, we moved them into the yard. My father set off a plot behind the garden and "together" we built a chicken house and put up a wire fence. Within the year, those chickens were providing us with both eggs and meat. And eventually, they would even provide me with education.

Since my parents had had bad experiences with country schools, they decided to send me to the parochial Catholic school in town, and since we were Protestants, the school charged us tuition. We didn't have the money, five dollars per month, but my mother resorted to barter. We provided the nuns with eggs, and they provided me with schooling until the sixth grade when we finally moved and I entered the public schools.

However, it was the *meat* aspect of the chickens that I remember most vividly. My father had taught me to hunt, but it was a black woman named Etta who taught me the art of executing barnyard animals. Etta helped my mother periodically, especially during canning season when both women would pool their vegetables and work away in the one hundred-degree Carolina heat of my mother's kitchen to provide winter food for their families. And when it came time to select and prepare a chicken for Sunday dinner, my mother would ask Etta to do it. Of course, at first, the idea of killing one of my chickens was horrifying to me. I had raised them from fluffy biddies, after all. I wasn't going to have it! But my mother began to persuade me, as only she could do. "We need to use our animal produce just as we use our garden produce," she told me, pointing out that although I loved those live chickens, I also loved good fried chicken. And I came to see that there was only one way to get it. I think, however, that the business of the chickens introduced me for the first time to conscious questions of ethical and moral paradox: how can a person both love something and exploit it? How can one—either man or God—nurture something beautiful into life and then kill it arbitrarily? How can one love both the life and the death of the loved object? These were emotional questions rather than questions that I could have phrased rationally. But they were very real and very palpable.

I managed to sequester a few of my favorite older chickens in one corner of the chicken house, and then I reluctantly let Etta have her way with one of the others those first few times. But it wasn't long afterward that my dilemma about killing chickens was permanently resolved.

I had a rooster named Freddy. I don't remember why I named him Freddy or exactly where I got him, although I know I had raised him from a chick. He was different from the other chickens, maybe part bantam, with deep red body feathers melding gradually into bronze and green around his head. He had a very rakish comb and top knot and spurs that were longer than those of any other rooster, and compared with the cookie cutter sameness of the white leghorns or the Rhode Island reds, he was a "matinee idol." (I knew that term from listening to the radio soap opera, *Mary Noble, Backstage Wife*, which began each episode with the question of whether or not Mary Noble could "find happiness with a matinee idol adored by a million other women.") In any case, Freddy was the life of the chicken yard, the first to crow in the morning and last to fly to roost at night, and I enjoyed watching Freddy keep his hens in line and strut around the place as though he owned it. Then it all changed suddenly one afternoon when I went down with my daily bucket of cracked corn to feed the chickens. I sprinkled the corn on the ground, and then, overcome by sudden need, I decided to take a quick pee into the bushes behind the hen house. I was engaged in this when Freddy walked by. I remember very clearly how he cocked his head to one side and studied me very thoughtfully with his beady eyes and then, without the slightest warning, flew up and pecked me very hard right on the head of my six-year-old penis. It hurt like hell! I kicked at Freddy. I chased Freddy. I threw the feed bucket at Freddy until finally he flew up into a tree where I couldn't get to him. But my outrage consumed me. Not only had I raised Freddy from a chick and been his friend, but I had saved him from Etta the executioner for several weeks on end. Now it would be different. I had been betrayed! As far as I was concerned, from that day forward, all chickens were merely meat, unreliable turncoats deserving slaughter. And the next time Etta came to catch and kill a chicken, I asked her to show me how to do it.

Etta had a son named Teeny who was just my age and who frequently accompanied his mother to our house. And over the next few weeks, Teeny and I would catch chickens together. We would be the cowboys chasing the bad guys, galloping our make believe horses across the garden and into the chicken pen to corner one of the cowardly varmints and bring it to justice, the way they did it on the *Gene Autry Radio Show* or on *The Lone Ranger*. Of course, the one we wanted most was Freddy, the leader of the "bad guys," but he was always smarter than the others and always able to fly over the fence and into the trees before we could get him. So we would settle on another chicken and bring it to Etta for our weekly lesson.

Her favorite method of execution was to wring the chicken's neck, and no ballet dancer was ever more adept. She could hold the chicken in one hand, stroke it to calm it, then grasp it by the neck and with a single turn and a snap, send the body of the chicken in one direction and the head in another. I tried it, but even in my outrage against chickens, the feel of their neck bones turning under my fingers made me shy back and hesitate. So Etta said, "Let's go to the woodpile." And there she showed me how to make the chicken lay its head on the chopping block as she held the axe at its heft with one hand and let the blade fall, neatly severing the neck. This was more my kind of thing, especially when I thought of taking revenge against Freddy. And soon, with visions of bloody vengeance dancing through my head, I replaced Etta as the family executioner, assigned each week to kill and pluck our Sunday dinner.

Freddy, however, cheated me one last time. Before I could get to him, that greedy and arrogant bastard, insisting as always on trying to eat all the chicken food before the others could get it, succeeded in choking himself to death in an attempt to eat the dry "laying mash" that I had put out espe-

The author's log cottage home, 1940.

cially for the hens. The justice, no doubt, was poetic, but I felt robbed and the edge of my excitement over raising chickens was dulled forever.

Now, in the late 1930s, although our domestic financial situation seemed static and totally unable to change, the world outside of rural North Carolina was, in fact, changing very rapidly. Aviation, for example, was advancing just as my father had predicted. The Douglas DC-3 was in service, suddenly transforming the possibilities for domestic commercial aviation. The Martin 130 Flying Boat, remembered as the China Clipper or the Lisbon Clipper, was in service, opening air travel to Europe and the Orient. By late 1938, both the Bell P-39 and the Curtiss P-40 fighter planes had been developed, and I'm sure my father felt that he had somehow ended on the sidelines of the world he loved most. His brother Robert, a Marine officer, visited us on his return from assignment in China in 1937 and brought us an eyewitness account of the Japanese attack on China and of their atrocities in Nanking. The American gunboat *Panay* had been attacked by Japanese aircraft in the Yangtze River, and both my father and my uncle were convinced that it would be only a little time before we were at war with Japan.

It was about this time that General Claire Chenault's Flying Tigers—The American Volunteer Group—was being organized to defend China using the new Curtiss P-40B pursuit planes, and over the weeping objections of my mother, my father volunteered. I remember their heated debates far into the night. "It's insane," my mother told him. "You're nearly fifty years old."

"I'm rotting in the woods of North Carolina."

"You've never even seen a P-40, much less flown one. You'll be flying against pilots in their twenties."

"They're paying a king's ransom."

"What good is a dead king, ransom or no?"

In the end, it was all taken out of his hands. On September 1, 1939, Hitler's army marched into Poland, and before the month was out, President Roosevelt had invited all interested reserve officers to apply for unlimited active duty with the armed services. My father jumped at the chance. First, he was assigned as executive officer, second in command, of Pope Field. And then came the dispatch from Washington: General Hap Arnold, the Chief of the Air Corps, whom he had known in 1917 when they were both young officers, had requested him as a member of his staff in Washington. In terms of the 1990s, it was for my father comparable to Vaclav Havel moving from prison to the Presidency of Czechoslovakia in six months time. From the woods of North Carolina to the capital of the nation and the nerve center of what would become the most powerful air force in history!

But he went to Washington with one more downside. One week before his departure, on a routine training flight to maintain his flying status, he flew an army observation plane, an O-49, known familiarly by the pilots as a "ball roller" because the landing gear were so close together that it was extremely hard to control on the ground. I remember when he came home at the end of that day. His face was bruised and he was limping, and he said to my mother, "Now I know why they call it a 'ball roller.'"

"What happened?"

"I came in to land and it got away from me," he said. "I literally rolled it into a ball at the end of the runway."

The accident called for a new physical exam and the doctor discovered both a slight heart irregularity and vision that no longer met the revised air corps requirements for flying.

It wasn't serious enough to keep him out of the service, but he was permanently grounded and removed from flying status. And I remember that when he finally left for Washington, he was savoring the full bittersweet flavor of the occasion. "I'm a damned kiwi," he said. "A grounded bird. I'm on my way to help command the greatest air corps in the world, but I'll never again be allowed to fly in it."

The author with his father and cousin, Mary Alexander, 1934.

Chapter Four

So when my father prepared to leave for North Africa in 1943 after his tour in Washington, there was more whizzing through my twelve-year-old brain than I could possibly process or understand. The mood was definitely upbeat, but at the same time filled with the direst apprehension.

During the three years with General Arnold, my father had been promoted to the rank of major and had been at the center of planning for the strategic aerial war of 1940 to 1943. The Air Corps had become the Air Force, completely separate from the Army, and my father had been assigned as part of the planning group for a new section known as The Ferry Command whose mission was to transfer planes in the fastest way possible to the war zone. Short-range fighters, of course, had to be ferried by ocean freight—exposed for the entire time at sea to attack from German submarines. But long-range bombers could be flown, and it would be my father's job, as commander of an airfield in North Africa, to prepare the way.

On the positive side, I felt enormously excited for him and proud. He was out of the woods of North Carolina and back in a position of centrally important command. He had risen from the disaster of his Fayetteville airport and now would command a much larger airport capable of handling any plane ever built. I was delighted to see him vindicated. But at the same time, I was fully aware of the dangers of war. My family had followed the daily radio news detailing the conflict from the fall of Paris to Dunkirk and on to the attack at Pearl Harbor, the Bataan Death march, and the battle of Corregidor. We had listened each night to the voice of Edward R. Murrow saying, "This is London," and then providing us with the daily toll of death and destruction during the blitz under the Luftwaffe. So I had no illusions about the dangers of war, even for a pilot who would spend the bulk of his time on the ground. And I knew when he departed overseas that it was entirely possible that I would never see my father again.

My mother and I accompanied him on the train to his embarkation point at West Palm Beach. By that time, my parents had paid off their Depression debts and bought the little white house near the Veterans Hospital (I remember that they paid three thousand dollars for it in 1941) where we were living when I had met Alfred earlier that year, and I remember that I was the one who locked the front door as we left the house and went to the railroad station.

We remained in Florida just long enough for my father to go through final processing, and I remember that the three of us went to dinner the night before his departure. It seems to me now that it was a very quiet dinner—so many things to say and so many things unspeakable—and that my mother even accepted a glass of sherry, which she rarely did. And then, half way through dinner, my father turned to me and said, "You know what your job will be while I'm away, don't you, son?"

And I said, "Yessir, I think so."

"Your job is to take care of your mother," he said. "You'll do that for me, won't you?"

"Yessir, I will."

"I know you will. You're the man of the house when I'm away. You defend the home front while I'm at the battlefront. We'll be fighting the war together."

We watched him board the heavily loaded Douglas C-47 at 5 A.M. the next morning. He hugged and kissed both of us at the fence and then strode briskly out through the pre-dawn chill and up the ramp, turning only once at the door to wave before the engines started.

When we got back to our rented car, my mother was weeping. I hadn't seen her cry since my first haircut, and now she was just sitting there behind the wheel in the semi-darkness with tears streaming down her cheeks. I felt like I was supposed to *do* something, but I didn't know what. Maybe I wanted to cry, too, but I wouldn't have dared let it happen because I knew my father would be ashamed of me. So I just sat quietly for a long time as though I were sitting in church while someone else was praying. And then finally she turned to me and said, "Hug me. Just hug me."

I did. And then, as the sky began to brighten, I said, "He's going to be all right. He's going to be just fine. We've got a war to fight."

It may have been adolescent bravado, but it got us through, and that afternoon, we began the long train ride back to North Carolina to go on with our lives in the new house.

We did get V-mail letters from my father, but most of them were so filled with censor's blots that we could hardly read them. We learned he had arrived, seemed healthy, that he loved us and prayed for us, but little concrete information about his exact location or the war. His letters to me were filled with encouragement of all kinds—to do well in school, to defend the home front, to take care of my mother. I was the best thing in his life, he told me, and he knew I would never let him down. I couldn't possibly appreciate the enormity of this burden at the time, but I took all his admonitions with great seriousness. I had to be educated, brave, courageous, bold, truthful, protective, and a force for making the world a better place, and no question about it.

My first job was to be "man of the house," and defender of the home, and I remember taking on that job with deadly seriousness because it was about this time that Alfred alarmed the entire neighborhood by shooting at an intruder. I wasn't there when it happened, but the police were still at Alfred's house the next morning when I stopped by on my way to school, and I saw the hole in the window screen where the shotgun blast had torn through. "It was a nigger," Alfred told me. "I could see his head against the light. He was trying to look into my room and then when he tried to unhook the screen, I just picked up my shotgun from the corner and unloaded at him."

Apparently, the shot didn't hit anybody and no other damage was done, but a 12-gauge shotgun blast in a quiet community at 2 A.M. has far reaching echoes. Although the crime of burglary was almost unheard of in those days, there were thousands of strangers in town as a result of the war effort, and we realized anything could happen. I think the entire neighborhood was suddenly on alert. And it was only about three days after Alfred's adventure that I myself was awakened at 2 A.M. by the sound of our front door opening. There was a bright moonlight that night and I could see the open front door from my bed. Slowly I got up and stood for a time listening in the darkened doorway of my room. *Suppose there was an intruder in our house,* I thought. And there was no doubt in my mind what I would have to do. Quietly, I opened the drawer of the desk in the hall where my father's pistol lay, and I remember that the feel of the cold steel in the darkness gave me a sense of great power. I would not hesitate to use it if necessary. But in this case, when I got to the open front door, I found only my mother walking alone in the yard. When she saw me, she said simply and without surprise, "Do you suppose that same moon is shining on Daddy tonight—wherever he is?" And then, as the hall clock struck 3 A.M., she hugged me suddenly, quite fiercely. "You're so wonderful!" she said. "Just like your father. I don't know what I would ever do without you."

Chapter Five

My mother's 3 A.M. embrace in the moonlight left me with a host of conflicting feelings and thoughts. On the one hand, I could see that she loved my father and she missed him, and at that level her comments to me were very re-affirming, assuring. At another level, however, her comments left me with a feeling of enormous embarrassment, as though something just was not right, as though she were flattering me, as though her late night embrace was offered to prepare me for some role that I had not yet agreed to play. And part of me wished it had never happened.

But a healthy adolescent boy is not going to spend all of his time in thoughts of high seriousness, even in a time of war. So in spite of the sometimes-dangerous aspects of our friendship, Alfred and I continued to have good times together. And in addition, as spring came on, I, for the first time in my life, fell madly in love with a girl named Ruth Ann who had moved in about three blocks away and who—with her friend Darlene—rode the school bus each day with Alfred and me.

Ruth Ann was not the first girl I had ever been interested in. Indeed, I think I was born with an interest in girls. I remember that at three or four, when my mother took me to Sunday school, I wanted to sit with the girls—not because I wanted to be one, but because I thought they were so beautiful. At age four, there had been Jonaleen, whose father ran the gas station near my father's airport. She and I had played together regularly until one afternoon, in a burst of mutual exploration, we decided to pee for each other behind the airplane hanger. This idyll ended when my father discovered us and called me to him. He didn't want me to play with Jonaleen anymore, he said. "She's just not appropriate." I didn't know how to counter this, so I lost her—although I continued to remember fondly our puddles in the sand.

Then there was Marian in the first grade that I had kissed regularly, causing all the other kids to giggle and snicker, when the teacher's back was turned. In later years, I was less demonstrative, but there was always some girl who was smarter or prettier than the others, or who was a good ball player, or a good singer whom I singled out as my, by then, more silent love. Ruth Ann, though, was totally different. She was about two years older than I and she had red hair. In addition, she was the first girl I'd ever known to possess a fully developed woman's figure, and I thought she was sublime.

At first, since she was older and often talking to other boys at the bus stop, I felt very timid about speaking to her and only glanced pleasantly in her direction. But eventually, she seemed to appreciate my reticence and spoke to me. And from that day, I came to think of the trip to school as a trip to paradise, especially when I was lucky enough to get a seat beside her. The only problem was that if my arm or my hip would rub against hers, I would inevitably get an erection, which was very difficult to hide in my thin cotton trousers. I started bringing home more schoolbooks to help cover this embarrassment, but some of the other boys, especially Alfred, had seen and began to taunt me. I would get off the bus holding my books in front of me, maybe limping slightly at first from the adjustment, hoping to walk quietly beside Ruth Ann that final block to school. But Alfred, like a devil from hell, would walk in front of me, calling back all along the way, "Come on, come on. You're gonna be late. Why don't you walk faster, huh? You got a bone in your leg or sump'm?"

Ruth Ann, however, apparently had not seen, and I hoped she never would, because my love for her had long ago transcended all earthly and fleshly limits. I would think of her first on waking in the morning and last before going to sleep at night. I thought heavenly and ineffable thoughts, but still, in total contrast to the purity of these conscious thoughts, on both occasions, my troublesome penis would rise throbbing in salute, and I was sure that it possessed a mind of its own.

Now, to paint a complete picture, I have to review here a brief *conscious* history of my recalcitrant member. Understand that no little boy thinks about his penis any more than he does his fingers or his toes. They're all just parts of his body as long as they work right and don't hurt and nobody calls attention to them. This certainly had been true for me, until the fateful age of about three—around the same time I was having my first haircut and before my fateful confrontation with either Freddy or Jonaleen—when my gentle organ suffered its first serious assault. I don't know how the decision came to be made, but given my parents' inheritance of 19th century theology, which held that Christians were the spiritual descendants of Old Testament Jews, and given my mother's view of me as the reincarnation of an Old Testament prophet, my parents apparently agreed that I should be circumcised. I suspect that my mother spearheaded the whole thing. In matters of this kind, my father rarely opposed her. After all, even Shakespeare's Othello had had some pretty rough things to say about that "uncircumcised dog that beat a Venetian and traduced the state." So it was decided that I have a general neatening up. Nobody seemed especially concerned that where the Jews performed their circumcisions when the baby was eight days old, I was at a more conscious and impressionable age. And not only that—in the interest of Protestant economic efficiency, I was to have my tonsils and adenoids removed at the same time.

The operation was performed at the Presbyterian Hospital in my mother's hometown of Charlotte, and I believe the doctor's name was Faison. These are things indelibly imprinted on my mind. The adults carefully explained to me beforehand that removing my tonsils would keep me from having so many colds and sore throats, and they promised me unlimited amounts of ice cream when I came out of the operating room. Nobody ever mentioned circumcision.

I felt quite confident going into it—that is, until the nurse came forward to put the mask for anesthesia over my face. And then I lost it all. As vividly as this morning's breakfast or last night's nightmare, I remember fighting and struggling against my captors, gasping and screaming in total horror as things went black and I could inhale only the cold and offensive fumes of ether against the back of my throat.

Afterward, I don't remember being conscious of a sore throat at all. I just remember waking with a scream, crying at the top of my voice, "My tee-tee hurts!" It was for me, at that age, certainly, the most traumatic event of my life.

My mother explained to me then, as she would do often when I was better able to understand it, that circumcision was a sign of our relationship to God. She later read and told me Bible stories, including the story of Abraham, and pointing out that circumcision was a physical symbol of Abraham's covenant with God and of the Christian covenant of accepting the same grace that God had granted Abraham. "Circumcision was there," she told me, "to remind a man to use his body wisely, that he was a child of God, and that he had a responsibility to promote God's kingdom on earth."

Such teaching was not all bad, of course, but it was an enormous burden to place upon such a rebellious member as the human penis.

Understand though, that when I met Ruth Ann, my knowledge of sex was still very much in a kind of twilight zone. I *knew*, but I didn't know—or maybe just didn't want to know—although certainly, I had been given the graphic, though shocking details, more than once.

The first time was over a long weekend at my Aunt Norma's house in Belmont, North Carolina. I was there with my mother and I was about eight. The mystery of erection had suggested itself to me in a rather mild form earlier. But suddenly, there at my aunt's house in the middle of the night, a force over which I had absolutely no control seized my usually docile tee-tee. It was standing as upright and rigid as a miniature Washington Monument under the sheet. The problem was that it wouldn't go away and it was beginning to hurt. My mother had told me about the Petrified Forest and how normally soft things could turn to stone, and I wondered if this was happening to me. I didn't want to call my mother because by this time in my life I had become quite modest, even where she was concerned. But at length, I could bear it alone no longer, and I called her. I told her I was hurting and I pulled aside the bedclothes to reveal my problem. For a long moment she just stood there straight-faced and looked at me. And then she said, "Um hum," the way a thoughtful doctor does when he hasn't got the slightest notion of how to deal with the problem at hand. "I think I should call your Aunt Norma," my mother said. Now, I wasn't especially overjoyed at the thought of having two ladies examine me, but I didn't object. Aunt Norma was older than my mother and had two sons much older than I, so she must have encountered my problem somewhere along the way. But I know now that she was no less Victorian and squeamish about matters of sex than anyone else in my mother's family. So picture, if you will, these two middle aged ladies positioned beside my bed and gazing down studiously on my involuntary, but embarrassing monument. To both their credit, I have to point out that neither one of them offered the slightest smile. "Um hum," my Aunt said, just as my mother had done. And then she said, still straight-faced, "Maybe we should put some Tetarine on it."

Now I don't know whether Tetarine is still sold over drugstore counters or not, but in those days it was widely used as a disinfectant, and I believe it contained such things as oil of eucalyptus and wintergreen. Anyone who has ever touched wintergreen to sensitive skin knows what my immediate new problem was. People say it offers a cooling sensation, but we receive and sense it as *heat*. And the immediate effect on me was electric. My poor distended penis may have hurt from inner pressure before, but that was nothing compared to the scalding sensation caused by the medication. Pain has always served as an absolute anti-aphrodisiac to me, so my erection subsided almost immediately. But I spent a good bit of the rest of that night in various stages of agony while those two ladies bathed my poor pitiful prick in warm soapy water and assured me that everything was going to be all right.

But, of course, nothing was going to be all right at all, certainly not for a very long time. And it was going to get worse even before the weekend was out.

The following day or the day after, I was playing with my cousin Craighead and a young black boy named Sam in the basement of my aunt's house. It was a wonderful basement with a dry earthen floor and filled with firewood, coal, canned foods, wagons, and wheelbarrows. And it gave off an incredibly delicious aroma of smoked ham combined with cedar and oak. Beneath the window near the corner stood a large wooden worktable where I could lay out the blueprints of the model airplanes I was beginning to build. And I was showing Craighead and Sam the balsa frame of a new model when somehow the subject of penises and erection came up, probably because the model blueprints had been published in England where they referred to a *propeller* as an *airscrew*. We all snickered at the word *screw*, of course, not quite knowing why, and then Sam—who was two or three years older than Craig and I—asked us if our "peckers" ever got hard in the middle of the night. I have always found it difficult to discuss this subject, but we both agreed that they did. And then Sam unloaded upon us the forbidden fruit, "That's so you can stick it between a girl's legs."

"What?" I asked. "Sam, that's crazy!"

"That's what men and women do," Sam said. And he made an obscene gesture with the finger of one black hand sliding into the fist of the other.

"That's disgusting!" I said. "Nobody decent would do a thing like that."

"Don't you know nothin'?" Sam asked. "That's the way people gets babies."

"It is not!"

"Yeh it is. Yo' daddy had to do that to yo' mama before they could get you."

"Now you just shut up, Sam. Shut up!" I said. "My parents would never do a thing as sickening as that!" My outrage at Sam was total. I hadn't been so infuriated by anything since Freddy had attacked me, and I'm sure I would have punched Sam in the jaw if he hadn't been so much bigger and stronger than I was. "You just shut up, Sam," I said again. "I don't want to talk anymore about it. It's ugly. And I don't want to play with you anymore either," I said. And I took the frame of my model airplane and went upstairs to play by myself.

But my life would never be the same after that day. It was rather like coming upon a bloody and deadly accident on the highway. You don't want to look at the gory and dismembered bodies, but neither can you force yourself to look away. Except that these horrifying pictures were figments of my own imagination, and I had little or no external experience to help guide me through them. I had seen the piglets suckling the mother sow on our neighbor's farm, and I had seen Mr. Slocumb's bird dog nursing her pups. I had even once seen Mrs. Bullard nursing her new baby. So I knew about breasts and nipples, and that was all very fine. But as for the rest of it, I felt that I was standing on the edge of a dangerous abyss. I knew that girls were different from boys and that they didn't have penises, but the only female pudenda I had ever seen was that of Jonaleen at age four, and a quick snapshot view it was. Why were boys and girls different in the first place? Suppose it was just possible that Sam was telling the truth . . . but no! It couldn't be. No decent person would do that. The very idea was revolting! And I tried to push the serpent back into the basket of tricks that my mind held waiting to play on me. I just wouldn't think of it, I decided. I would live and act as though Sam had never spoken.

But that was not to be. In the days that followed, my mother apparently realized that I needed more education on reproduction and also that she was totally unprepared to provide it. My father was away on active duty somewhere, so it was all left up to my mother. She went to the library and brought home pretty books on nature, all speaking of the need of fertilization between male and female to produce new life, but all carefully avoiding the specifics of sex beyond pictures of bees with pollen on their legs. Then, with admirable dispatch, my mother went to the army hospital at Fort Bragg and persuaded one of the young doctors, Captain McCoy, to give me an elementary course in the physiology of sex. He was a very nice man and I remember sitting in his office as he gave me a very matter of fact description of the basics and I realized with horror and total dismay that Sam had been right and that the world was not the place I thought it was.

Still, my mother was not content to let my generally subdued demeanor speak for my serious reception of this mystery.

As we drove home from Dr. McCoy's office, she added an important footnote to my sexual education. Sex, that is to say, "Human reproduction"—I cannot imagine her actually using the word sex—was not something a person should ever allow his mind to dwell on. And of course, one was never to tell any dirty stories about it. Further, I was not to start thinking of girls in terms of their bodies. Their minds and their souls were the important things, not their bodies. Reproduction was part of the sacred rite of marriage, she told me, "A sacred thing, ordained by God to be practiced only within marriage and for the purpose of having children." To engage in these "intimacies" outside of marriage was a violation of the Seventh Commandment, and anyone who did that would go straight to hell when he died.

Of course, at age eight, I was not even remotely tempted "to engage in these intimacies," but her comments surely confirmed my feelings: this stuff was dynamite and I wanted as little to do with it as possible.

So, even in the face of irrefutable science, when I met Ruth Ann four years later, I was continuing to hold on to one corner of hope: that while most people had to resort to the crude exchange of bodily fluids in order to reproduce, surely the good and the beautiful could find a different way. Surely *some* people, through embracing and kissing and speaking their love, could transmit the magic power of life without such indignity.

So in those moments when my body took over and my autonomous penis rose in throbbing excitement at the thought of Ruth Ann, it disgusted me. My love for Ruth Ann was a pure and unearthly thing, something sublime, everlasting and spiritual. In my English class I had read Poe's poem about Annabel Lee and their "kingdom by the sea," and I knew it had been written for Ruth Ann and me. Perhaps one day—some far off, heavenly day—our love might be consummated with a kiss, but there was *nothing* I wanted to do to her with my penis. After all, I realize now, I had inherited from my father the ideal that my life's work would be to protect the honor and beauty of women, and I would have gladly died before allowing the slightest stain to sully Ruth Ann's purity.

But I was soon to discover another problem altogether. Ruth Ann was a Catholic. Now I had never considered this a problem with either the girls or the boys whom I had met at Saint Patrick's School. But Ruth Ann was something different. Already in my strict Presbyterian Sunday school and from my mother I had learned that we were staunch Protestants. I had learned about Martin Luther, John Calvin, and John Knox. And I had been told clearly that the United States would never have existed in its present form if it had been settled first by Catholics because, where Protestants acted on their own responsibility, Catholics deferred everything to the Pope and allowed the priests to tell them how to live. *How,* I wondered, *could I love someone who would run to a priest rather than think for herself?* But then, in a burst of illumination, I settled on a wonderfully happy plan: I would *convert* her! My love would be no ordinary thing, but a force extending even to the saving of Ruth Ann's soul.

So my passion for her increased as I looked for her at the bus stop, walking down the halls of the school, or maybe best of all, just watching her from a distance as she walked ahead of me in that swinging fluid motion that set her apart from all females on earth and made her *my life's purpose.*

In the spring of that year, Alfred met a boy by the name of Cecil Early who lived on a farm not far from us. I don't know where Alfred met him because, at sixteen, Cecil had already reached the legal age of decision and dropped out of school. But Alfred brought Cecil to my house one afternoon, and from that time on, we became regular visitors to the Early farm.

Standing at about six-feet-four-inches, Cecil was taller than either one of us, but he weighed only about 120 pounds, and when he worked around the farm wearing his blue denim "overhauls" and carrying a pitch fork or a shovel, he looked rather like a young version of *American Gothic*. Sometimes we would go fishing together and I remember that Cecil kept us laughing with his personal brand of country humor in which he compared almost everything to some portion of the human anatomy: "Be careful, boys, this river bank's slippery as a soap maker's ass." Or, "No use tryin' to fish over yonder 'cause that water ain't but pecker deep." But we would have fun, and back at the farm we liked helping Cecil slop the hogs, feed corn to the scrawny mule, and round up the cows from the back pasture at milking time. It wasn't all one way, of course, since Cecil also had a part-time job as ticket taker at the Carolina Theater. So whenever he was on duty and Alfred and I wanted to go to the movies, we just walked in to see Cecil, and he would pass us right on by, without tickets, to see the show.

Anyway, one afternoon that summer when we were out back of Cecil's house slopping the hogs, we realized that there were still lots of unharvested watermelons in Mr. Early's field and that something ought to be done about it. So the next day we harnessed the old mule to the wagon, painted a sign, and set up shop to sell watermelons on the side of Raleigh Road. It was there that Ruth Ann found us while riding her bicycle with Darlene on a Saturday afternoon.

For some reason, Alfred was not with us that day, but I was sitting on the wagon with Cecil in the sparse shade of a tall pine when the girls came riding by, and we pointed to the melons and shouted, "Come on over and we'll cut one for you."

When they got to us, I was stunned almost to silence. Ruth Ann was wearing very short shorts and a halter-top, which was hardly more than a large bandanna tied at the back. She was barefooted, and her toes were so perfectly and delicately formed that I couldn't take my eyes away. Never in all my rampant imagination had I dreamed that such beauty existed on this earth. And no sooner had she stopped and leaned her bicycle against the wagon than my enigmatic penis leaped forward several inches down the leg of my khaki colored shorts. It was like having another person in my pants, someone who was determined to embarrass me and ruin me at every turn. I had been taught meticulously never to curse or use profane language in any way, but on that day, I remember gritting my teeth and whispering to my penis, "You son of a bitch, I'm gonna kill you!" just as Ruth Ann dismounted.

"Hi!" Ruth Ann said.

She was standing directly in front of me, and my perch on the side of the wagon had placed my crotch almost at her eye level. I smiled as radiantly as I could, but I felt hotter with embarrassment than anything the ninety-degree summer heat could provide because my damn penis had ignored me completely and was continuing to grow and throb away happily half way down my thigh. "We've got some of the best watermelons in the state right here," I said. And I pointed flamboyantly toward the back of the wagon, trying to distract her. "I was savin' that big one back there just for you, wasn't I, Cecil?"

"Sure was," Cecil said. The girls naturally had to look at Cecil as he uncoiled his beanpole length from his seat in the shade. "This big 'un here," Cecil said. He patted a melon. "Won't no mor'n a minute ago we agreed we was gonna save this'un for that red-haired gal and her friend from up the road."

He winked and made the girls giggle, and this gave me a chance to slip down without being immediately discovered. But then I realized I had an even more prominent problem. Maybe if I stood facing the wagon and talked over my shoulder, everything would be all right, I thought. Maybe after I stood up for a minute the damn thing would go away without being noticed. But then, on the moist summer air, I caught the scent of Ruth Ann's lipstick or sweet smelling soap and I realized it was never going to happen.

Cecil was still patting the melon. "Damn," he said. "This'un's hot as the back of a stove. Let's see if we can find a cooler one on the bottom of the pile."

"What?" I said.

"Come round here and help me."

"Oh." I knew I couldn't walk toward the girls without being discovered, so I decided to duck under the wagon. Unfortunately, just as I did it, the girls decided to walk around closer to where Cecil was, and they were standing there looking at me when I came out the other side. There was no doubt what they saw. I might as well have been trying to conceal a workman's flashlight in my shorts. Darlene began to giggle immediately, and Ruth Ann put her hand to her mouth in surprise, but then, even she began to snicker. And I felt a kind of sick wave of heat surging across my entire body, scorching my ears, burning my eyes, making my scalp feel like it was being incinerated. But at that point, I knew that the only thing to do was behave as though nothing were happening. "Now, let's see if we can find a nice juicy one," I said.

"Oh . . . well," Ruth Ann said. "I guess we'd better go."

"No, no," I said. "I've got something good for you." And of course, this made the girls giggle even more.

"It's getting late and all," she said.

But by this time, Cecil had rolled a melon to the tailgate, and I forced myself to smile above my fury as I touched it and reached for the large butcher knife that was wedged between the boards of the wagon. "Not too late for this," I said. And I stabbed the melon and sliced downward.

Actually at that moment, I think I wished I could slice the offending prick all the way off my body. But instead, I just drove the knife up to its hilt and pulled the blade along the length of the melon until I heard the hollow pop as the melon opened, revealing its crimson heart. "You can't walk away from a piece of that now, can you?"

Somehow the thought of the knife and the action of cutting had the desired effect. When the melon rolled open, perfuming the air, my erection vanished as suddenly as it had appeared. I sliced again and again, removing a large sliver of heart. And then I turned full front toward Ruth Ann and held out the fruit with its juice dripping from my wrist. "You'll never find a melon better than that," I said. She took it from my hand, and Cecil handed Darlene a piece. And then, still laughing to themselves, the girls rode away into the slanting afternoon light.

Afterward, I helped Cecil take the melons back to the barn and unhitch the mule before I finally rode home, sticky with watermelon juice, just before dark. I found my mother waiting beside the back door as I rode into the yard, and from the cast of her body and the stolid look on her face, I knew she was not pleased. "Where have you been?" she said.

"At Cecil's."

"And where else?"

"Just there."

"Who else was there?"

I told her what we had been doing.

"I called all over the neighborhood," she said. "I was worried."

"I'm sorry."

"Don't you have any consideration for me at all?"

"Yes, of course."

"Didn't you remember that I had bought steak?"

"No ma'am."

". . . that I had spent the extra ration stamps and the money to give you a specially nice dinner? And you didn't appreciate it even enough to come home for it!"

"I forgot."

"You forgot. Well *I* didn't forget. You wouldn't like it at all if I forgot, would you? Your supper has been waiting for an hour."

"I'm sorry."

"You have no consideration for me at all. You run around with that stupid Cecil and flirting with the little Catholic hussy from down the road, but you don't think of me at all. *You* have *your* friends all the time, but I'm here all *alone*. Do you understand what that means, *alone*? Your father is away, heaven only knows where, but you seem to have no sense of responsibility whatsoever. I need company, too, whether you realize it or not. And I think your father would be very disappointed if he knew how you're behaving. Now go wash your hands so you can eat your cold supper."

In that moment, the intensity of her anger and hurt became the most painful experience of my entire life. There were no words to describe the depth of my despair. I think I saw myself then as a total failure, a total infidel, totally unreliable, moved by forces that I could not control. I had failed myself and my love for Ruth Ann; I had failed my mother and forgotten my promise to my father, and in so doing, I had even failed my country and the war effort. I knew, of course, that Ruth Ann would never be able to see me again without a slight derisive giggle in her heart. *But then maybe it is all right,* I thought. *Maybe it is as it should be. Maybe I deserve punishment, deserve it for not being able to control my damned prick. And surely, I deserve punishment for letting Ruth Ann and my friends lead me away from my basic duty to my parents and the world at large.* And I think, for that night at least, I almost hated Ruth Ann for her power to tempt me.

I sat through a cold and silent supper with my mother, and afterward when I went to bed, I just lay there weeping at the thought of my worthlessness. I would do better, I resolved. I would. Somewhere deep inside, I felt that I had been burdened with more responsibility than was rightfully mine, but wasn't that true also for the men on the battlefield and the prisoners being tortured in concentration camps? The job was *to measure up*, no matter what the burden. I remember pressing my face into the tear-wet pillowcase and praying for forgiveness. I would do better. No matter what. I would take better care of my mother. I would never disappoint her again. I would find a way to make my father proud when he returned from the war.

Chapter Six

And almost immediately, out of my cloud of shame and chagrin, I began to make a major effort toward rehabilitation. For weeks I stayed close to home, doing penance, waiting and available to answer my mother's every call. I did yard work. I didn't even see Alfred except at those rare times when he would bring the lawn mower from his house to help me with the grass. And then, by that time, my mother was growing flowers, and she had me on my hands and knees cultivating and fertilizing, watering and pulling weeds while she supervised. She even got Alfred on his knees a couple of times, but he was always good about hearing his own mother's *call,* and he didn't stick around long for that sort of thing. Then, as the fall came on, my mother had me cleaning the house and polishing furniture. God, how I hated it! But I said nothing. I polished away. It was my duty. And I was a good Southern boy. My father had often quoted General Lee's dictum that, "Duty is the sublimest word in the English language." And I accepted it without question. I knew that I was not cut out to be a *homo domesticus,* but I framed everything in the context of the war: soldiers in the field obeyed orders whether they liked them or not; prisoners of war suffered torture rather than reveal military secrets. It was the least I could do to obey my father's orders and keep my mother happy by polishing the furniture or doing anything else she thought necessary to fight the war on the home front.

I didn't see Ruth Ann again until school started in the fall, but my mother did arrange for me to attend a church conference for young people at nearby Flora MacDonald College for several days while she went to visit her sister. I don't remember that I learned much about the Presbyterian Church or the Christian religion at the conference, but I did enjoy immediate relief from what Washington Irving called "petticoat government," and I did encounter three things that would influence my whole life.

One was that I met a number of very pretty girls from other parts of the state, and I was able to talk with them and enjoy their company. I wasn't in any way unfaithful to Ruth Ann, of course. But these girls allowed me to see that if Ruth Ann were unable to forgive the inappropriate intrusions of my wayward pecker, at least Ruth Ann was not the last girl on earth. There could still be hope after disaster. By this time, I had learned to control my penile problem by wearing tight Jockey shorts under my pants or a jock strap under my bathing suit when I went swimming. So, even though I was not always quiescent, especially when surrounded by pretty girls in skimpy suits at the pool, at least I was able to keep my embarrassment safely out of sight and myself out of trouble. Second, I met John, who, with Alfred, would become one of my very closest friends. We shared a room together for those few days, but even beyond that we tended to gravitate toward each other. We told the same kinds of silly jokes and made puns, and I came to realize that although John had two brothers, he—like Alfred and me—was very much an outsider. Except for my cousin Mary, he was the first person I had ever met whose parents were divorced. His older brother, Jack, whom John admired very much, had become a state champion field and track athlete and had already graduated from high school and was serving in the navy. His younger brother was living with his mother, and John was living with his father. I remember that we lamented together the death of one of Jack's closest friends who had become an Air Force pilot and had recently been shot down over the Pacific. We talked late into the night, speculating about the direction our own lives might take. We wondered if the war would still be there to involve us when we were older. And whether it was or not, we both wanted our lives to make a difference in the world. Just to disappear without making some kind of contribution seemed such a waste. *What could we do,* we wondered, *to make the world a better place?* I don't know whether or not such high-minded introspection was part of the plan of the conference organizers, but the air of the place was full of it. *Could we best serve as doctors, lawyers, writers, missionaries, teachers, or military leaders?* we asked. And whatever we became, the question was already prominent in our minds: *Who would be our mates? Who would be the girls and later the women who would share our lives?*

We didn't realize the significance of it at the time, of course, but we also shared very similar tastes in women. I had found a color photo of movie actress Maureen O'Hara taken as she came off the set after making a movie with Tyrone Power or Errol Flynn, and I stuck it on the wall for us to admire. There she stood with her red hair, flaring nostril, and heaving bosom, and we both thought she was divine. *Even with the red hair, Ruth Ann didn't look at all like Maureen O'Hara,* I thought, but then Ruth Ann was only a girl and I was just a boy. Maybe in a few years I would look more like Errol Flynn and Ruth Ann like Maureen O'Hara and we, too, could seek adventure, gold, and glory along the Spanish Main. Of such are the contradictory ideals and dreams of boys.

I was also awakened to another ideal during that brief church conference. It was the ideal of music—or I should say, music as I had never before heard it.

⟩ Now, I had listened to music from the radio all my life. I had learned the popular songs—especially those with a western motif—and sung them in my child's soprano. And later, after my voice had changed at age eleven, I had started singing the popular love songs of the era in my developing baritone— all for my personal pleasure, of course. It never occurred to me to sing for anybody else, unless maybe it was for my parents, and for them I only sang the cowboy songs or the funny songs that Spike Jones and his City Slickers or Phil Harris might turn out. This of course, was the era of Frank Sinatra, Bing Crosby, Ella Fitzgerald, Glenn Miller, the Dorsey brothers, Woody Herman, and Nat King Cole. It was also an era when a totally different world of music was easily available on commercial radio. At least once a week, NBC would present the NBC Symphony Orchestra conducted by Arturo Toscanini in full concert. On Saturday afternoons, we had a full Metropolitan Opera broadcast, and on Sunday afternoons, the Metropolitan Opera baritone, Robert Merril—often with Roberta Peters and Lili Pons—would present an hour of opera and light classics.

My mother had insisted that I take piano lessons when I had attended Saint Patrick's School. Although I'm sure I was an indifferent student, I had dutifully submitted to the teaching of a stern faced nun and had learned notation and a few easy pieces to play on the piano that my mother had inherited from her Aunt Annie. So we weren't exactly deprived of music. We just didn't have much chance to hear it in live performance. But that situation changed for me during that conference week.

Flora MacDonald College had a very good music conservatory and a dean named Robert Reuter who, when he was not teaching, traveled from town to town presenting piano recitals. There were no college students in residence during the summer, so Dean Reuter spent the time practicing and preparing the recitals he would perform in the winter. He was a gaunt and intense man who wore dark, form-fitting clothes and walked with a slight Byronic limp. For the first few days, I saw him only when he came in to provide accompaniment for one of the worship services. But one evening toward the end of the conference, I was walking by the conservatory with a dark haired girl named Jane McNair when we were both brought up short by the sound of the piano from inside. What was this? We moved quietly up the steps between the Doric columns that supported the porch, and there, through the window, we could see Dean Reuter alone beneath a single light on the stage of the empty auditorium, and I don't believe I have ever been privileged to observe greater spiritual concentration. The man was simply pouring his soul into the piano as he rehearsed a Chopin ballad. Later I think he played Debussy. But I had never heard anything like it. And I think it was on that night that I got my first glimpse of what great art can be, that it has the power to transport us into spiritual realms that we cannot reach any other way. And I knew that I wanted to be part of that world if I could possibly achieve it.

This was a lot of discovery for one brief period of less than a week, but I was twelve years old and hyper-tuned to everything that was going on around me. At the end, I truly felt like a different person. Yet there was one more event that I encountered that week that I was not quite able to process, and I'm not sure I can process it and reach any reliable conclusion about it even today. My mother was waiting to meet me at the church along with other parents when our conference group returned, and on our way home, she told me that she wanted to stop for a moment by Mr. Wiseman's office to pick up an insurance policy. I knew Mr. Wiseman. He was a member of our church and was pleasant to everybody, but he had always amused me because, with his large ears, he reminded me of Mickey Mouse with gray hair. He nodded frequently in agreement, even when nobody had said anything to agree with, and his eyes blinked as though someone had just surprised him in the dark and turned on the lights. Anyway, when we arrived, he greeted us warmly and invited us into his office where he laid out an insurance policy on the table and proceeded to explain the details. It was a policy on *my* life, it seemed. "And very inexpensive," Mr. Wiseman said, pointing out the advantage of buying life insurance at an early age. It was a mutual policy, he said, and "double indemnity"—which I understood to mean that it paid double if I happened to be killed in an accident or if I lost an arm or a leg. And he smiled when he said it. My mother, of course, was the beneficiary. "I'm buying this for you," she told me, "as a form of saving so you'll have an estate when you grow up. By then, it'll be all paid up, and you can decide whether you want to keep it, cash it in, or borrow from it in order to help with your education." This was all perfectly reasonable, of course. There was nothing that I as a twelve-year-old boy could say against it. Certainly, I had no illusions about my mortality. But there was something about it that made me feel very uncomfortable, even embarrassed, in the same way I'd felt uncomfortable on the night my mother had embraced me in the moonlight and told me how wonderful I was. But I couldn't name what it was, so I think I just smiled and mumbled in response. But I always saw Mr. Wiseman's Mickey Mouse smile somewhat differently after that, and I remember that I ended that eventful week with even more questions than I had possessed at the beginning.

Chapter Seven

The good news at the end of that summer was that Ruth Ann had not cast me into eternal outer darkness because of my childish lack of control. In fact, when school started, she actually seemed glad to see me. She came to greet me warmly on that first day when she saw me at the bus stop, and we sat together on the bus and walked together to school—without embarrassment. I think I felt rather as Lazarus must have felt when he was raised from the dead. Without a word being spoken, it was clear that my sins had been forgiven and that I had been granted a second chance. It was especially nice too, since Darlene seemed to like Alfred, and in the days and weeks that followed, the four of us formed one of the happiest groups I have ever been a part of.

Often on those golden autumn afternoons, we would meet after school and walk home, delighted to be out in the open surrounded by the turbulent colors of the trees and free of the noisy bus. We would walk first along the streets of the town, sometimes stopping at the Carolina Soda Shop, where all the older kids hung out, for a coke or ice cream. Then, we would walk on along Hay Street to the Market House and down Greene Street beneath the elms and the water oaks and on past the James Hogg Monument until the city street

The Fayetteville Market House.

turned into a county road, talking and laughing and telling stories for the length of the full four miles. And often, certainly while the afternoons were long, we would go and sit on Ruth Ann's front steps or on Darlene's porch until the very last minute before we *had* to go home.

Of course, I did not tell my mother about spending so much time with Ruth Ann. Her angry reference to Ruth Ann as that "little Catholic hussy" had stung me badly. Catholic Ruth Ann might be, but *hussy*—whatever the word meant— she certainly was not, and I did not, under any circumstances, want to hear my mother speak of her again. My desire to protect Ruth Ann from all enemies, public and private, included even my mother. I was outraged at her comment. But how does a twelve-year-old boy defend a girl against his own moth-

er—especially in time of war, during his father's absence—
when he is duty bound to honor, protect, and defend his
mother? In such a childhood question is found the basis for all
serious moral questions, those which force one to choose—
not between a good thing versus an evil thing, but between
two opposing *good* things.

However, at about this time, I came to see very clearly a
problem, which I had felt for my entire life—the conflict
between my mother and girls. She didn't talk about it to me
directly, but in hundreds of ways, whether by indirect comment or just by attitude, my mother had always led me to feel
that she just didn't want me to have anything to do with girls.
Time after time, in one of the stupid teasing ways in which
adults molest children, people—usually older men, but
women, too—had asked me in my mother's presence, "Who's
your sweetheart?" or "Have you got a sweetheart in school?"
And even before I would have a chance to hang my head and
mumble a response, my mother would interrupt as deftly as
though she were snapping dead buds off a flowering plant and
say, "We don't have *sweethearts*, Mr. Slocumb. We just have
friends, don't we, son?" And she would fume about this to me
afterward. "It's so silly even to *think* about children having
sweethearts." Up until the first grade, I had had no special dif-
ficulty letting her handle the problem of sweethearts. But
then, in the first grade, if you remember, I had met Marian
and my heart had been conquered, at least temporarily, as I
looked forward each day to kissing her on the cheek when the
teacher's back was turned. There was no doubt in my mind
then that Marian was my sweetheart, so if some adult buffoon
should challenge me with his silly question, I was fully ready
to chirp, "Marian, she's great." Except that my mother continued to impose her objection to the whole idea: "We *don't*
have 'sweethearts'!" I kept quiet, but it was then, I think, that
I first came to see that in some areas of life, my mother just
didn't know what she was talking about.

She had a set question, which I saw as the ultimate put-down and which she could direct toward anyone new that I happened to mention, but which she directed toward girls with particular venom: "What's *her* title to glory?"

It was the sort of question for which I, at eleven or twelve, could find no conceivable answer. I didn't really know what "glory" was or if the person concerned was entitled to it or even how one got a title to it. The question always reduced me to stumbling, speechless shrugs, so early on, I tried to avoid it by mentioning my friends as rarely as possible.

There was another dimension, however, that had crept in over the years and filled my heart with a kind of panic—my mother seemed to expect me to think of *her* as my sweetheart. She admired my father's brother, Brooks, who had never married, but had remained at home on the family farm taking care of his widowed mother. She delighted in telling me how Brooks would come in from work, pick up his mother, whirl her around, kiss her, and call her "his sweetheart." She thought it *so* romantic that my grandmother would "dress and primp" at the end of every day in order to look pretty for Brooks when he came in. "Just as though she were waiting to meet a new beau," my mother told me approvingly.

This was a quaint story, I felt, but it horrified me for reasons I was not yet able to put into words. And it horrified me even more when my mother would tell me directly how she looked forward to a time when I would grow to manhood and the two of us could travel together around the world and how I would always be there, like Brooks, to take care of her in her "advancing years." I don't know what she planned to do with my father while the two of us gallivanted around the globe. But as I remember it, these fantasies would come upon her most strongly when he was away from home somewhere on active duty. Maybe she was afraid that some day he would not return. But whatever the case, it became clear to me that *I*, no less than the contract on Mr. Wiseman's desk, was being prepared to serve as her insurance policy and that my life was being planned for me, without consultation, by forces that did not necessarily have my best interests at heart.

So I think it was during those few brief months of enjoyment with Ruth Ann that I began darkly to perceive of my mother as my enemy. She was kind to me, yes. She fed me, clothed me, and comforted me when I was sick, dressed me in nice clothes, and gushed over me when she showed me off to her friends. But somehow I felt that she was at war with a fundamental part of my makeup, a part that I had to defend whatever the cost. The words *eroticism* and *sexuality* were not words that I would have used at six or twelve. God knows, the idea of sex as a physical relationship was troubling enough all by itself. But the idea of *fidelity* was not difficult at all. It was certainly central to a nation in time of war, central to a boy or to any person seriously concerned about his religion and his relationship to God, or to anyone who loved another person. It was just that now, it seemed that I was being asked to be faithful to two opposing systems of value.

At six, when someone had asked me if I had a sweetheart, it had been a question of my mother versus Marian and I remained silent; at twelve, it became a question of my mother versus Ruth Ann. I still remained silent or tried to hide the relationship altogether, but in truth, I felt that it was really a question of my mother versus my *self*. And my decision, even at six, had been—regardless of my silence and no matter how many times I may have forgotten it in my life—that my fidelity to my *self* was more important than my fidelity to any other person or thing on earth. My mother was simply wrong; children *did* have sweethearts and they loved them very much. My mother was wrong, and she was opposed to something I felt to be precious. But even with her error, I would still have to honor her, obey her, and protect her. I would not, however, let her error keep me from loving someone else—a thing that seemed even more important to my life than loving my mother.

Of course, looking back now from the advantage of years, I believe I understand some of the unconscious forces that worked away in my mother. They made her at one and the same time both my preserver and my enemy. It was, at its simplest, an overwhelming fear of abandonment and loss. In 1901, when my mother was ten years old, her father had died, leaving behind a pregnant wife and seven children on the family farm. Within a year of his death, my mother's brother John burned to death after backing into an open fireplace and catching his clothes on fire. Their mother (my grandmother), who had already lost two other children, then bore her final child and immediately, for all practical purposes, lost her mind. Today we would say that my grandmother receded into profound depression, but for years she was totally incapable of functioning as a parent at all. This effectively meant that the children became orphans and that other members of the family had to see that they were taken in and provided for. My mother went to live with her Aunt Annie who by then had a growing medical practice in Charlotte and who saw that her brother's children were educated. My mother's survival with her aunt, then, appeared to be rather comfortable as she lived in the large city house on North Tryon Street and eventually graduated from one of the best woman's colleges in the area. But I believe that the profound collapse and loss of her family, combining in some strange way with her inherited Victorian reticence, influenced everything my mother felt and did for the rest of her life. This caused her to operate on what seemed to be two levels of existence at once: the attempt to grasp and the attempt to liberate. She hated my father's flying and had once asked him to stop because of its dangers, but she gave him her inheritance for his airport. She actually allowed me a lot of freedom, but she took out insurance policies on my life with herself listed as beneficiary. She apparently wanted me to have friends, but never wanted to lose me to another woman, especially not to "that little Catholic hussy from down the road." So, she planted in me the little capsules of venom that made me feel horribly unfaithful if I even looked admiringly in the direction of a pretty girl. My mother's childhood trauma and loss influenced everything she felt and did, but clearly those losses were beginning to have a ripple effect on everything that *I* felt and did, as well.

Of course, I understood nothing of all this at age twelve, and even if I had, it wouldn't have mattered. I would still have had to defend myself. But our unspoken yet palpable conflict filled me with enormous guilt. At one point, I even wished that my mother would die and release me from the pain of divided allegiance. And then I felt even worse. What a totally worthless human being I must be to allow such thoughts even to enter my mind! I wished my father would come home and take the pressure off. Maybe if he were there she could spend her energy on him; he would distract her, take care of her, and leave me free of the burden. But that was not to be for a good while yet. I was going to have to handle this one on my own. And as is the way of all weak or unenfranchised creatures when confronted by superior force, I resorted to deception.

Mind you, however, I did not lie—certainly not overtly, in any way. I couldn't have done it. My father had drilled into me from my earliest years always to tell the truth, no matter what the cost. The worst name you could call a man was *liar*. I couldn't have made my mouth speak a lie. But clearly, I saw also that *all* truths did not have to be told all the time. One could remain silent. And one could use tactics to divert an enemy. I think I learned a lesson directly from the wild birds that I had watched at nesting time, seeing a mother thrush flap and drag her wing on the ground, pretending to be injured in order to lure and divert a marauding cat away from her nestlings. So too, by dissimulation, I would protect my freedom and protect Ruth Ann from my mother's insults. I would also protect my mother from knowledge of my defection and myself from her anger. Thus I would deceive in order to be true. I would, in short, become a double agent in the service of love.

The turning point came at Halloween. These were the years before Trick or Treating was invented and most neighborhoods were on guard against the tricks that would inevitably come. Often on the morning after Halloween, people were likely to come out to search for their morning newspapers and find their yard furniture hanging from nearby trees and their car windows soaped with occult warnings or naughty words. I remember once that someone stole a goat and slipped him into the schoolhouse where he was found the next day eating notices off the bulletin boards. Nuisance stuff mostly. I don't remember anyone doing anything truly destructive. But one way to avoid the nuisance was to have a party for the neighborhood kids, and that year, the party in our neighborhood was held at Darlene's house.

It was nice, and my mother had no problem with my going to a nearby Halloween party. She was not an evil woman in any way, and actually, in another sharp contrast to her darker side, she approved of my having a social life. But of course, to avoid any possible embarrassment, I pointed out that I was going to the party with Alfred—which I did. Alfred and I went to Darlene's house together after first stopping by to pick up Ruth Ann on the way. I wore a mask and a cowboy hat like The Lone Ranger, and Ruth Ann wore a rhinestone tiara, a beaded dress, dark red lipstick, rouge, and mascara, and I thought she was the most beautiful thing ever created.

It was a warm October night with a full moon and absolutely cloudless skies. (I will carry these details clearly to my grave.) Eight or ten of us assembled in Darlene's backyard for the party. We roasted hot dogs and marshmallows over an open fire, drank cokes, and bobbed for apples in a galvanized tub. Some of us were even brave enough to try dancing to the music of Darlene's 78-RPM phonograph, which was hooked up by extension cords to a table on the patio. It was a lovely party, and I remember as I tried to dance with my hand in the small of Ruth Ann's back, that I felt I was becoming truly a man of the world.

It was the sort of party you wanted never to end, but since most of us were only twelve or thirteen, Darlene's mother began to wind things up about 9:30 or 10:00 P.M. Alfred, Ruth Ann and I stayed later than the others to help clean up, and then we persuaded Darlene's mother to let Darlene join us while we walked Ruth Ann home. She set a curfew and we told her we would walk Darlene back home on time, and off we went. What we did not tell her, of course—or anyone else for that matter, since they were strictly illegal in the state of North Carolina—was that, even when he was leaning over the open fire to cook hot dogs, Alfred's jacket pockets were loaded with firecrackers.

We told Darlene and Ruth Ann as soon as we were out of the house, and they thought it was *great,* giggling and dancing around in a circle the way teenaged girls do. And we immediately selected our targets and planned our tactics. We would go up to a house, ring the doorbell, and then as we heard someone coming to answer, we would light a firecracker and run for the shadows. When the timing was right, it was wonderful. The unsuspecting victim would walk seriously to the door and open it just as the fuse reached the firecracker—and BAM—it exploded right at his feet. Watching from the shadows, the four of us would go into paroxysms of laughter and run further into the darkness as our target's impotent curses trailed after us through the night.

Finally, the last target was best of all—Mr. Lyons' house. Mr. Lyons was a guard at the Veterans' Hospital, and on several occasions he had rather rudely ordered Alfred and me off the hospital grass. "I hate that son of a bitch," Alfred had told me one day. And this Halloween night seemed the perfect time to take our revenge. We had seen Mr. Lyons getting out of a car in front of his house, so we knew where it was and we went directly to it. "This one's all mine," Alfred told us. "Wait for me here behind the shrubs." Alfred also had some Lucky Strike cigarettes in his pocket, so first he lit a cigarette to have available for lighting the fuse, and then we followed the glowing coal as he moved forward in a low crouch as though he might have been a marauding Indian. For some reason, Mr. Lyons didn't have his front light on, and this made everything easier. Alfred laid the entire final string of firecrackers across the doorway and peeped through the glass panel as he rang the bell. After a moment, even from our hiding place at the street, we could see Mr. Lyons coming through the house dressed apparently in bathrobe and slippers as Alfred touched the glowing tip of his Lucky Strike to the fuse and disappeared into the darkness.

It was perfect! No sooner had Mr. Lyons opened the door than the first firecracker went off, and Mr. Lyons leapt straight up about two feet in the air. "God Almighty! Jesus Christ! Son of a bitch!" He was screaming and cursing and whirling around like a dervish with loose bowels as the next firecracker went off, and then the whole string started to go: BAM BAM BAM, rat-tat-tat-tat-tat-tat-tat-tat like a machine gun assault. Mr. Lyons tried to stamp out the rest of the firecrackers, but it was too late, and we could hear them continuing to go off under his feet as the four of us burst from the sheltering shrubbery and disappeared into the pine thicket across the street.

I don't believe I ever laughed more in my life. You would have thought we had won the war single handedly. And five minutes later when we reached the Confederate breastworks that ran across hospital property, we were exhausted. We just flopped like a litter of puppies on the pine tags and lay there gasping for breath in the moonlight.

An old pine forest is a wonderful place anytime. The pine tags have a way of subduing the undergrowth, creating the effect of an extended brown carpet—soft, fragrant, and silent.

On that October night with the distant hint of wood smoke in the air, as we gradually subsided from the roil of our laughter, I think it was the most wonderful spot in the world. We had fallen into a hollow, which, nearly a century earlier, had been scooped from the earth as a defilade emplacement for Confederate artillery. It was especially soft from the years of collected pine tags, and I wonder sometimes now what old General Johnson would have thought if he could have looked into the future and seen four mischievous teenagers finding rest and shelter in the moonlight where once his cannon had waited to blast marauding Yankees into smithereens. I think I must have sensed the irony of it all even then, but there was absolutely no time to think about this dimension of our existence because in a very brief time after our arrival, Ruth Ann rolled over and laid her head on my chest.

For a few moments, I was stunned to *total* speechlessness. My heart was pounding even more rapidly than the rat-tat-tat of the firecrackers under Mr. Lyons' feet. My lungs were suddenly constricted, and for a long time, in the dreamlike atmosphere of it all, I didn't dare move. Something enormously important was happening, and looking back on it now after half a century, I can truly attest that *that* was one of the transforming moments of my life: Ruth Ann had laid her head on my chest! Gradually, I developed sufficient courage to look down. She was still wearing her tiara, and it sparkled and glistened in the moonlight. In the unworldliness of the moment, I could well have been Theseus or Oberon or even Bottom the Ass lying spellbound beside Titania, Queen of the Fairies in Shakespeare's forest of Athens. On the opposite side of our artillery position, I could see Alfred lying with *his* head on Darlene's chest, but they were just talking away as though completely unaware that something magical was taking place around them, and I gave them no more thought.

Ruth Ann's head was in the hollow of my shoulder. I could smell the fragrance of her hair, rich and clean like the newly cut hay in Mr. Early's field, and cautiously, as my courage increased, I allowed my right arm to close gently around her shoulder. She didn't jerk away in indignation as one might have feared; she actually seemed to like it and snuggled closer, and she looked up at me expectantly, her face such a scant few inches from mine that I was further overwhelmed by the scent of her lipstick.

It was *the* moment of decision, and for a brief time, I was paralyzed with fear. I had seen men and women kiss with great passion in the movies, but I also had seen and heard many stories of how women slapped men's faces or simply rose in indignation and left the scene forever when a man presumed too much. What if I should lose her by going too far and not showing enough respect? And then, as though abandoning thought altogether, I leaned down and kissed her on the lips.

I swear to you, I saw lightning, zigzag yellow bolts of lightning streaking through the boiling clouds that now filled the space where once my brain had been. I might have kissed Marian on the cheek when I was six, but never in my life had I kissed a girl on the lips, and I thought I had entered heaven. Ruth Ann not only remained comfortably where she was, she actually threw her arm tightly around my neck and pressed my lips even more firmly against hers.

Mind you, we were children. Our lips were closed tight and our kisses dry as the Sahara desert. The moist sexual invitations of older lovers would have horrified us both and would remain something to discover far in the future. But I think that at age twelve, even with dry kisses, the passion and intensity of that moment was no less than the passion and intensity of adults. And I know beyond a doubt that on that night, on a carpet of pine tags in an abandoned Confederate gun emplacement, beneath a canopy of long leaf pines backed by a hunter's moon, my life was changed forever by my first discovery of passionate correspondence.

For the next month, Ruth Ann became my *total* preoccupation. Oh yes, I continued to go to school and do my homework. I continued to take the piano lessons that I had resumed in the fall. I continued to play the trumpet—inspired by Harry James—which I had begun to play in the Junior High School marching band. I even continued to go hunting with Alfred, and now that football season was over, John came out and joined us on our forays into the woods. But through and beyond and beneath it all was the image of Ruth Ann's tiara adorned face, firing and inspiring an excitement to my activities that they had never before possessed. And I saw her as often as I could—not only before and after school, but also in the evenings after dark. It was difficult to arrange, but we were inventive, and we were helped by the fact that Ruth Ann had begun babysitting for the children of the doctors who worked at the Veterans' Hospital. Her own father was an army doctor who also held a specialist's appointment at the veterans' facility, so the local families came to know her and call on her often. Frequently on our way home from school, she would tell me she was scheduled to sit for the Highsmiths or the Greenbergs who lived close by. "I'll call you soon as I get the kids to sleep," she would whisper close to my ear.

So I would work early, finish my homework and my piano practice, and be ready when her call finally came. And when it did, I would disguise my enthusiasm and try to make my voice sound perfectly neutral, if not actually laconic or bored. Then I would turn to my mother and say, "Mom, I'm going up to Alfred's for a few minutes. I'll be right back."

Since my homework and chores were finished, and since these sojourns rarely lasted more than an hour, she usually had no objection, so off I'd go on my bicycle. And I *did* go to Alfred's. I always went where I said I was going. But I just stayed there long enough to give Alfred the Greenberg's phone number and tell him to call me if my mother checked up on me. The whole circuit lasted no longer than ten minutes. And then I would appear at the Greenberg's door where Ruth Ann would greet me with enthusiastic kisses and lead me to the sofa where, for the next twenty minutes, we would be locked in such racking embrace you would have thought that the entire future of the globe depended on our being together. Then, always punctual, I would interrupt our still pristine kisses, check the Benrus waterproof watch that my parents had given me for Christmas, say an agonized farewell on the Greenberg's front steps, and arrive back at my own house in plenty of time to run my still trembling hands casually over the piano keyboard once more before I told my mother good-night.

We played several variations on this scheme. Sometimes Ruth Ann would call Alfred, and he would then call me or even walk down to get me. And since he was running this same kind of caper with Darlene, we served each other well, keeping watch, running interference, and covering for each other whenever we needed it.

And then it all ended. Not quite overnight, but almost. I found Ruth Ann slumped in a seat of the school bus one cloudy November morning right before Thanksgiving, and she was looking so gray and deflated that I knew in an instant something was wrong. She wasn't even wearing her usual rose-colored American Beauty lipstick. "What's the matter?" I asked. "Are you sick?" And she just shook her head. She tried to smile, but couldn't quite make it work.

"We've been transferred," she said.

"What? When?" Since Halloween, I had been so intense-ly focused on Ruth Ann that I'd almost forgotten the war and that both our fathers and, consequently, *we* were involved in it. But now it hit me again with all its vengeful fury.

"My Dad's been ordered to Fort Sam Houston in Texas," she said, "to work in the hospital there. He's supposed to report next week."

"Are you going?"

She nodded. "The army's going to move us."

For a moment, I thought I was going to faint. I saw spots in front of my eyes and everything looked kind of watery. I wanted to say something, but my mouth just wouldn't work and it was probably just as well because all the combined volumes in the local library could not have begun to express what I was feeling at that moment. We had always carefully avoided showing any outward sign of our affection in public, but on that morning, the only form of communication I could muster was to let my hand fall over hers on the seat between us. I remember that her fingers were ice cold, and I remember that we did not speak again during that entire trip to school.

We all assembled to say goodbye when Ruth Ann's family moved out ten days later. Darlene, Alfred, and I sat on the steps or stood around trying to make jokes with Ruth Ann as the moving men loaded furniture and household goods into a van. And then Ruth Ann's house was empty. We all just stood there and shrugged. Her brothers were in the car, and her mother was calling from the curb as Ruth Ann lingered with us in the yard. My arms and my chest were quite literally aching to crush her to me in one final embrace, but standing directly under her mother's watchful eye, I simply couldn't do it and neither could she. I think maybe our fingertips touched as I handed her my mailing address.

"I don't know our new address yet," she told me, "but I'll send it to you as soon as I get there." And then she was in the car, waving and throwing us collective kisses as her mother turned in the driveway. "I'll write," she called. "I'll write." And then we just stood and watched the car as it grew smaller and smaller in the distance.

When they were at last out of sight, Darlene said, "Why don't you guys come on by my house for a coke, and maybe we'll listen to some records or somethin'."

But I didn't much feel like it. "No thanks," I said. "I guess I need to get on home." And I left them there and walked on across the hospital property and along the Confederate breast-works, feeling the pine tags slick underfoot and lingering for a moment by the fateful gun emplacement, seeing Ruth Ann with her tiara as she had been on Halloween and seeing her now anew as she waved from the departing car. "I'll write," she had said. "I'll write."

But she never did.

Chapter Eight

I went through the rest of that fall in a kind of daze, a state of numbness. I did my schoolwork, I practiced my music, and I spent a lot of time in the woods. But the shine had vanished from everything. And I think that neither my mother nor Alfred nor anyone else had the slightest idea what I was thinking or feeling. It was just not the sort of thing a person talked about, after all. What would I have said? "I feel desolate?" And what does another person say to a twelve-year-old boy who feels desolate? Maybe, "Try some warm milk and cookies and you'll feel better in no time." I would rather keep it to myself, thank you. So I read more and I began to write things.

In my English class we were reading the short stories of Edgar Allan Poe, and I became fascinated with his bizarre syntax and vocabulary and, ultimately, with the music of his language—"The Cask of the Amontillado," "The Fall of the House of Usher," "Ligeia," the poems, "Ulalume," "Annabel Lee," "The Bells," and of course, "The Raven" with its "lost Lenore." Poe, it seemed to me, knew what lost love was all about. I had no real idea of the complexity of what I was reading, of course, but I knew it spoke to me in a very profound way, and I suddenly wanted to write something of my own. I had begun writing verses and rhymes at about age seven or eight, but now I wanted to write something different. And I began to write long effluences, which were driven totally by emotion. I wouldn't call these pieces either stories or poems in the usual sense—maybe "tone poems" would fit them better because they were tied directly to music. Often on a Sunday afternoon, I would listen to Toscanini and the NBC Symphony with a notebook in front of me and write page after page in my looping circular script as long as the music possessed me. And the best part was that afterward, I *liked* what I had written. Of course, I was trying to imitate Poe, but we all imitate somebody to start with, and I thought Poe was a pretty good model.

At about this same time, I also began to investigate some of the old books in my parents' bookcase. My mother had kept her school copies of Milton and Shakespeare, both of which were printed on glossy pages and contained numbers of steel engravings. I especially remember an engraving of Satan in *Paradise Lost*, which depicted Satan gazing in longing at the glowing gates of Heaven, which he would never again be allowed to enter. And in the Shakespeare book, there was an engraving of Venus, bare breasted, raising her arms in lamentation for Adonis, whose lifeless body lay across her lap forming a kind of pagan *Pieta*.

All of these stories and pictures of separation, longing, and loss tore me to the backbone. I identified with each of them. I even saw Satan as the beautiful fallen angel he was and pitied him his loss of Paradise. But the soft flesh of the lamenting goddess of love moved me in ways I had never before imagined—highly erotic, highly spiritual, and deeply painful all at once. It was almost more than I could bear. The vision of female suffering seemed somehow even greater than male suffering. But all in all, I think that in some miraculous way—

which is the province of art—these stories and pictures worked together to sustain me in my own silent world of lamentation. And then there were my two friends.

I did not become a totally retiring introvert. Both Alfred and John joined me from time to time for trips into the woods. And I remember that once, even though winter was coming on, we went on a camping trip along the Cape Fear River, walking first northward along the Rockfish and Norfolk railroad to a point where Carver's Creek flowed into the river. It was a good fishing spot in summer and a quiet watering hole for game year-round. I remember that one of us shot a rabbit on the way up, which we skinned and cooked over an open fire for supper. But the real quarry that we brought home from that trip was Indian arrowheads and pottery shards. The rain had fallen heavily in those early days of December, and the banks along the watershed to the Cape Fear had washed, unearthing a trove of Indian artifacts, suggesting that there might once have been a village on the very spot where we were camping. None of us had ever even heard of Indians living along those shores of the upper Cape Fear, and now we were holding in our hands the fragments of pottery, arrowheads, tomahawk heads, and spearheads—the remnants of a vanished people. "They weren't included in any history book I ever read," John pointed out. And I realized that, so far as our world was concerned, it was as though these people whose work I held in my hands had never existed, that they had been born to live their own lives and create their own form of civilization and disappear from the earth leaving no trace beyond their broken cook wear and their beautifully etched weapons.

We washed the mud off the things we had found, and then that night after we had eaten our rabbit supper, we sat there and looked at our trophies beside the campfire. It was a kind of spooky time for all of us, I think, as though we were in the presence of very real, but unseen forces, and I remember feeling jumpy and nervous over any unexplained sound I heard in the woods around us. One arrowhead was razor sharp, made with a jeweler's precision from nearly transparent flint, and I held it up against the firelight. "How did they do it?" I asked. And we speculated about methods of chipping or dripping cold water in a pattern on hot stone. But no theory seemed adequate to explain the precise edging and sharpness. "What makes a people disappear?" I asked.

"These," Alfred said. And he held up another arrowhead and a spearhead on the other side of the fire. "They might have been good enough once, but they couldn't stand up against gun powder."

"You think we killed 'em?"

"Sure we killed 'em," Alfred said. "If you ain't got the right weapons, you ain't got shit. Just ask the guys goin' up against the Japs and the Germans."

"Is it always gonna be that way?" John asked.

"What else is gonna keep the Japs and the Germans from takin' over the world?"

"That's not what I meant," John said. "I mean, are we ever going to be able to talk to each other instead of killin' each other?"

I would learn over the next year that such a question was pure John, the peacemaking middle son sandwiched between two brothers on one side and two warring parents on the other—a boy always looking for the middle ground of peace. And yet, I had glimpsed another side of John bursting forth almost frighteningly on afternoons when Ruth Ann and I had watched the junior varsity football practice. We had seen him charging through the line and knocking opponents aside with such ferocity that one might have thought the entire national war effort depended on his carrying the football across the goal.

"I mean," John said, "one day the war will end. How do we keep it from happening again? And how do we do something that has lasting value so we won't just disappear like the people who made these arrowheads?"

"We *are* going to disappear," Alfred said. "One day we'll be just as dead as they are."

"Unless we create something that outlives us," I said.

"And what's that gonna be?"

"You love music," John said to me. "Maybe you can create lasting music. But Alfred and I don't have talents like that. What are *we* going to do?"

It was a new way of thinking for me. Of course, all along I had wondered which way my life would go, whether I would be a soldier, a cowboy, a pilot, or a doctor, things like that. But I had never thought of myself as having a "talent" that anyone else could notice. I just did things I liked to do. But John's statement made me feel kind of strange. Both of them were older than I, and yet he was saying I had something they didn't have. I wasn't sure I wanted to be pointed out as *different*, at least not by them. These were my friends, after all, and my pleasure was in finding ways we were alike.

I'm not sure how we resolved that conversation, if indeed we ever resolved it, but I remember that so much of the time we spent in the woods—both then and in later years when we traveled up the river by boat—would be spent in this kind of metaphysical speculation. What was valuable? What would last? Where would we invest our lives so that we, too, might last? And at this stage—although Ruth Ann still occupied much of my thought—there was very little talk of girls. That would come later.

But all of these things—the music, the writing, the literature, and our contemplation of a vanished people in the forest—all worked together to help cure the wound left in me by Ruth Ann's abrupt departure and by my father's continued absence, which I realize now had left me feeling defenseless. Maybe it all worked together to make me feel humble, maybe it introduced me to a new understanding of life's reality, but at the very least, it showed me that I was not alone and that others before me had loved and lost even more than I had. So I began to see my life with a new perspective. And I valued my beautiful flint arrowhead as though it had been encrusted with diamonds.

Chapter Nine

A few days after we returned from our camping trip, John came to visit me driving his father's 1941 Ford V-8. I knew he had only his learner's permit, so I was surprised to see him driving alone. "How'd you get the car?" I asked.

"Oh, my dad's gone to a party," he said. "So I thought I'd take the car and go visiting."

I rode with him up to Alfred's house, and Alfred was very impressed with the Ford. He already had his driver's license, but his family owned only a 1938, six cylinder Chevrolet, and this Ford was one of the hottest cars on the road. "Let's take it out for a spin," he said. And he talked John into letting him drive.

The wartime speed limit was only thirty-five miles per hour, but in a matter of seconds, Alfred had the Ford's speedometer touching eighty. "Wahoo!" he yelled. "Now that's power!" But John calmed him down, and we cruised back home at a more sedate speed. "What did you do, steal the keys from your dad?" Alfred asked.

And John said, "Yeah. Sort of. I took them out of his coat pocket when he was getting dressed. But he knows I've got 'em."

"What do you mean 'he knows' you got 'em?"

"I drove him to this party and promised to pick him up."

"And he let you drive without a permit?"

"He didn't have any choice," John said. "See, last year, he totaled a car on the way home, and we found him upside down in a ditch. So this year, I told him he had to let me drive or I'd throw the keys away."

"Oh."

And then John changed the subject abruptly, "Listen, I've got a job working at the House of Flowers florist shop for the Christmas holidays," he said. "They need more people, and they're paying forty cents an hour. Why don't you guys come to work there?" It was a thing I had never considered, but forty cents an hour in 1943 seemed like a king's ransom. "We could have a good time," John said.

Alfred said he couldn't do it because he was going to visit his grandfather in Virginia for Christmas, but I thought it would be a great idea. "I'll ask my mom," I said. "But I'm sure it'll be all right."

And then it was time for John to go pick up his father. "You want us to go with you?" Alfred asked. And he said it in a way that made me feel like he knew something I didn't.

"No," John said. "That's all right."

"Come on," Alfred said. "We'll keep you company, and then you can be our chauffeur and drive us home. Besides, since I've got my license, it's legal for you to drive with me in the car."

"Okay," John said. "Okay. Maybe that would be good." So I called my mother to tell her what we were doing and we headed for town.

The Collier's house on Oak Ridge Avenue was brightly lit with Christmas colors, and when we arrived we could hear music from inside. "Sounds like they're havin' a good time," Alfred said.

"Yeah," John said. "I'll go get him. I hope it won't take long."

"It's not cold. We'll wait," Alfred said. And then, after John was gone, Alfred lit up one of his Lucky Strikes. "I'm not gonna give you one," he said to me. "You're too young."

"Aw, I've smoked before."

"Yeah, well you didn't get it from me. Maybe after you turn thirteen next week I'll give you one."

I shrugged and we waited. And then, after no more time than it took Alfred to smoke that cigarette, we could see John coming out of the house holding his father's arm, escorting the stumbling man toward the car with the force and dispatch that a policeman might use to evict a trespasser.

John's father was what might be called a congenial drunk. And I would learn over the years that his drunken congeniality was actually an extension of his sober congeniality. He liked everybody, he was polite to everybody, and he was cordial to everybody. I'm sure he was a successful real estate and insurance salesman because he had the ability when he was sober of concentrating on a person with such intensity that he made you feel like you were the most important person in the world. And then, when he was drunk, he not only liked everybody, he *loved* everybody. He wanted to hug people and show them how much he loved them. It was as though he was afraid that one day his friends would go off and leave him and his life would collapse if he didn't embrace them. But on that night, I could hear him complaining to John all the way across the yard, "John, it's too early! I haven't seen everybody yet. I'm not ready. I don't want to go!"

"Come on," John said. "You're going."

Although I had only seen drunkenness depicted in the movies, I had no doubt what I was seeing in John's father. Yet both Alfred and I got out of the car and stood respectfully to meet him as though nothing were wrong.

We shook hands, and then, reeking of Jack Daniels or Wild Turkey, Mr. S___ had to hug each one of us. "Boys, boys," he said, "I'm so glad to see you at last!" He spoke with a mellifluous and carefully polished Southern speech, "John has told me about you. And I'm so glad you're getting him out in the woods. Every boy needs to spend time in the woods."

John opened the passenger door and pushed his dad into the seat with probably a little less ceremony than I thought he might deserve, and we headed toward John's house with his father lighting up one cigarette after another and gently railing the whole way: "You know, John, I'm really mad at you for doing this—embarrassed me in front of my friends."

"Yes sir," John said.

"I mean, you're my son and you're supposed to do what I tell you."

"Yes sir."

"You live in my house.

"Yes sir."

"You're driving my car. And I'm the one who says what happens in my house and who drives my car."

"Yes sir."

"And I'm Goddamned mad at you for doing this to me."

"Yes sir. I know."

When we arrived at the house, Alfred and I followed the two of them inside with Alfred following as though he might have been a backup policeman just behind John's dad. Where Alfred got his experience I never found out, and in all the years I knew him, he never revealed the slightest hint.

"It's time for you to go to bed," John said to his dad.

"Like hell it is! I'm going back to that party."

"No you're not," John said.

And he folded his dad's arm in a chicken wing hold behind his back and pushed him toward the bedroom, with his father shouting all the way, "I am not going to bed, Goddamn it! You let go of me! How dare you treat me this way in front of your friends!"

Alfred and I looked at each other and let them go on down the hall by themselves, and then in just minutes, everything was silent. After a time, John came back alone and just stood there, pale, in the hallway looking at us. "He passed out," he said. And then he said, "I'm sorry." And in spite of everything he could do to fight against them, there were suddenly tears streaming down his cheeks.

"Aw, you haven't got anything to be sorry for."

"Why does he do it?" John asked. "Why does he do it? Goddamn it! I love the man. You understand that? I love the man. He's a wonderful guy. And then he does this!"

I don't remember what Alfred and I said then. I just know we stood there making noises, trying to be helpful until John finally got hold of himself and said, "Come on, I'll take you home."

"Give me the keys," Alfred said. "I'll drive." And John handed them over without even a hesitation. "And you're going to spend the night at my house," Alfred said.

"No, I can't," John said. "I've got to come back. He may need me."

"No he won't," Alfred said. "If he wakes up, he'll only hassle you. And if he finds the keys to the car . . ." He shrugged. "Let me put it this way. If you want to get these keys back tonight, you'll have to fight me for 'em."

Oh, the anguish of boys over their fathers! My own time would come far sooner than I knew, and I wouldn't have anything so visible as a bottle to blame for the problem. But on that night, as Alfred flipped the keys in the air and challenged John to fight him for them, we all laughed suddenly and then went home. And as with so many other things that happened during those years, I don't believe any of us ever mentioned that night again. But I went home knowing far more about human love and friendship than I would ever be able to put into words.

Chapter Ten

Two days after my thirteenth birthday, I began work (My very first job!) at the House of Flowers. In many ways, it was for me the beginning of a new era. Not only would I be discovering the freedom that came with earning my own money, but I was also about to meet people totally unlike anyone I had ever even dreamed of before. I was also about to discover, in those closing days of 1943, that in the eyes of some people at least, I was little more than a piece of convenient meat.

Now, for the sake of full understanding, I need to describe myself at that time. And suffice it to say, I was not at all what I appeared to be. I was by then a good five-feet-ten-and-one-half inches tall and I had begun shaving. In addition, during the previous year and without ever having to go through the traditional "squeaky" stage, my voice had fully changed into a baritone that pleased even me. And to the basic framework, I had done a lot to develop my own body.

Though I'd never been overwhelmed with a passion for athletics as such, I did admire individual feats of strength and skill such as those displayed in field and track events. I had done some pole vaulting and high jumping and rope climbing, and I had thought I was pretty strong. But during the previous year when I had heard that an upperclassman nicknamed "Brute" could actually do 120 pushups, I had taken it as a personal challenge. And without telling anybody, I had begun a private program of daily exercise to beat "Brute." I started by doing ten pushups and then adding one every day or two. And although I still had a long way to go before I would reach my eventual goal of doing 125 pushups every morning before breakfast, I was already well on the way, doing about 50 each morning, when I started work at the House of Flowers.

All this is by way of saying that while I was in fact a naive and callow thirteen-year-old on the inside, many people looking from the outside just assumed I was seventeen or eighteen, and I never corrected them. When I applied at the House of Flowers, Jack Jordan, the owner, didn't even ask if I had reached the legally required age of fourteen before putting me to work. Nor did he ask if I had a driver's license. He just assumed these things. And the first time he tossed me the keys and told me to take the company truck and drive to the Point Sandwich Shop to pick up lunch for everybody, I thought I was in heaven. Oh, I had driven the family car—mainly in the driveway of my parents' house, driving backward, forward, and turning around and occasionally driving around the block with my mother in the car. But being liberated to drive alone on the public highway was like being released from prison. And I knew I was going to love my new job.

I didn't get to drive a lot, since there were older and more experienced workers there who took care of most of it, but I felt like part of a team. I was available for anything, whether it was helping with deliveries, meeting customers in the front of the store, trimming flower stems, or helping decorate churches. I had never imagined how busy a florist shop could be during a holiday season, but that wartime Christmas, the

House of Flowers was operating nearly twenty-four hours a day, filling orders not only for the normal number of funerals and holiday parties, but also adding to that the demands of literally hundreds of additional weddings being celebrated by couples who found themselves in a world at war, which no longer allowed them the luxury of long engagements. There were three full-time floral arrangers, and they produced new arrangements as fast as the rest of us could get the supplies to them and load the truck for deliveries.

John and I worked together some of the time, but it seems to me now that I rarely saw him except on afternoon breaks when we would go next door to the Merita Bakery and buy a loaf of hot bread right out of the oven for ten cents. We would sit out back and slather that bread with butter we kept in the cooler at the back of the store, and then we would wash it down with a pint of milk.

I soon realized that at the same time John and I were eating our afternoon bread and milk in the back of the store, Jack Jordan and the florists would be opening an afternoon fifth of whiskey at their work stations in the center of the store. That first bottle would last them until about suppertime when Mr. Jordan would order food brought in for everybody who was working late, and then he would start on the second bottle of the day, this one mainly for himself. It was as though an alcohol burner fueled his energy for the entire holiday season, at least until about 9 P.M. when he would order a "Bromoseltzer" to put out the excess heat. I remember watching him shape a corsage of delicate cymbidiums while his "Bromo" bubbled and fizzed on the table beside him and then frothed down his chin and arms as he drank it.

Now although these were certainly busy and rushed times, I would often find myself alone at the back of the store during the afternoons when the others were out making deliveries. My job was to cut flower stems and wire them with wooden spikes to keep them upright, and to help relieve the tedium, I would burst into song to entertain myself. It was a time when "Spike Jones and his City Slickers" was a popular comic band—certainly with us twelve and thirteen-year-olds—and I had learned all of "Cocktails for Two," complete with sound effects as performed by Spike Jones. So while I trimmed flowers with one of the wickedly curved box cutter knives that Mr. Jordan had provided for us, I would sing away in the back of the store. Until one afternoon when I thought I was alone and I suddenly heard Jack Jordan yelling from his work station up front, "Who the hell is that singing back there?"

It was about 4:30 P.M., so he had just opened his first bottle of the day and was feeling kind of mellow, and he charged back with his stained green hands full of roses and said, "Is that you?"

And I said, "Yes sir."

"Well, hell's bells, don't keep it all in the back of the store. Come entertain the rest of us," he said. And he grabbed my sleeve and pulled me up to the worktable where the other florists were slaving away. "Now," he said, "we're gonna take a break while we're entertained by Mr. Spike Jones himself." And he poured the others a shot of whiskey and they all stood or sat back and watched expectantly as I began.

I don't know where I found the chutzpa to do it. I must have been in one of my silly thirteen-year-old moods, but I plunged fully into "Cocktails For Two" with all the sound effects: "In some secluded rendezvous that overlooks the avenue—putta put, put, putta put, put put!" I gave that song a full dress burlesque presentation from one side of the room to the other. Even when I heard the other guys coming in from their last delivery, I didn't let them distract me, and by the time I finished, Jack Jordan was literally rolling on the floor with laughter. I've never had a more appreciative audience. There were tears streaming down his face and he was holding his sides. "God damn!" he said when it was over, "I'm gonna call you up here to do that and cheer me up every time

I feel pissed off about something." And he did, as a matter of fact. From time to time all through the rest of that season, he would find me in the back and beckon me up to the front of the store. "Sing it," he would say.

"What?"

"Hells bells! Just sing it!" And I would belt away. It was sort of like Rick and Sam in the movie *Casablanca*: "Play it, Sam. Just play it."

I learned some other Spike Jones tunes to keep things interesting, but "Cocktails For Two" was always Mr. Jordan's favorite. Even years later, he would see me somewhere and say, "Come on, just one line, just sing me one line of "Cocktails For Two."

So I was feeling pretty good by the time I finished my first stint as court jester and went back to trimming flowers that afternoon. But I was about to discover a whole new world of complications resulting from my one moment in the spotlight. As I came through the doorway into the back room, Clarence, the only black employee in the store, was leaning casually against the wall picking his teeth with a match stick and looking at me with a flat gaze that conveyed nothing less than total hatred. The look in his yellow eyes alone was enough to set me back, but when he spoke just above a whisper in a voice that only I was able to hear, I felt a chill all the way down my backbone. "You think you some kinda smart-assed white boy, don'tcha?"

"What?" I said. I couldn't believe what I had just heard. I had hardly even realized that Clarence was black, and I had never heard anybody speak to a person of another race and point out the racial differences. It just wasn't polite. And then, Clarence repeated himself: "I said, 'You some kinda smart-assed white boy, ain'tcha?'"

It was another one of those questions for which there is no answer, like my mother's favorite question of, "What's her title to glory?" To respond to it is to make yourself look stupid, but to ignore it is to offend the questioner. It's always a challenge. And in this case, I realized that the challenger was just waiting to be offended.

In my confusion, I think I just shrugged and said, "No," and started to walk away, but Clarence wasn't going to let me off so easily.

"No, what?" he said. "You ain't a smart-ass or you ain't a white boy?"

I raised my pink-fleshed hand and looked at it. "I ain't a white boy," I said. "What do you think?" And I kept on going.

But that challenge from Clarence had instantly changed everything around me. My cheeks and ears were suddenly hot and my heart was pounding. Every muscle of my body was electrified and alert. And suddenly as I went back to work, I felt a strange new sense of protective comfort as I closed my fingers around the handle of my work knife and sliced downward with its hooked blade. Surprise. Anger. Confusion. I sliced through whole sheaves of flower stems and sent their stalks shooting across the floor like small spears. *Had I acted like a coward or had I done the right thing? And what was the right thing?* I wondered. *Should I say anything more or just let it go? What if it happens again?*

My father had always told me that most bullies were cowards and that if anyone tried to bully me, I should just haul off and punch him in the jaw as hard as I could. And indeed, I had successfully ended several confrontations with other boys in the schoolyard just that way. But this was not a schoolyard and Clarence was not a boy. He was twenty-three years old and he had massive shoulders and thick, powerful hands, and he walked with the flat-footed and self-confident truculence of a prizefighter, like a middleweight Mike Tyson.

And had he actually bullied me, anyway?

Of course, these questions and feelings followed me home at the end of the day. I replayed the scene again and again as I rode the bus. I was so preoccupied at dinner that I could hardly carry on a conversation with my mother. My thoughts kept me tossing and sleepless far into the night, and then, after I finally did manage to fall asleep, they woke me up again and again and forced me to imagine every possible scenario that could play out between Clarence and me. But nothing was solved, and in the morning, all my misgivings were assembled and floating over my shoulder like a dark and foreboding cloud of apprehension as I reluctantly caught the bus and returned to a job, which only one day earlier, I had approached with a sense of joy.

Just why Clarence had focused his venom on me I could not imagine. Surely, I knew that from the beginning I had not liked Clarence because he was surly and profane in the extreme. But I had not done anything knowingly to show my dislike, and during the first days of my job at the House of Flowers, we had worked side by side without any trouble. Yet, in his constant flow of obscenity, blasphemy, and tales of mayhem, Clarence was clearly different from any other black person I had ever known.

Looking back now with the benefit of years, I realize that for a white boy growing up in the American South, I had actually known very few black people. But—starting with Etta, Teeny, "Uncle" Sandy, and including even Sam, the purveyor of shocking sexual news—the black people I had known had been kind and gentle. And in truth, at an earlier age, I think I was hardly aware of color difference at all. Etta taught me a lot and Teeny was my first playmate. I loved Teeny, and often Etta had taken me with them to their unpainted tenant house on the outskirts of the Stubbs' farm where Teeny and I played in the woods. I think if anything, I was more conscious of dialect difference than of color difference, but that didn't bother me because even the neighboring white people spoke a dialect different from my parents, so it seemed normal. I enjoyed visiting Teeny's house because there I could do a number of things that I couldn't do at home. Teeny's father,

Henry, was a kind and easy man who humored both of us. I remember that on hot days when we came in from playing, Henry would pull back the cover of the open well on the back porch, and he would let me unroll the winch that lowered the well bucket into the black waters far below. I could see my reflection in the water at the bottom as the bucket went down. When the bucket was filled, the three of us would crank away at the winch to raise it again to the surface where we would take turns drinking ice-cold water from a tin dipper.

Henry, also, was the first man to let me shoot a real gun—a thing that even my daredevil father had not allowed me to do at age five. Henry owned a short barreled, single shot Springfield .22 rifle that he kept on nails above the front door of the cabin, and one fall day, he lined up tin cans on a fence behind the house and let Teeny and me have a go at target practice. I thought it was the most wonderful thing in the world to hear the crack of that rifle. I even hit one of the cans and knocked it off the fence.

And in the winter—it must have been the year we turned six—after an especially heavy snow, Teeny and I would play like we were wild horses. The black child and the white child magically transformed into horses and galloped across the still unblemished countryside behind Etta's house, totally oblivious to all the cruelty and pain in the world as we ate snow from the generous, low hanging bows of long leaf pines.

And then, as seems to be the case with everything in this world, that too had come to an end. And my father drove the beginning wedge of change. (Remember, he was a child of the Reconstruction, inheriting and bringing with him into the new century all the prejudices, hatreds, and fears of that turbulent period, in total contrast to the gentle and courtly exterior with which he met the world.) I remember that in the spring of that year, Teeny and I were wrestling on the grass in front of our log cottage when my father came home and saw us there. We were tussling in total good humor, the way children do, and my father watched us for a moment before he called me. I'm sure I was sweating, breathing hard, and covered with grass stains as I broke free and ran to him, and he gave me a moment to catch my breath. Then—with his back to Teeny and his hands on my shoulders—he spoke in a low voice so as not to be overheard, "I don't want you to play with Teeny that way anymore."

"But why, Daddy?"

"It's just not . . ." And I remember that he used the same word he used when he had discovered me peeing with Jonaleen. "It's just not *appropriate* for you to be wrestling with a colored boy that way. Now stop." His voice was low and calm, but very firm, so I knew there was no appeal.

"Yes sir."

"You don't have to tell Teeny what I said. But I expect you to obey me."

It was like lowering a shade across my innocence. I had never thought of Teeny as a "colored boy" before. He was just my friend. But now suddenly I couldn't see him any other way. It was the very first time I can remember that racial separation or racial difference had ever been mentioned in my presence. For all of his life, my father was solicitous and courteous in the extreme to every black person he ever spoke to. And yet now, I had been introduced to another reality and its corresponding confusion, which I suppose, is the cost of growing up.

I never told Teeny what my father had said. I didn't wrestle with him anymore, but we continued to play together through that summer, and then the following September we each went off to our separate segregated schools, and I never saw Teeny again. His parents, Etta and Henry, moved away, and I heard later, long after the fact, that Teeny had cut his foot working in Mr. Stubbs' barn and that he had died of blood poisoning. It was my first experience of the death of anyone from my childhood, and since Etta and Henry were no longer a part of our lives, the news came to me as from a great distance. But though I couldn't possibly have understood all its implications at the time, I think that in my own childish way, I lamented more in Teeny's death than just the death of a friend.

The point is, that given my benign early experiences with black people, I had no place in which to fit Clarence who clearly thought of himself as a black man and of me as a smart-assed white boy and hated me for it. Apparently, Clarence spent his nights in a section of Fayetteville known locally as "Little Harlem" where everything to satisfy fleshly appetites seems to have been available. Regularly, Clarence would come in hung over and entertain the older guys—or anyone in earshot—with stories of how he had spent the previous night playing with Suzi's titties or Viola's pussy. "Man, she had the biggest titties I ever seen in my life!" Or, "She had little bitty titties that wouldn't fill the palm of my hand. But she had some kind a' tight ass." Or, "Her cunt looked like a dollar watermelon with a fifty cent slice cut out." Or, "She was a screamer. Sounded like a stuck pig when I fucked 'er."

The older guys would laugh or nod sagely at these scurrilities and try to give the impression that they, too, knew what went on in the exotic back rooms of Smokey's Tavern and in the adjacent buildings of Little Harlem. But I simply could not respond in any way. These stories horrified me. They made me want to leave the room. But I knew instinctively that leaving would make me the laughing stock of the whole group. And the idea of being ridiculed and treated like "the baby" was even more horrifying than Clarence's stories. So I stayed, heard, and said nothing. But I'm sure now, looking back, that my dislike must have been imprinted on my face like the reaction to a bad smell.

In any case, I remember that one morning Clarence had come in with a cut under his eye, and Eldred, one of the older guys, had started joking with him about it, "Ran into a little trouble last night, did you?"

"Yeah, well let me tell ya'. I'as gettin' a piece a' ass," Clarence said. "Good ass. I met this gal at Smokey's, see, and I could tell right off she wanted to fuck, so I followed her to her place, and I'as gettin' into it pretty good—ya know, really groovin', when her husband walked in."

"Looks like he did more than walk in."

"Shit! Son'va bitch! Take a mighty poor man if he couldn't hit another man when he's fuckin' a woman and his back's turned. But when I rolled off that bitch an' grabbed my box cutter, the dumb bastard learned sump'n." Clarence reached with one fluid motion toward his pocket, and an instant later, as illustration, his hooked blade box cutter was open and just inches from Eldred's nose. "Muther-fucker's a lot worse off than me this mornin', I promise ya'."

And suddenly Eldred was not laughing at Clarence anymore. "Yeah," he said. "I see what you mean." And he had walked into the next room as Clarence put his knife away.

So my resolution after the "white boy" incident was to have as little to do with Clarence as possible. It was a situation I simply was not prepared to face. And of course, there was nobody I could talk to about it. All the younger males would have thought I was a coward (which I secretly suspected, anyway) and Jack Jordan would have laughed me into the street. "Called you a 'white boy'? Well, hell's bells, tell me, just what the hell else are you?" He liked Clarence. Clarence might come in hung over, but then so did all the rest of the adults around there. Clarence knew the work and he did his job well, just as they did. And he was polite as pie to the boss. He and Mr. Jordan joked together. And against these odds, I knew there was nothing to be done.

So I contrived to avoid Clarence. My daily job suddenly became an elaborate tactical operation to work in a part of the store where Clarence was not likely to be. I shuffled to go out on deliveries with other drivers or to work as long as I could outside the store helping one of the florists decorate a church or arrange flowers and potted plants for weddings. And some of the time, when things were especially busy, I managed to work in the front of the store greeting customers and writing up orders with a clerk named Alma. Alma was a very pretty and flirty young woman in her twenties who seemed to like me a lot. I had agreed to work only until Christmas, and this way I thought I could make it through those last few days.

Then late one afternoon when I was with Alma up front, Mr. Jordan called me and waved me to the back beside him. "This order's got to go out to the Honeycut Development right away," he said. "It's a big order and this woman's drivin' me nuts." He slammed his car keys down on the table. "Everybody else is out on delivery, so you take my car and these flowers and go shut her up for me."

"Yes sir," I said. And in less time than it takes to tell about it, I had loaded the boss' car and was on the way to Honeycut in a state of literal bliss. Not only was I out of the store and on the open road behind the wheel of a big Chrysler automobile, but it was also another day home free. And I had only one day left before my job ended on Christmas Eve!

So I was feeling pretty good by the time I got to Honeycut. It was just after dark then, but I finally found the right apartment and carried the first load of flowers with me to the door where I didn't have to wait more than ten seconds before I was met by a highly made-up young woman wearing a soft dressing gown. "Thank God!" she said. "I was afraid you were gonna leave my house all drab for the party tonight."

"No ma'am," I said. "Mr. Jordan really worked hard to get these flowers here in time."

"I bet he did after I yelled at him," she said. "But come on. Put 'em in here."

She led me into the living room, which was already beautifully decorated for the party. The lights were low, soft music was playing on the phonograph, and the aroma of spicy food was floating through the air. As I placed the last spray on the table where she showed me, I caught the scent of perfume emanating from her dressing gown. "Oh, that's lovely," she said. "This is gonna be so great!"

"Yes ma'am," I said. "The house looks really beautiful."

"You think so?" she said. "You're sweet." I smiled and was about to go, but she took my arm. "Wait a minute. Let me get you something."

She went into the bedroom, which opened off the hall, and a moment later she returned with money in her hand. "This is for you," she said.

"Oh, no ma'am. Thank you just the same."

"You mean you don't want a tip?"

"No ma'am. Mr. Jordan pays me. You don't have to give me a tip for doin' my job."

"Well you're very unusual. And you're cute, too. You sure?"

"Yes ma'am."

"Well, at least stay and have a drink with me," she said. "It's gonna be a while before the party starts." She grabbed my arm again and pulled me toward a table covered with bottles, glasses, cheeses, and hors d'oeuvres of all kinds, but I held back.

"That's nice, but I think I'd better be gettin' on back to the store," I said. But then suddenly she was holding my arm even tighter than before and pressing it into her bosom, and I realized with sudden blinding clarity that she was not wearing anything at all under her dressing gown and that she wanted me to know it. At that close range, I caught the aroma of whiskey on her breath, mingling now with her perfume and creating a heady concoction indeed as she moved my arm from one side to the other just so I'd be sure not to miss anything. "I really ought to be going," I said.

But she moved her face close to mine and spoke very softly. "Are you sure you don't want a little something here first?"

It was a hard moment, and even now I don't know whether I was more horrified at the thought of leaving or at the thought of staying. But finally, it was another situation that I at thirteen was not even prepared to think about, and with a sense of mounting panic, I began to pull away toward the door. "Ma'am, thank you," I said. I didn't want to be rude. After all, she was offering me considerable hospitality. "But you know, I'm workin' and I've got other deliveries (I lied), and . . . and I need to get back to the store."

"Oh," she said. At this point, I was at the door holding the knob. "Then I guess you'd better go," she said. "I'm sorry. But you're a good boy. A real good boy. Merry Christmas."

I nodded, and a moment later I was out in the clear December air walking toward the car with my heart pounding nearly out of my body and the scent of her perfume clinging to every fiber of my clothing.

I started the car and quite literally raced out of Honeycut Development and into the highway. *Oh my, oh my! This sexy woman had pushed my arm into . . . oh my, oh my!* I couldn't forget the soft and ever inviting pressure of her breasts rolling freely from side to side beneath my upper arm. Oh my! In a mere thirty seconds, she had offered me everything that I had always been taught would send me straight to hell. Oh my! And I had wanted it! Oh my! And then I was horrified at my admission. No, of course I didn't want it, not really. I had left, hadn't I? But in all truth, I knew that there was a part of me that never wanted to leave that beautiful room. "As a man thinks in his heart, so is he," I remembered the words of Jesus. *But I ran,* I thought. I didn't do it. I ran. Like Joseph from Potiphar's wife. Surely that counts for something. But Oh! Oh! Oh! By the time I reached the center of town, I was able to settle down and concentrate on my driving. But I was not the same boy who had left the store an hour before.

I parked Mr. Jordan's car in the alley behind the store, managing to knock over two garbage cans and create a great clatter as I did it. And then I just sat there in a kind of after shock. How was I ever going to get that woman out of my mind—the feel of her body, the scent of her perfume, the seductive sounds of Claude Thornhill's orchestra in the air, and the ripe aroma and flashing color of flowers in candlelight? This was something my mother and father had never told me about, something, indeed, that they seemed not even to know about at all. *Have I lost my soul?* I wondered. *Was that all it took? A moment of temptation and it was over? There's nothing I can do about it now,* I thought, *except to be the very best boy I can be. Maybe God will forgive me, yet, if I can just stop thinking about it.*

But I was not going to have a long wait before I received a strong antidote to my lascivious longings. There was only one light on in the back of the store as I went in, and the place was deserted—except for the hard working florists up front. So, still thinking of the woman at Honeycut, I went into the closet to pick up the coat I had worn that morning. The closet was dark, and I was fumbling to unhook my coat from the nail on the wall when I heard a sound behind me and turned to find Clarence standing at the back of the closet grinning at me. "Hey, white boy," he said. "I bin waitin' for you."

I jumped in total surprise at the sound of his voice. "Oh!" I said. "Clarence. I didn't see you."

"Yeah, I could tell that," he said. And then as he moved out of the shadows, I saw far more of Clarence than I had ever wanted or needed to see. His pants were unzipped and he was holding his fully erect and very large penis in his hands and pointing it toward me. "I'll give you a dollar a' hour to hold this for me," he said. "How 'bout it, white boy?"

I had seen lots of naked boys in the showers after gym class at school, but never in my life had I seen another male, much less a black male, totally erect. And I think that for a moment I was completely stunned as Clarence stood there stroking his penis and pointing it at me. "Come on and hold it for me," he said again. "'Les you want to put your lips around it and that'd be okay, too."

That's when I bolted. "Clarence, shut up! Go to hell! Leave me alone!" I shouted. And I jerked my coat off the wall and headed for the lights at the front of the store where I escaped into the street without speaking to anyone at all.

Needless to say, that night was another one of those turbulent nights filled with a combination of illusion, image, and outright hallucination. I knew it was going to be sheer hell, because nothing that had happened during the day would leave my mind. I dreaded going to bed. On the one hand, there was the woman at Honeycut, fragrant, sexy, desirable, and seductive, holding my arm and leading me into that bedroom off the hall where—in scene after scene—I could envision myself untying and opening that scented robe as she lay on her bed. Oh God help me! At first, I would not even allow my imagination to depict what I might reasonably expect to find revealed there. But gradually, all her parts filled in. I could see her in full nakedness, and I felt a strange combination of desire and hatred. I didn't *want* to want her; I didn't want to be filled with the desire to see her, and yet, that desire throbbed through all my semi-conscious dreams and fantasies.

On the other hand, there was Clarence, exposed, leering, and aggressive. In my dreams, I wanted to bash his face in, and yet, I didn't want to get too close for fear I might touch that protruding penis. I wanted—and my fantasy began to portray it in slow motion—wanted to pull out my box cutter and, in one clean swipe, whack that prick clear off his body. At first, I saw only the cut, the curved blade swinging down in surgical sterility and leaving his penis writhing on the floor like the severed body of a black snake. And then, reality began to click in, and the scene, including my own body, was suddenly awash with blood.

If I fell asleep, I dreamed of seduction and mayhem; if I lay awake, I imagined it. And by the next morning, I was totally exhausted. I didn't want to return to the House of Flowers at all. Even though it was Christmas Eve and supposed to be my last day at work, I didn't want to face it even one more time. I almost called in sick or, worse, almost asked my mother call in for me. But I knew that such a solution would be weak and cowardly, and I felt like I had to regain something of my self-respect. So I went. I forced myself to walk through the door, smile at people, and go through the motions of whatever I had to do until Jack Jordan, in a sudden wave of Christmas spirit, closed the store at mid-afternoon. He paid us all off so he could get down to some serious holiday celebration. "It's been a good season," he said. "But I'm gonna need some of you part-time guys to work until New Years." He asked me specifically if I wanted to get in a few more hours before school started again.

"No," I told him. "No thanks." I told him I needed to spend a little time with my mother.

"Well, that's a good thing to do," he said. "I suppose that's a good thing. But, Hell's bells! I was expecting you to sing 'Cocktails For Two' for me on New Years Eve."

"Yeah," I said. "Well maybe next year."

I picked up my pay and went out into the cold air to catch the bus home. I would, in fact, spend most of the remaining Christmas season with my mother. But in my heart, I knew there was only one place I really wanted to be, and that was in the woods, because it seemed to me then that it was only in the woods that anything made any sense at all.

Chapter Eleven

Somewhere in his *Essay on Man*, Alexander Pope tells us that human happiness depends upon a combination of our hope, our ignorance of the future, and our ability to live each day to the fullest, and certainly that idea proved true for me in the winter of 1943. I *did* get to spend a lot of time alone in the woods, and as always, the forest worked its strengthening magic. But even though my hope of making sense out of things was not realized, in the woods or anywhere else for that matter, I was able in my ignorance of the future, and in spite of the continued absence of my father, to achieve a sense of happiness as 1943 went out and before the turbulent year of 1944 had fully revealed itself. To start with, my mother gave me a chemistry set for Christmas, and in a bizarre way, I combined chemistry with my trips to the woods. I had cut our Christmas tree in the forest and helped to decorate it in our living room, and when I found the chemistry set beneath it on Christmas morning, I was overjoyed. A chemistry set! I would be launched into the new age! I would transform the world.

The author with friends on the streets of Fayetteville, 1943.

I immediately thrust myself into a program of reading and experimentation, and before long I had succeeded in filling the house with noxious vapors. My mother made me take my laboratory onto the side porch in order to spare the house, and for a while—even in the chilled air—I continued my experiments, like Dr. Jekyll, unabated. But then suddenly, I became badly sidetracked—or maybe I should say, "very narrowly focused" in my investigations when I discovered one bright December morning that my chemistry set included supplies of sulfur, potassium, and charcoal, the components of gunpowder! *Wow!* I thought, *I'm really in business here!* My father had taught me long before that one of the reasons why Harper's Ferry, where John Brown was hanged in 1859, was so strategically important was that it was the location of a large potassium mine and that potassium was important to the making of gunpowder. And then my father—not the Gilbert chemical company—had given me the formula.

I'm sure that somewhere there is a clever theologian who can make a convincing case proving that God must be male simply because He set the universe in motion with a big bang and now continues to do a great deal of His creative work with other Big Bangs such as volcanoes, earthquakes, and thunder storms. In any case, every little boy I know loves a big bang, especially if it's not too close and if he can control it, and I was no exception. I set out immediately to make gunpowder and to use it in every conceivable form. First, I tested it in an open space by putting a match to it and watching it flare. Then I proceeded to enclose it in various containers and make firecrackers. I found that a reinforced toilet paper core, stuffed with gunpowder and provided with a sufficiently long fuse, could make a wonderful big bang. And from the hollow core of a paper towel roll, I made a skyrocket, which, although its guidance system needed considerable improvement, did in fact get off the ground. It whizzed in ever increasing loops and concentric circles around the backyard until it finally self-destructed over the neighbor's dog pen, causing quite a bit of excitement among the liver and white pointers.

I also found that I could buy the separate ingredients for gunpowder in eight-ounce canisters at the drug store. In a eureka-like flash of discovery, I realized that as a hedge against the shortage of shotgun shells that had been brought on by the war, I could start reloading my own shells—which I did. It was lovely! Once I had assembled all the components— primer, powder, wads, and shot—I became a one-boy armament factory. Not only would the shotgun shells provide me with the aesthetic value of a big bang, but they also had a practical value as well when I went hunting.

So I saved all my expended shell casings for re-loading, and I worked very hard, measuring my ingredients, tamping each component firmly into place, and then crimping it all together with pliers around the rim of a shell. By a day's end, my hands would be so black with charcoal that my mother almost despaired on Sunday morning of getting me clean enough to present myself properly "before the Lord." But it was all worth it. By New Year's Eve, I had amassed a half dozen black powder shells. And then I went into the woods.

This would be the big test. I was very excited about the possibilities, but at the same time I was somewhat nervous and apprehensive. I knew that modern manufacturers had long since abandoned black powder in favor of a faster burning white powder propellant, but the nearly half a million deaths toted up by black powder during the Civil War had left me no illusions about its lethal capacities. Suppose I had overloaded my shells? I had heard of cannon blowing up and killing their crew. Suppose the shotgun blew up in my face and killed me or worse, maimed me for life? I remembered my father once telling me about a pair of Heidelberg dueling swords that he had inherited. He explained to me how the Heidelberg students in fact coveted a dueling scar on the cheek as a badge of honor. *Maybe if the gun blows up, I will get just such a badge of honor,* I thought, *a scar on the cheek to make me "interesting."* (Oh, the corrupt creative mind of youth!) I could see myself attending some social engagement in a far off romantic capital long after the war. I would be standing aloof on the fringes of a dance floor with my interesting scar and looking rather like Errol Flynn in *Dawn Patrol,* when I would be approached by a young woman looking rather like Maureen O'Hara in *The Black Swan.* "Did you suffer terribly from your wounds?" she would ask. And I would reply with a tone of great mystery, "Really, My Dear, it's something I've promised myself never to discuss." (Believe me, when James Thurber came out with Walter Mitty, I felt that I had found a soul mate.)

In any case, I decided that my experiment would be well worth the risk, and on the last day of 1943, I picked up my father's 16-gauge double-barreled shotgun and headed for my firing range far in the woods. Mind you, I had been every bit as secretive about my endeavors as were the atomic scientists preparing for the really big bang at Los Alamos, because I knew that if my mother had ever found out, she would have stopped me. So I was highly elated to be free and alone to accept the results of my work, whatever they might be.

It was a damp, cloudy day with the temperature in the mid-40s, and I remember it vividly because the weather contributed a great deal to the spectacular results. I had started wearing one of my father's identification "dog tags" along with my flint arrowhead on a chain around my neck that fall, and I remember touching these magic things beneath my shirt as I reached the clearing in the forest where I loaded one of my black powder shells into the left barrel of the gun. Then I said a kind of prayer, pressed the stock firmly to my shoulder, lifted the muzzle to the sky, and squeezed the trigger.

Ka-Blam! The blast was enormous, kicking the gun back hard against my shoulder and ultimately bruising it considerably. But Balboa himself could not have been more exuberant when he discovered the Pacific than I was at the moment of that big bang. A column of flame erupted from the barrel of the gun, a cloud of smoke filled the winter sky, and I could hear shot slamming into the trees across the clearing. It was a success! I loaded a second shell and fired away—Ka-Blam! And again, flame and smoke belched heavenward. It was truly beautiful. I couldn't have been more elated if I'd been firing a 155-millimeter howitzer. I fired a third shell as final proof that I was on the right track. Everything worked perfectly, and I knew I would continue to load my own shells as long as I could get supplies.

I sniffed the acrid, but delicious bite of gunpowder smoke on the winter air and turned toward home with the expanded chest of success and in a virtual state of ecstasy. But it seems to me now that at another level, my joy came from the fact that with my explosive Christmas adventures, I achieved a wonderfully curative and cathartic effect on my own soul. I was able to escape from my memories of Ruth Ann, my turbulent thoughts of Clarence and the woman at Honeycut and to send them all drifting away with a blast of fire and smoke into the permanent cloud of my distant memory. Those thoughts were too personal, too frightening, too embarrassing, and finally, too incomprehensible for me to deal with anymore. But with my shotgun and my black powder, I had achieved planning, discipline, execution, and bang-up results, and it seemed to me that *that* was the shape of happiness. And even before the day was out, I would begin to milk it for all it was worth.

On that December 31, 1943, I was invited to my first New Year's Eve party. It was held at Ann Byrd McArthur's house on Oak Ridge Avenue, and it included maybe a dozen of us eighth graders. I remember it being a relatively orderly and rather sedate affair, but fun nonetheless. All the boys wore jackets and ties. The girls wore pretty dresses or sweaters and skirts to mid-calf with maybe a string of pearls and of course, saddle shoes for those girls who had not started wearing heels for dress-up occasions. We danced to the music of Glenn Miller, Tommy Dorsey, and Harry James and felt very sophisticated, even with several parents present to watch over us. But going into it, I knew that I was going to be the life of the party. I had done things during the Christmas holiday that none of my classmates had even come close to, and as I told about them, excluding, of course, my confrontations with Clarence and the woman at Honeycut, I felt that I had suddenly become "interesting" to my friends—even without a scar on my cheek.

Among the boys, I remember that John was there with Rudolph Singleton, among others. The boys seemed very interested in learning my formula for gunpowder, how I made my fuses, and where I got my ingredients. Somebody even nicknamed me "The Mad Bomber"—which I enjoyed and which fortunately didn't stick with me beyond that night.

The girls—among them Martha Lazenby, Carolyn Simpson, and Ann Blackwell—seemed more impressed with my ingenuity and the danger, especially the part about my going off into *the dark woods* alone to carry out my experiments. Remember, it was an era in which girls, for the most part at least, appeared to be content to experience their adventures vicariously by attaching themselves to brilliant and adventurous males. In order to do this, they instinctively found ways to make the males feel wonderful by praising their exploits: "You were *so* smart to do all that. Weren't you just scared to death—out there in the woods all by yourself?" Or, spoken while looking deeply into one's eyes, "I could *never* have done that. It's *so* dangerous!" We were in the American South, remember, and Scarlet O'Hara was not merely a figment of Margaret Mitchell's imagination. Nevertheless, it all worked wonders on the male ego and made me feel that 1944 promised to be a wonderful year indeed.

However, it was also at this party that I met a girl who had a totally different take on things. Her name was Nadine Whisnant. Her father was an army officer stationed at Fort Bragg and her family had just moved to Fayetteville during the Christmas holidays. I didn't know then, of course, that over the coming year she would prove to be a source of great delight as well as great despair for some of us. But, I was struck with her immediately because in addition to her natural good looks and knockout figure, she was the first girl I had ever met who expressed any kind of professional ambition. Oh, she was charming enough and seemed duly impressed with the story of my holiday adventures, but she immediately countered with the question, "Have you read Martha Gellhorn's latest article in *Life*?"

"No," I had to confess. I hadn't read much of anything since the Christmas vacation began.

"Well, I read her latest report from the battlefield in North Africa," Nadine said. "I think she's *so* wonderful—she and Margaret Bourke-White both. That's what I want to do when I finish school—be a journalist."

"You do?"

"Yes!"

At the mention of Africa, I was tempted to tell her that my father was stationed somewhere in Africa. But I remembered just in time that his location was a military secret, and I held back as Nadine continued in a voice of high excitement, "Can you imagine anything more thrilling than being sent around the world as a reporter?"

My Aunt Norma was a reporter, but all she ever reported was the social news of Gaston County, which didn't seem so thrilling to me. However, now I had to admit that after listening to Edward R. Murrow's radio reports from London, I too had thought about being a journalist one day.

"Oh, I don't mean *just* being a journalist and nothing else," Nadine said. "I want to write *everything*. But journalism can send me to all these exciting places." And then Nadine told me that Martha Gellhorn's husband, Ernest Hemingway, had recently written a novel about the Spanish Civil War.

Now at this stage of my life, I had hardly even heard of Ernest Hemingway, much less what he wrote about. However, I had heard of the Spanish Civil War and the way General Franco had allowed Hitler and Mussolini to test their war materials against the Spanish people in support of fascism. And I realized instantly that talking to Nadine was a radically new experience for me. My parents, of course, respected the literature of the past. But aside from my English teachers, the only other person I knew who had the slightest interest in writing was a boy in my class named Jack Crosswell who had read a lot of Zane Gray and Jack London. Nadine, I would soon discover, liked the older writers, too, and loved Poe and Hawthorne as much as I did, but she was clearly conscious of the continuing relationship between writing and the world.

"I was always interested in the Spanish war," I told her. "My father thought it was the Axis preparation for the war we're in now."

"Really?" Nadine said. "Well, they've just made a movie of Mr. Hemingway's book. It's called *For Whom the Bell Tolls* and it stars Gary Cooper and Ingrid Bergman, and oooshe-poo, is it good!"

I would soon learn that *oooshe-poo,* spoken with a rising inflection and sometimes with a little squeak at the end, was for Nadine roughly equivalent to Scarlet O'Hara's "Fiddly dee!" But at thirteen, I found nothing wrong with it, and I found a lot *right* about Nadine. She was the first girl I had ever met who had a conscious *content*.

Now, I don't mean to insult anybody by that statement. I'm sure that many girls of my generation contained ideas and ambitions, and I would certainly meet them later. But in our early teenage years, the girls I knew had never expressed their ideas or even hinted at their ambitions to me. Even Ruth Ann who was a full two years older than I. It was as though the girls were willing to be blank slates on which the boys inscribed *their* own ideas and ambitions. But Nadine was not willing to be anybody else's blank slate or mirror. She could be as flirtatious and cute as the next girl, maybe more flirtatious and cute than most, but she would inscribe her own ideas and pursue her own ambitions in her own way, thank you.

To me, this was like a cold, clear drink of water on a hot day—a girl with ideas and ambitions. John, Alfred, and I had talked about our ideas and ambitions and the direction of our lives, but when we talked about girls—although we might love them—it was rather like discussing a foreign and unknown creature. Girls didn't have to be concerned with ideas and ambitions, did they? Unless it was somebody like my great Aunt Annie, the doctor, or someone like Amelia Earhart. All the rest of them just seemed to wait until *we* focused our ideas and ambitions, and then, if they liked us and found our ambitions attractive, one of them would marry us. But Nadine was a girl who could be one of us, a girl whose ideas and ambitions gave her substance and content to deal with! I was also delighted and surprised to learn that Nadine lived only a short distance from me and that we would be riding the same bus when school started again at the end of the week.

So I went home that night seeing the world in a totally different way, and I was anxious to tell Alfred about our new neighbor when he drove up in his parents' car full of high excitement after his return from his grandfather's house a few days later. "Let's go dove hunting," he said, even before entering the house. "The season ends tomorrow and I know where they're flying."

"Okay," I told him, and he came in and talked to my mother while I got ready.

"There's a big corn field up at Little River," he said when we were in the car. "I don't think anybody ever hunts it, and it ought to be just right this time of year." Little River was a good distance away and it was already late in the day when we started out, but although Alfred was eager to get into the field and inclined to drive very fast, I was glad for the chance to see my friend and to test my black powder shells in an actual hunting situation for the first time.

We did, in fact, have a very successful hunt. My shells, complete with the great plume of black smoke, worked perfectly, and we managed to bag enough birds to make a good stew the next day. But it was just after sundown when we left the field, and if Alfred had felt like speeding on the approach earlier in the afternoon, he felt like flying on the return through the gathering darkness. This, of course, was long before seat belts, air bags, and flashing turn signals. I remember sitting there and watching the speedometer of that old car inch upward past seventy as we flashed by the site of my father's now abandoned airport with its empty hangar sitting isolated and sad on the edge of the field. There was only one other car on the road in front of us and Alfred eased into the left lane in order to overtake and pass it. Then through the dusk, when we were probably less than fifty feet from the other car, I saw the driver's arm extended horizontally from the window making a left turn signal, and it was obvious that Alfred did not see it. There was not even time to shout a warning before that other car was dead in front of us, fully perpendicular to our line of travel and leaving us absolutely nowhere to go.

It has always surprised me that we were not all killed in the crash that followed, but our survival is strictly due to Alfred's quick reflexes and driving skill. In the split second remaining, he braked and swerved sharply to the left so that we skidded sideways and struck parallel to the other car with the impact being absorbed by the sides rather than head on. Still, it was violent. When the sound of squealing tires and crashing metal finally subsided, I was on the floor and Alfred was in the passenger seat where I had been. When we looked outside, we discovered that we were in the middle of a cemetery surrounded by grave markers, and everything was very quiet.

My door was jammed shut, hard up against the side of the other car, but Alfred's door was okay, and as soon as we realized we weren't hurt, Alfred was outside and heading toward the other driver who had been thrown against his passenger door. This was the part of Alfred I always admired. Although he could be aggressive, careless, and totally reckless in one moment, he could be the coolest and most responsible person imaginable in the next. And during an emergency, he was at his best. In an instant, he was beside the other car trying to open the door for the driver, who was an older man and obviously rather stunned. "I'm sorry, sir. I didn't see your signal," Alfred said. "Are you all right?"

"Just groggy," the man said. Alfred helped him out.

"Maybe you'd better lie here for a minute 'til your head clears," Alfred said. And very quickly, he cleared a space between grave markers and spread his own coat for the man to lie on.

"I'll be all right," the man said. "I hit my head on the door." But he accepted Alfred's guidance and lay stretched out on the coat for several minutes.

"I'll go somewhere and call an ambulance," I said.

"No, no. I'm all right," the man said. He pushed himself up on his elbows. "My house is right over there." He pointed to a light far off between the trees.

"Then we'll help you home," Alfred said.

As it turned out, none of us was injured, and the cars, although badly damaged and twisted on the outside, would still run. Within the hour, we had pushed the cars out of the cemetery, accompanied the other driver home where he and Alfred exchanged insurance information, and were again on the road. We were riding at a kind of crab angle in a car whose rear wheels no longer followed directly behind its front wheels. "God damn! My old man's really gonna be mad about this," Alfred said. "He doesn't even know I took the car."

"Well, good luck," I said as he stopped and let me out through the driver's door when we got to my house. "Let me know how it turns out." And as he drove away, I realized that it was only the second time I had spoken through the whole experience.

It was another one of those things I did not tell my mother. I was late for supper, of course, but I explained it merely by saying that we had had car trouble. "Had to push it," I said.

"Well, I was worried sick," my mother said. "I was afraid something had happened to you."

"No ma'am, we were fine," I told her.

And we were. But that was to be another one of those nights in which troubling after-images came flooding back to haunt me once the lights were out. I would see the image of the other car turning sideways in front of our windshield, the two cars closing at high speed with no possible route of escape, the sound of squealing tires and the crash of steel and the sensation of being hurled by overwhelming forces against the firewall, realizing that if Alfred had not swerved as he did in that final second, we would have sliced into the side of that other car like the blade of a mattock, bending it into a crescent and throwing me through the windshield and the engine into Alfred's lap—scene after scene flashing by in both sleep and wakefulness. And I think it was then, during those sleepless after-shocks, that I first fully perceived the close proximity of the valleys and pinnacles of human life—that a period of great happiness can be succeeded in an instant by a period of great sorrow and that the difference between life and death at any age is no greater than a heartbeat and can depend entirely on decisions made and actions taken in mere fractions of seconds.

It was enough to sober a thirteen-year-old boy considerably, and while I was not totally paralyzed by my new awareness of the unseen dangers and instabilities that constantly surround our lives, I did proceed into that year of 1944 with a sense of enormous gravity and responsibility, a feeling that I wanted to control everything that happened in my own life and protect the lives of those around me.

My mother reinforced this new feeling of responsibility one morning the following week as I started out to school. She handed me a note for my principal and told me that she was going to take me out early that day. "I have an appointment at Fort Bragg hospital," she said. "I want you to go with me."

"Are you sick?"

"I haven't been feeling well, and I'm going for an exam," she said. "But I may need you to drive me home."

I had noticed that she had seemed rather dispirited through the Christmas season, but I thought it was because of my father's absence and the long silences that fell between his letters. I think that in fact he wrote to her almost every day and to me once a week, but the letters—most of them blotched with countless censor's smears and slices—seemed to get backed up in the system for weeks at a time.

The news of the war coming back from Europe told us that he—or at least, the Ferry Command—was certainly doing its job of ferrying war planes to Europe because during late 1943 and early 1944, the European skies had been filled with U.S. bombers. The submarine pens at St. Nazaire had been blasted into oblivion by B-17s. The column of smoke rising over the Ploesti oil fields after visits from B-17s and B-24s had been reported at over sixty thousand feet. The disastrous raid on Sweinfurt had cost the United States sixty bombers and their flight crews in one day. We knew that my father was somewhere in Africa and not at the air raid staging areas in England, but we also knew that the Nazis were not passive in their resistance and that they would do anything in the world to cut the aviation supply lines of which he was a part. So over everything we did—no matter how personally intimate, pleasant, or disturbing it might be—there was always this other cloud of worry and concern over my father's safety. We might hear nothing from him for a month and then receive a whole packet of ten letters at once. And in every letter that he sent to me—along with his declaration of love for me and his prayers for my safety—there was his command to "take care of your mother."

"Sure," I said, when she asked me to go with her to the hospital. "I'll be waiting for you in front of the school." I didn't look forward to spending the afternoon in a hospital waiting room, but the prospect of driving the car legitimately was always pleasing, and my father's repeated reminders of my responsibility to my mother left no doubt as to what I should do.

I went with her that day and on a number of succeeding days. I spent hour after long hour in the doctor's crowded waiting room, reading or doing my homework, or alternatively, walking around the hospital grounds and watching the low flying planes as they flew out and returned from their training areas. One of the drop zones for the 82nd Airborne Division was very close to the main fort, and often I could see the long strings of paratroopers spilling from a flight of C-47 transport planes barely fifteen hundred feet above the ground. More and more troop carrying gliders were in evidence—sometimes as many as three trailing behind a single tow plane, and the rumble from the artillery range at the back of the fort seemed to go on continuously.

Several times a week, I would accompany my mother to her appointments and afterward, drive her home along the country road that was a short cut to our house. And then one afternoon in late winter as we arrived home and parked beside the large camellia bush in the side yard, my mother just sat for a long time in the car without opening the door. I remember that the sky was milky white with a weak winter sun barely shining through the thin overcast, and that she herself seemed extremely pale and nervous as she laid her hand on my arm. "I have to tell you something," she said. "I have to have an operation."

"You do?"

She nodded, and I could see she was struggling to hold back her tears. "I know you're only a boy and I hate to bother you with this sort of thing, but you're the only person I have."

"I'll do whatever I can," I said. "What's the matter?"

"I've been bleeding," she said. And then there *were* tears streaming down her cheeks.

"Bleeding?"

"Hemorrhaging," she said, "the way women do, but so much more. I can't seem to stop. It's been going on for weeks."

Maybe it's true at any age, but for me at thirteen, the idea of bleeding, *hemorrhaging*, was frightening in the extreme. And the idea of hemorrhaging in combination with my mother's tears produced a greater sense of despair and terror in me than I can possibly put into words. At age seven, I had fallen off my bicycle and cut the large artery inside my left hand on a bottle that I had broken with my BB gun. The sight of my own blood pumping into the air like a fountain with every beat of my heart had been truly horrifying. That bleeding had been controllable with pressure and a tourniquet that my mother tied around my wrist before taking me to the hospital. But *hemorrhaging*? How had she continued to live? How had I not seen? "I'm sorry," was all I could manage to say. "I didn't know."

"I tried not to leave any sign to worry you," she said. "But I was filling one sanitary napkin after another, all day long. The doctor says I must have a hysterectomy—that my uterus, my womb, must be removed," she explained.

Thinking about it now, I realize that each of these words struck me like a blow to the head. Bleeding. Hemorrhaging. Sanitary napkin. Hysterectomy. Uterus. Womb. Yes, I had received my one-hour course in sex and reproduction from Dr. McCoy that afternoon when I was eight years old, but *menstruation* was only a word to me, a word that had to do with some aspect of the mysteriously complex female body. And it was an aspect I felt it was better not to think about. Bleeding was a frightening thing. And the thought that women bled regularly through their genitalia as a routine part of their adult lives was something that my male child's mind just could not yet accommodate. To say nothing of thinking about it in relation to my mother! I had seen her supply of sanitary napkins in the bathroom closet. But the vision of these things applied to my mother's body and soaked with her blood was a sight that simply made the circuits of my mind shut down. I didn't want to think about it in any way. Outside, at thirteen, I possessed what appeared to be the body of a man: beard, pubic hair, and a deep voice. But inside that body was a frightened child, closing his eyes, covering his ears, and running away in panic from the unthinkable, from the unseeable. Edvard Munch caught it perfectly in *The Scream*, his drawing of the panicked child. I think I had managed to perceive of my mother as a sexless creature. The things that applied to other women just did not apply to her. But now being forced to think of her blood, her womb, the secret recesses of her body that had formed me and nurtured me into life made my temperature drop to serpentine levels. Somewhere Freud says that no man becomes truly free until his father dies. To that I would add that no male child becomes truly a man until he is able to contemplate his mother's menstrual blood without panic. And I was about to learn.

That day, the child inside me ran screaming blindly into the forest of his panic. He left me, the ice cold boy-man, sitting immobile behind the wheel of that 1941 Chevrolet, looking directly into my mother's eyes. *What would my father have me do?* I thought. Suddenly, I heard my own voice, dry but surprisingly calm, almost as the voice of a stranger, saying, "When are you planning to have the operation?"

"Early next week," she said. "I'll need you to be with me and help me."

"Of course," I said. "Just tell me what you need."

Our memory of events, which is to say the bulk of what we call *consciousness*, is created by shock: pain, pleasure, loss, surprise, moments of fear, and moments of revelation. And if the intensity of an experience is not so violent that it shocks us completely into *un*consciousness, then the greater the intensity, the more vivid the memory and the greater the consciousness. I believe I first became conscious of my own mortality during the summer of 1935 when I was four years old— the same year that my father conducted his Great Gala Air Show as his last hurrah to civil aviation. It was the summer I learned to swim.

With the fires of the Great Depression scorching our American nation into a new type of fiscal and social consciousness, the country club near our house had been forced to abandon its exclusivity and open its lake to the public at large. And we were able to go there at a price of ten cents for kids and twenty-five cents for adults. It was a beautiful lake of dark, but sweet water with a white sandy bottom and surrounded—on three sides at least—by tall trees and forests that rolled up and over the nearby hills unmarked for miles by human habitation. There was a long pier built out into the water, rafts anchored near and far, and diving boards, both high and low, on the main pavilion. And my parents would take me there several times a week.

They would lure me, objecting at first, but gradually beginning to trust them, out into chest deep water where they would hold me horizontally and encourage me to paddle and kick as they scooted me back and forth between them. My father tended to lose patience when I didn't learn to swim as quickly as he thought I should, but my mother was more long suffering. She was not a strong swimmer herself, but she knew enough to teach me, and she persuaded my father to just let me play between our lessons. It was the right thing to do. More than anything else, I wanted his approval, and I was willing to work for it on my own. So at our very next session, between exhortations to "Look at me! Look at me!" I pushed off from the sandy bottom and swam the ten feet to my father without touching.

I got the approval I wanted. We were all delighted, and I set out immediately to extend my range. My father taught me other strokes beside the dog paddle, and by halfway through the summer—before that year's polio epidemic closed so many public facilities to children—I was using the sidestroke and swimming beside my father all the way to the raft.

It doesn't take much to convince a four-year-old boy with a new accomplishment that he is invincible. My mother took me to the lake almost every day, whether my father was able to join us or not, and my aquatic ability increased with almost geometric proportions. I was diving, swimming under water, and trying every new thing I could think of.

And then one day in mid-summer, my mother's youngest brother, Howerton, came to visit us. (This was the brother who was born the year their father died.) As an escape from the windless July heat, he volunteered to take me swimming. I was delighted. A new audience! "Look, Uncle, watch me swim under water! Watch me dive off the pier! See how far I can swim!" And this last was the exhibition that changed everything. I started out from the shore, headed for the near raft, a trip I had made often with my father. But where on previous afternoons I had climbed routinely onto the raft for a rest before swimming back to shore, on that afternoon the temptation of a new audience was greater than my wisdom, and I didn't even hesitate at the raft. I had to show off my boundless strength. And instead of stopping to rest, I simply changed course and headed for the pavilion—a distance at least twice as far as my previous swim and over much deeper water.

I was about half way to the pavilion when I realized that it was going to be a long voyage indeed. Suddenly my arms just did not want to take one more stroke and my legs didn't want to make one more kick. And I knew that the fun and games were over, that swimming was not about showing off, but about saving your life when you had nothing else going for you. Many years later, I would experience the same sense of sub-surface panic in an army airplane when the fuel gauges were dragging *empty* and a long distance still remained between me and the nearest airfield—that sense of, "What do you do now, Buddy? It's all up to you."

In the country club lake I took another stroke. And I gave another kick. And I took another stroke. They were coming slower and slower and I was gasping for air. But I forced it. I was making progress and I kept on making progress until I reached a spot about ten feet from the ladder at the pavilion. I then had absolutely nothing left and I went down in about twelve feet of water, drifting down, rather like falling asleep, unable even to stir until my feet touched the smooth sand and I thought, *I'm too young to die!* and I gave one last powerful push off the bottom with my legs. When I broke the surface, my fingers were actually touching the rungs of the ladder at the base of the pavilion. My uncle from the shore had seen my distress and had yelled to alert the lifeguard, but the lake was noisy and the lifeguard hadn't noticed until I actually touched the ladder, when he jumped in to help me. I suppose I was glad to have company at last, but I think my main feeling was one of anger and disdain. I had made it on my own, and I didn't want to be robbed of my victory. But resting on the pavilion afterward, I was a changed child. It would take me years, maybe a lifetime, to disentangle all the things that I had learned during those few brief seconds. But foremost then and ever afterward was that sense of my mortality—and not just my own—the awareness, again awakened by the car crash with Alfred, that we are all, in a real way, very temporary creatures. Along with that realization came a nearly crushing sense of responsibility: "What do you do now, Buddy? It's all up to you." This was exactly the conundrum that I faced sitting in the car with my mother when she told me about her upcoming operation.

I know now that in a real way we were both facing the same issues. She had a number of acquaintances but no truly intimate friends, and her one sister was hundreds of miles away tending their aging mother, while my father was thousands of miles away making the world safe for democracy. I know that she must have been feeling the same sense of isolation that I had felt, alone and exhausted in deep water. For her, it must have been like reliving the sense of abandonment she had felt at age ten when her father had died and her mother had retreated into that cloud of shock and depressed estrangement from which she never really returned. We may have been mother and child genetically, but in truth we were two children fighting our fear of abandonment as we confronted our mortality in the white light of that winter afternoon: 'My life's blood is running out; what do I do now? It's all up to me.'

She went into surgery the following week at the Fort Bragg Army Hospital, and I was there with her. The staff was very good to me. They even found me a bed in the children's ward and let me stay there. In the mornings I caught the bus to school with the other "army brats" that lived on the base at Fort Bragg. Then in the afternoons I would return to visit her in her room and, after a few days when she was stronger, to walk with her holding my arm as she began to move slowly about the halls of the hospital. Everything was slower in 1944, and surgery patients were not forced out of the hospital as fast as they would be later.

But in truth, I have to admit that once I thought my mother was going to be all right, I found a certain pleasure in my independence for those few days. In the evenings I could slip out of the hospital after visiting hours and go to the movies with all the soldiers at the nearby post theater. And one night, I alarmed everybody by disappearing completely and going home to sleep at our empty house in my own bed.

But I was there when she was discharged—still very weak—to drive her home. And that's when my nursing duties began. Now, I believe that this was the first time in my life in which I found myself in a truly paradoxical position, a situation in which duty and emotion were violently at odds, in which public honor and private personal integrity could hardly occupy the same room together. It was the first time that I remember passionately wanting two diametrically opposed things at once. For, remember, if you will, the inherent conflict that had existed between me and my mother from very early in my life, that feeling that I wanted to be free of her. The fact that I loved and respected my mother and wanted to help her changed this feeling not at all. I had wanted my freedom from the time she had curled my hair and treated me like her doll. Her doctoring me when I wasn't sick, her grooming me to be her caretaker, her driving a wedge of guilt between me and any girl in whom I ever showed the slightest interest all created in me a desire to break away. Patrick Henry himself never wanted liberty from a tyrannical England more than I, at thirteen, wanted freedom from my mother. And yet, I had a responsibility to her and for her. I had a duty to perform. She was, of course, my lifeline to food, shelter, and life itself, and for those things I was grateful. In helping her I was helping myself. But beyond any practical concern, there was my father's expectation that I would do my duty without fail and with good humor, and I would never have violated that. So I embarked upon my nursing duties feeling that while I was doing things that were honorable, true and good, I was at the same time entangling myself more and somehow working against my own desire for freedom and independence.

For the first few days after returning home, she seemed to suffer a setback and was unable even to get out of the bed. With her guidance, I prepared and served our food. And then I brought her the bedpan. Never disparage hospital orderlies or nurses who perform these services routinely. They are truly the saints and martyrs of the medical profession. For if I had been panicked earlier merely by the *thought* of my mother's bodily fluids, you can imagine my state when confronted by them in fact. But confront them I did—with clenched jaw and eyes averted as much as possible and with something approaching a sense of shame at looking upon that which I should not be seeing. But I think it was then that I came to believe—and adopted it as an article of faith, rightly or wrongly—that the way we feel about something is absolutely irrelevant, that it is only what we *do* that is important because survival depends upon action.

Of course, during all these "intimate" moments, my mother took the opportunity to show me the physical traces of her ordeal. I remember one day as I was bringing her a basin of warm water and a washcloth for bathing, she said, "You want to see my scars?" and before I could say anything, she began lowering the waistband of her pajamas.

I know I did not say *yes*, because in fact, there was nothing that I wanted to see less. But I felt that saying *no* would be rude or offensive in some way, and so I just stood there holding that basin of warm water and mumbling unintelligibly as she revealed her distended lower abdomen. "That," she said, pointing to a vertical white line below her navel, "is the scar I received when you were born. They lifted you right out of there."

"Um," I said.

"I almost died when you were born."

"Yes Ma'am."

"But I'm not sorry," she said. "I could never be sorry. It's the best thing I've ever done. You understand that, don't you?"

"Yes Ma'am."

"And *that*," she said, pointing even lower to an angry horizontal cut with several stitches still in place, "is what they just did."

"Yes Ma'am," I said again.

"I thought you should know what I've been through."

"Yes Ma'am." And then, surrounded by a cloud of guilt and shame over all my earlier rebellious thoughts, I excused myself to empty the washbasin.

I did not faint, but things did start to go gray. I remember sitting for a long time on the edge of the bath tub, hanging my head down in order not to pass out, as she had taught me to do years before when I had cut my hand so badly. After a few minutes, I rallied and brought her the basin of rinse water. "What took you so long?" she said. "What were you doing?"

"Oh, just getting the water temperature right," I said. "I think it's okay now."

Her turn to serve as nurse would come sooner than either of us suspected, but in the meantime she began to recover quite rapidly. And though I had to drive her to the hospital to get her stitches removed and for subsequent check-ups, by month's end, she seemed almost normal, and I was once again living as a mere school boy.

Chapter Twelve

I think that during this time of nursing my mother through her recovery, it was Nadine more than anyone else who gave me sustenance. I would regularly detour by her house and walk with her to and from the school bus, and the mere sight of her eternally curious eyes and the boundless good humor of her smile were enough to enrich me for a whole day. She was pretty and sexy beyond measure, and I was certainly conscious of those charms, but—maybe because of my remembered pain over Ruth Ann's departure or the daily practical physicality of my mother's femaleness—our relationship was more like that of brother and sister. We were a pair of only children—army brats—with common interests, and beyond that, Nadine—or "Deanie" as I came to call her—taught me things.

Where my interest in literature had been in the recognized writers of the past, as read by my parents or my teachers, Deanie kept up with things that were being published in current magazines and books—often quite frivolous things—but she seemed not to mind. She consumed them all. *Life, Look,*

Collier's, The Saturday Evening Post, the old *Cosmopolitan* with all its short stories, *Time*, even the *Saturday Review of Literature*. She read the modern romances—*Rebecca*, Shellabarger's *Captain From Castile*, Daphne DuMurier's *Frenchman's Creek*. "Oooshe-poo! Is it good!" she would tell me with an irrepressibility I've rarely met anywhere. And of course, to keep up with her, I had to read them, too.

And then she taught me to listen to the popular music of our day in a brand new way. Although I enjoyed the big bands of the 1940s (especially Harry James after I heard his recording of *The Flight of the Bumblebee* and *The Carnival of Venice*, which I was trying to play on my trumpet), my main interest had continued to be in classical music and the works of the classical composers and performers. But Deanie listened to every popular musician available—Frank Sinatra, Bing Crosby, Dinah Shore, Ella Fitzgerald, Peggy Lee, in addition to the big bands. Her main concern, however, was with words, phrases. I would drop by her house and she would play the latest 78-RPM recording by Frank Sinatra for me—*Night and Day, All or Nothing at All, There's No You*. At first, I was not convinced that I should even bother to listen. My ear had been tuned to the virile strength of Robert Merril, Ezio Pinza, and George London, and compared with them, I thought the early Frank Sinatra sounded like a starveling. "He has no voice," I would say. "Without a microphone, no one would hear him beyond the footlights."

"But he *does* have a microphone," Deanie would tell me, "and listen to what he does with the voice he's got."

So I listened, and gradually I had to admit that he did have something. He might never be able to sing *Don Giovanni, The Barber of Seville*, or *Faust*, but when it came to addressing the feelings of private people "In the Wee Small Hours of the Morning," he really had no equal. Not that I abandoned my interest in classical music at all; I just expanded my interests, and this expansion would radically change the focus of my life over the next several years.

Now, strange as it may seem for someone who listened to as much music on the radio as I did, there was no phonograph in my house. So among the first things that I did for myself that spring was to take my earnings from the House of Flowers and buy a portable record player. That's when I truly began to memorize the songs of the day. I also bought the sheet music and learned to play many of the songs on the piano and on my trumpet, although neither my piano teacher nor my band instructor seemed to have the slightest sympathy for this foolish waste of time. I know I must have driven my mother crazy, and many a day she made me take the record player into my room and close the door. But the payoff for me was that I could talk knowledgeably with Deanie about the styles of various singers and even sing snatches of songs for her on the way to the school bus. We were like two explorers, each of whom wanted to find some new and exciting thing to share with the other every day. Just how important this new tapestry of friendship had become for me was something I probably disguised and hid even from myself. I just enjoyed it. Deanie and I seemed almost to breathe in passionate rhythm with each other, and yet, I never labeled it or ever so much as held her hand romantically. And then it was all radically interrupted in early spring by a case of mumps.

I don't know whether it really had any connection with my disease or not, but one afternoon in early April, Alfred came by my house with Buck, his fox terrier, and we went for a walk in the woods. Alfred had not been allowed to drive his parents' car since the big accident in January, so he walked or rode the bus everywhere. I remember that we walked down to one of our favorite spots along the Cape Fear River where, with the leaf cover still off the trees, we found a previously undiscovered grape vine that had attached itself to the highest branches of an oak, which jutted out over the water. "Wow!"

Alfred said. "I bet we could make a good swing out of that." And without hesitation, he took the long corn knife that I often carried in my belt like a machete and hacked the vine off at the ground. A moment later, he had tested it and was swinging like Tarzan from the top of the bank far out over the water and back. It was truly a delightful ride. We were like monkeys. He would take a half dozen swings, I would take a half dozen, and then we'd trade off again until about an hour later when I was high in the air above the river, the whole structure gave way without warning and sent me plunging into the still icy water with about fifty feet of grape vine trailing after. It was cold! But I managed to disentangle myself and swim to shore where Alfred, laughing like an idiot, tried to help me up the muddy bank.

We went directly home then, but April or not, I was deeply chilled. Even after I got into the house and sat in front of the stove, it took me a long time to warm up. And by the next morning, I knew that I was sick. My throat hurt, my head ached, and my mother took one look at me and said, "I think you've got mumps."

We tend to laugh at the physical distortions of people with mumps, and surely by the end of that day my jaws and neck were expanding to look comically like the jowls of a plump Berkshire hog. But I wasn't laughing. I was feeling terrible, and when my mother took my temperature, she found it spiked at 105 degrees.

It was then that we realized how much the world had changed in a mere matter of weeks. Where earlier in the winter the army hospital had found space and time to accommodate both of us, now all the military facilities were filled to bursting with wounded and ill men returning from the battlefronts. From southern Italy across to North Africa and east to the Philippines, we had service men and women locked in mortal combat, and the carnage had been enormous. Many of the civilian doctors who normally served the city of

Fayetteville had been called to active duty—and at a time when Fayetteville itself was overflowing with the families of service men stationed at Fort Bragg. In short, medical aid was suddenly at a premium and usually available only after waiting many hours with other sick people in a crowded waiting room.

After many efforts and a seemingly endless wait on the telephone, my mother was able to reach Dr. Verdury, the same doctor who had sewed up my sliced hand when I was seven, and he seemed quite alarmed when she told him about my high fever. "Shall I bring him in?" she asked.

"No," the doctor said. "Don't move him under any circumstances. Mumps is more dangerous than we like to think." And then he told her to give me aspirin and apply ice packs to bring the fever down. "I'll be there to see him," the doctor said. "It'll take a while, but I'll come to the house. Just get the fever down and keep him quiet."

The keeping quiet part was going to be easy, I felt. I could hardly lift an arm and I was as close as I've ever been to becoming delirious. But the thing that worried me most at the time was that I would miss my usual daily discussion with Nadine. She wouldn't know what had happened, and I didn't want to talk about her with my mother.

As it turned out, Deanie called that night to see what had become of me. She had never had mumps and she was not about to visit me, but politically adept as she was, she played the Southern Belle so well on the telephone that she was able to disarm and charm even my mother. "She's a nice young lady," my mother said after their conversation. "She volunteered to pick up your school assignments so Alfred or John can bring them by." And that's what happened eventually. But before I was even remotely able to concentrate on a school assignment, I had a much darker road to travel.

In many ways, I think physical illness is worse than physical danger. Danger tends to be intense and short-lived, and there is always the chance of taking some action to change things. But illness saps our will and autonomy. And I think it was with the attack of this "mere" childhood disease that I first experienced the horror of feeling that I had absolutely *no* power to control my own life. It had all been taken out of my hands—and this at the same time that I had just come to believe that I was the one responsible for everything.

Why do all the big issues of life—the awakenings, the successes, the failures, the pains, the pleasures, our health, and even our consciousness itself—all revolve around or affect us through our sex? Was Freud essentially right, after all, when he implied that we are at core merely living manifestations of our sexuality and that if one is to be attacked, then the best place to create devastation is through one's sex? If so, then the disease of mumps knew how to attack me with the greatest devastation. By the time Dr. Verdury arrived at our house at 7 P.M. the following day, exactly thirty-six hours after the initial call, my disease had announced itself fully. It had progressed from my throat and the lymph glands beneath my ears, through the glands of my inner arms, down my sides to the inside of my thighs, and most cruelly settled in my testicles. By the end of that second day, it was as though my scrotum contained a pair of large tennis balls. Moving without pain was an impossibility. And to make matters worse, on that first night, for the first time in my life and to my horror and alarm, I experienced my first nocturnal emission. Such things are commonplace among adolescent boys and, as "wet dreams," they are usually spoken of with snickering and joking. But I had never even heard of such a thing before, and this, coming when it did and combining both pleasure and pain, was both frightening and deeply embarrassing. I remember that I was dreaming about Ruth Ann—not the dream, just the fact that she was in it—when I was struck by this spontaneous orgasm and woke to find the bed wet and my testicles grossly enlarged. *What is happening to me?* I wondered. *Am I being punished for the lustful thoughts I had about the woman at Honeycut or the ones I've struggled to suppress about Ruth Ann and Nadine? Am I dying? Is the power of helping myself being removed totally from my hands?* It was a long and frightening night, and I passed it drifting in and out of consciousness as my mother applied new ice packs to reduce my fever.

The doctor apologized when he arrived. He had been working for twenty-three hours without rest and had come as quickly as he could. And then when he examined me, I could tell from the expression on his face that mine was no routine case of mumps. He spoke to my mother in the hallway, speaking barely above a whisper, but I could overhear every word. "Normally I would recommend we take him to a hospital," he said. "But the hospitals are already overcrowded and the best thing is to keep him here." He gave her some medicine and wrote out a prescription for more. "This will help," he said. "But only time will change things. Keep using the ice, especially around his testicles. Keep the fever down. It's more dangerous even than the disease."

She went with him to the door. "Doctor," she said. "I haven't had mumps."

"Then you will probably get it," he said. "If you do, call me. But take care of yourself. Mumps is very hard on adults."

And so we waited for my disease to run it's course, with me lying flat on my back and ice packs piled around my throat and groin for long periods of time. And then about ten days later I remember waking at night in a heavy sweat and knowing that the disease had gone as far as it could and was now beginning to retreat. Not that I would be leaping out of the bed any time soon. It would be a slow retreat, and I would remain virtually bedridden and swollen for five long weeks, but I suddenly felt hopeful and again interested in the world. That was when my mother came down with it.

So imagine, if you will, the two of us alone, immobilized, and swollen, lying in our separate bedrooms and very conscious of the doctor's repeated warning, "Stay in bed. The more you move around, the more likely you are to develop painful and dangerous complications." But one of us *had* to move. If we ate, someone had to get the food and prepare it. And this is where my friends became enormously helpful.

Both Alfred and John had had mumps and they came to see me, but since Alfred lived closer, it was mostly he who went to the grocery store for us. My mother gave him a list and the keys to the car, and as was always true of him in times of emergency, he enthusiastically turned his hand to helping in any way he could. My mother also called our neighbors, the Herrings, from whom we bought most of our farm produce, and Mr. Herring regularly delivered butter, eggs, and home-made bread and canned goods to our door, along with the mail from the post office. But doctor's warning or not, one of us always had to get up to take a turn cooking the food.

Although her visible symptoms were not so great as mine, I think my mother was nearly as sick as I had been. She ran a high fever. She swelled enormously around her throat. She lost her voice and for weeks was unable to speak above a whisper. Whether this loss was a physical result of the disease or a hysterical reaction to stress, I never knew. Certainly she had been through enough that spring to produce a home front version of "shell shock" or combat fatigue in almost anybody. But for-ever afterward, in times of stress, her voice would be the first thing to fail—as when, at the age of twenty, I told her I was going to get married and she lost her voice and went to bed for a week. However, in 1944, we managed to survive our bat-tle, and by late May, still carrying hidden, but life long scars from the ordeal, we were again up and going about what passed for normal life.

But achieving a truly normal life in the spring and sum-mer of 1944 would prove difficult indeed. First, for me, even after I went back to school, looking somewhat emaciated after losing ten or twelve pounds, I was required by the doctor to wear a "suspensory bag" or modified jock strap to gird up my loins until all the residual swelling and sensitivity had disappeared. This device, in spite of my loose hanging clothes, produced for me somewhat the same silhouette as a cod piece in the trousers of a 16th century gentleman. Although no one ever said anything, I was aware of receiving frequent sidelong glances and hearing snickers from my classmates at what appeared to be my permanent erection.

Thanks to Deanie, Alfred, and John for bringing me my school assignments, I was not behind in my schoolwork, but this helpful cooperation on the part of my three closest friends produced probably the most painful and wrenching complication of them all. I remember walking down the hall after school one day in late May or early June of that year, walking routinely toward my locker as I did at the end of every school day, when I passed Nadine and John—which I also did at the end of every school day. Except that this time they were standing together and they did not see me. Indeed, I think that they did not see anything except each other. It was as though they had suddenly become electrified or infused with a kind of atomic radiation that encircled them with a golden halo and set them apart from everything and everyone in that gray hallway. Deanie was leaning back against her locker gazing up into John's eyes with such total adoration that for an instant I almost felt like apologizing for having intruded into their private sacred moment. They were not speaking—they were only gazing at each other. But I knew that the look in her eyes was one she had never even come close to turning in my direction, and I knew that my world was changing again.

Needless to say, for the next few days, the discovery of this passion between two of my most loved friends produced a jangle in me such as I'd never before confronted. It was like falling or sinking into deep water as I had done at age four, looking for a lifeline or seeking a solid bottom from which I could again spring up into the light. Deanie was not *my* girl.

There had never been any suggestion of that, and if anyone had asked me, I would have denied it. Yet in the six months that I had known her, she had become my most intimate companion in the world. She did not replace John and Alfred; they were my companions, too. Each of the three provided something that the others did not. But Deanie had become the closest. What would happen now? Deanie and John could never have the kind of relationship that she and I had. John had a philosophically speculative mind, and that was the area that cemented our friendship most. But though he had appreciation for the arts and literature, he was not an artist and could never meet her in that arena. Yet, after one glance at them in the hall, I needed no guidebook to tell me that nothing I could do would be sufficient to turn the tide of their passion.

The very next day, Deanie began to talk to me about John as we rode together on the school bus, telling me how handsome she thought he was, how well mannered, how brilliantly he conducted himself in class discussions. And John began to talk to me about Deanie—her beauty, her liveliness, her quick wit. And I could only agree. All this was true about both of them. How could I object in any way to the fact that one of my dearest friends loved another of my dearest friends? But in less than forty-eight hours, I had become a kind of go-between, with each of them confiding in me their deepest feelings about the other. And I found myself overnight the trusted repository of other people's confidence.

The interesting—and in a way, wonderful—part was that they never shut me out of their relationship. I dropped by Nadine's house on Saturday afternoon as I often did just to talk. And John was there. He had gotten his father's car and they were planning to go to the movies, but they both seemed glad to see me. "Come go with us," John said.

"You sure?"

"Yeah. Of course, I'm sure."

"Yes," Deanie said. And she took both our hands. "It would be *so* much fun!"

And I went. It was the beginning of a strange and passion filled triumvirate. I never had any doubt where the lines of force lay. Deanie leaned on John's shoulder, she held his hand in the movies, and she gazed into his eyes, all in ways she never did with me. But when we walked down the street, she walked in the middle holding both our arms. Later, when their relationship had really warmed, they might fall into periods of passionate kissing while I, with eyes slightly averted, sat beside them in the front seat of John's car. Since both of them had confided to me virtually every thought and feeling they had about the other, it was as though they included me as their emotional banker, keeping me close by for safety and support. It would become for me yet another experience of paradox—the experience of being totally inside and totally outside of a situation at the same time, of being both included and excluded by the same act, of both winning and losing in the same event, of joy and sorrow in the same moment, and finally, the experience of both loving and hating the same people at the same time.

And then, while these personal emotional whirlwinds continued to howl across the hills and hollows of my soul, the outside world exploded in a way that would change everybody's focus. I remember my mother's turning on the radio news before I left for school on the morning of June 7th and hearing the announcement—maybe in the voice of Robert Trout from CBS news: "Allied Forces, led by the United States, have invaded the Continent of Europe." We had all supposed it would probably happen someday, but on that morning we stood there in the kitchen stunned as the still limited news filtered through the airways. Allied Forces, commanded by General Dwight Eisenhower, had mounted on June 6 the greatest armada in history and now were laying siege to the coast of Normandy. There were still few details.

We learned only that every ship available to the United States, England, and the Free French Forces had been deployed in the battle, unloading wave after wave of troops against the defending Nazis, following heavy shelling and continuous bombing by the Air Force. We also learned that the 82nd Airborne Division and the glider units so recently training at Fort Bragg had been deployed in the early hours of the fighting.

Our thoughts, of course, went first to my father. Where was he? Had he been transferred to the European sector or was he still in Africa directing the flow of aircraft toward the fighting? Then there was the speculation about my first cousin, Alexander Stowe, whom we knew to be stationed in England with the Fifth Infantry Division, and about my mother's brother Howerton, the same uncle who had been with me on the day I nearly drowned, who had until recently been transporting troops and supplies in the campaign against Sicily. My two remaining uncles were stationed in the Pacific and so probably were not involved in this European thrust. But to have three members of the family involved with it was quite enough.

I think that for a time Fayetteville was as beleaguered a city as any in the world. It was, after all, the home of the 82nd Airborne. The families of the men in the 82nd lived there, to say nothing of the families of the men in every other unit based at Fort Bragg and now involved in the European campaign. And I would say that in two thirds of the homes in the Fayetteville area that morning, the wives and children of service men were gathered around the radios in their kitchens and all asking the same questions about their loved ones: "Where are they? Are they living? Are they dead? Are they suffering? Are they doing their jobs well so that this awful war can be brought to a close?" And of course, unstated, there was always that other question which silently soaked through our lives like an endless rain: "If the worst happens, what's going to happen to me, to us?"

It was a time of joy and fear, jubilation and sorrow, courage and sheer panic. Deanie's father was still at Fort Bragg, but John's brother Jack was in the navy, probably at sea, we knew not where. Alfred's Uncle Maury was in the Marine Corps and Alfred didn't know where he was either. My father's most recent letters—now nearly a month old—had told us that at least at that time, he was still in some jungle rain forest in Africa. He told us also that he had recently been in the infirmary, but was now back on duty. No other details, of course, beyond his personal desire to see us again soon. But from the European fighting, specific news began to reach us fairly quickly as the Allied forces consolidated their beachhead and moved further into France fighting for every inch of ground against reinforced German defenses now commanded by General Erwin Rommel. For days, the advance seemed stalemated at St. Lo and then at Metz. And then the news of casualties began to reach us. My cousin Alex was among them. We received the news late one night, less than a month after the invasion, when my mother received a call from her sister Norma. Alex had been wounded at Metz. As yet, there were no details beyond the facts that he was out of the fighting and had been evacuated back to a hospital in England. And I remember that my mother and I both offered special prayers for his survival and recovery before we went to bed that night.

But while individual casualties, wounding, and deaths struck many individual families across America that summer, it was probably the experience of our teacher, Ruth Howard, that focused the human dimension of the war most tellingly for the members of my high school class. Miss Howard was our most popular teacher, vivacious and pretty, in her early twenties, and with a reputation for being a demanding teacher of world history. But her strict demands seemed in no way to diminish her popularity among the students. The boys all fell in love with her and the girls all wanted to be like her. And when one day she was visited at school by a handsome young Airborne captain named Guy Jones, the whole student body had gone into a kind of collective twitter. For Guy Jones was the personification of the ideal American soldier—dark hair, even white teeth, tanned face, perfect build, and quick smile, wearing the jump boots and uniform of the 82nd Airborne which made its wearers all look like supermen to start with. Twentieth Century Fox could not have cast better. Miss Howard was with him often, and now all the girls fell in love with him and all the boys wanted to be like him. I think a lot of our youthful dreams and ideals somehow became focused and personified by this lovely couple. And when they married in the spring, it was a kind of confirmation for us all, telling us what we so much wanted to hear, that dreams could be realized, that everything was going to be all right, and that finally, true love conquered all. To be able to walk through life with the beauty and grace of Ruth and Guy, what more could anyone ask?

Of course, Captain Jones was shipped out with the 82nd when it left for Europe, and Miss Howard—now Mrs. Jones—took her place like Penelope among the thousands of American wives who waited for their husbands' return. When news reached Fayetteville that Captain Jones had been killed in action during the early days of fighting following the D-Day invasion, it was as though everyone at my school had lost a much loved older brother. This couldn't be happening! The universe couldn't possibly allow one so young and perfect to be struck down so cruelly! Yet in reality, we knew that it was happening around us and across America every day, but especially in Fayetteville where so many military families were concentrated. Of course, those youthful ideals which we had invested in Ruth and Guy Jones now were twisted and reshaped into enormous and frightening questions: "Could any dream actually be realized? Would anything ever turn out all right? Did true love have any power at all?" We had to go on living our lives, but somehow now, it seemed almost shameful to think of living our own lives when so much was at stake with so many whom we loved in other parts of the world.

Chapter Thirteen

My cousin Alex survived his wounds. Gradually we learned that fragments from a German artillery shell had hit him just outside the town of Metz. Since all the officers and senior non-coms had been shot out from above him, he was serving as acting platoon leader for what was left of his unit at the time he was hit. He told me when he returned to the states the following year that his life had been saved by a Luger pistol that he had taken from a German officer. He had slipped the Luger into his hip pocket for safekeeping, and when the shell went off directly behind him, the Luger had shielded him from the largest fragment. "It shattered the Luger," he told me, "but if the Luger hadn't been there, it would have taken my leg off and I would have bled to death before anyone could reach me."

But the biggest immediate change for my family was that my father returned to the states. Totally without warning. I simply answered the telephone one night and he was on the other end. "Son, I'm back," he said. And I must have deafened him with my shout of joy.

My mother came running, and after all the shouting, the crying, and the giving thanks to God for his safe return, we began to gather bits of information. He was in a military hospital, a center for tropical diseases in Miami. "Are you sick?" my mother asked.

"Well, I picked up something in the jungle. There were complications."

"But what is it?"

"They're not sure. They're testing."

"We'll come," my mother said. "We'll come now."

"No," he told her. "They may send me home on leave even before you can get here. Let me find out their plans."

And gradually in that first long phone call and in the calls and letters that followed immediately after, we began to get the full picture. He had been at Roberts Field, an air base near Monrovia, Liberia, which was technically an independent country, but in fact, a kind of U.S. colony, carved out of the jungle and designated in the 19th century as a place to ship emancipated North American Negroes. Liberia's strategic importance during the 1940s was as a source of rubber and hardwoods and as a staging area for shipping aircraft and munitions to Europe and other parts of Africa.

But in spite of its shipping, rubber, and logging activities, Liberia was hardly an industrial nation. It was a jungle. And the problem for my father began, it seems, with the fact that he had never been given the full course of inoculations that he should have received before being shipped to such a place. We tend to think of war as conflict between opposing armies of men who contend heroically for victory, but in truth, the most vicious enemies of field armies may not be men at all and may, in fact, be totally invisible and devoid of concern for geo-politics. Fungus, dysentery, hepatitis, cholera, malaria, yellow fever, dengue, anthrax, plague, dehydration, sunstroke, and the still mysterious affliction of "combat fatigue" can destroy an army even more effectively than artillery, bombs, and machine guns. And men suddenly uprooted from the relatively sterile environments of North America or northern Europe and thrust into the tropics without sufficient protection become walking targets. My father, without all his shots, apparently became host to every spore, spirochete, and insect borne disease available to plague human kind in the primitive tropical areas of the world. For the most part, he apparently tried to work through it, taking whatever medicines could be provided by the base infirmary and returning to duty. But in the equatorial heat and humidity, the duty itself had an enormous down side. It was not flying—the life's blood of every devoted pilot—but maintenance, repair, supply, and transit services, and of course, making sure that all the men assigned to the unit were able to perform all their duties all the time. Though there were half a dozen defensive fighter aircraft assigned to the base, the Ferry Command in North Africa depended primarily on the British for fighter and radar protection from German attack. So the job of the men at Roberts Field was—day and night—to ensure an unending flow of bombers for the major push against the Third Reich.

Finally, it had been dengue fever that brought him down. Headache, fever, delirium, skin rash, and in the middle of it all, the heart irregularity that had been detected after his crash in 1939 now burst forth as full fledged angina.

We knew none of this at the time. But the ravaging effects of his diseases would become painfully obvious within minutes after he appeared suddenly, unannounced on an afternoon in mid-summer. I remember that I was lying on the living room floor reading in front of the fan when I heard a noise outside and looked up to see him wearing dress "pinks" and a Sam Browne belt, standing in the doorway, and I ran, literally leaping in the air to embrace him. I had grown much heavier during his absence while he, having just risen from a hospital bed, had grown much lighter, and it was only the edge of the doorway that kept the joy of my onslaught from knocking him backward down the steps. But I could see in a moment, as could my mother when she came rushing in response to my shouts, that he was greatly weakened, almost emaciated from the effects of his illness. The shoulders and upper arms that I remembered as powerfully muscled were now bony, almost childlike to the touch. And the exertion of walking from the taxi to the door had left him winded. Of course, I was so over-joyed to see him that I didn't take in the meaning of all this at first. My father had returned! God had answered our prayers! A million thoughts—some altruistic and loving, some purely selfish—went surging through my mind all at once. But after my gratitude for his life, I think my most dominant feeling was my joy at being liberated. I would no longer have to bear the full load of being the "man of the house" and taking care of my mother. I was at last being set free to be just a growing boy without having to shoulder the burdens and dangers of the adult world at the same time!

Little did I know. My father had been reassigned to the Ferry Command headquarters in Miami, but he had been granted a month's convalescent leave. He would be at home for most of the summer, and after that, he told us, he wanted to arrange for us to join him in Florida. It all promised to be very exciting. Yet even before that day was out, I had calmed down enough to see my father more objectively, to see clearly the uniform that no longer fit his thin body and the deep lines of pain and worry etched across his face. And I remember thinking as I saw him sit wearily in the wing chair at the cor-ner of the living room that I was looking at a man whom I had never seen before in my life.

The first thing he wanted to do was to re-build his strength and endurance. And I wanted to help him. We began by taking short walks and stopping frequently to rest. He wanted to see quiet waterways, so we went to the country club lake, not so much to swim, but to sit on the bank and gaze at the water and to fish. And gradually, as his range of walking increased, we made it all the way to the river. He told me very little about Africa, but gradually bits of information began to emerge: the black people he had seen were all very short, he said, few of them as tall as five feet. And he never heard any of them sing. "It was very strange," he said. "We think of Negroes as being musical, but there they were all silent." He gave me a leopard tooth, drilled and hung on a thong for a souvenir. "There were many wild animals," he told me, "leopards and crocodiles and monkeys. I wanted to bring you a little monkey, but of course, I couldn't." And then one afternoon after a period of long silence, he stopped in the middle of the sandy road that ran along the border of the Veterans' Hospital property and said, "They ate one of my men." He was looking at me, and theoretically he was talking to me, but he had a look in his eyes that told me quite clearly he was seeing neither me nor anything else in the immediate area.

"What? Who?" I said. "Who ate one of your men?"

And then his eyes focused on me again as though he were coming out of a trance. "Driver ants," he said. "The driver ants ate one of my men."

Gradually he told me the story. It seems the American business community living in Liberia had welcomed the Air Force units enthusiastically. The Goodyear Rubber Company had a large operation there, one that was very important to the U.S. war effort. There were also logging and mining companies as well. And needless to say, this group of *colonials* had formed a fairly tight knit community—much as the British and French had done in their colonies. Early in the war, the Americans had feared German invasion, so out of gratitude for the U.S. military presence, they invited the service men into their colonial social world as much as possible, giving occasional parties and providing as much entertainment as they could. My father told me that it was after one of these parties that one of his men, walking back to the air base, had sat down to rest beneath a tree and apparently fallen asleep.

"We found his skeleton the next morning," my father said. "The ants ate almost everything except his dog tags."

Of course, I was never able to appraise the full importance of this incident in my father's life, but I think it was important because he referred to it more than once, later even giving me a short lecture on the life and habits of driver ants and how they plague the countries in which they live. And although he never said so, I think he felt responsible and embarrassed to have one of his men die in such a bizarre way.

Now certainly, within the first weeks after my father's return, I saw quite clearly the effects of his illness and the heavy emotional burden he had brought home. But I also saw that his physical strength seemed to be returning, and in my usual optimistic way, I took this to mean that everything was soon going to be okay, and I was determined to make the most of the freedom he brought me.

A Boy Scout camp had been scheduled for late summer at Lake Singletary about fifty miles from Fayetteville, and though I had wanted to go, I had not mentioned it to my mother because I didn't think I should go and leave her alone. But now with my father's return, everything had changed and I made plans. John was going to Scout Camp, too, but since we were in different troops, we wouldn't be likely to see much of each other.

I had joined the scouts mainly as a way of having a wider association with boys my own age, but for the most part, I had always found scouting rather bland. I admired the principles of boy scouting as stated in the Scout Law: "A Scout is trustworthy, loyal, helpful, friendly, courteous, kind, obedient, cheerful, thrifty, brave, clean, and reverent." And in the Scout Oath: "On my honor I will do my best to do my duty to God and my country and to obey the Scout Law; to help other people at all times; to keep myself physically strong, mentally awake, and morally straight." And the Scout Motto: "Be prepared." They were things I had tried to achieve for most of my life. But as one who had easy access to the forests and water-ways, I found for the most part that I could do more exciting things by myself in the woods than I could with a bunch of scouts around. The camp at Lake Singletary, however, was to be a different thing. It was to concentrate on water safety, and it was there that I could learn rowing, canoeing, and life saving under qualified instructors and win merit badges and a Red Cross life saving certificate that would qualify me to work as a lifeguard. Also, though I never admitted it even to myself, my eagerness to go was probably prompted somewhat by my desire to free myself finally from the last cloud of timidity about deep water that had hung over my shoulder since age four. So it was with great hoopla and excitement that I went off with our scoutmasters and about ten other boys to spend two weeks in the water during what had become a very hot summer.

Lake Singletary was a large, clean lake—about three miles across—filled with what appeared to be black water. Three feet beneath the surface, it was virtually impossible to see any-thing, and so we had to be especially alert. The first week was largely dedicated to conditioning and training. I learned to row and master the courses set up by our instructors. I learned to paddle a canoe, paddling on one side only, and then I learned how to swamp a canoe, empty it, and then get back in, all in deep water in the middle of the lake and without once touching the bottom.

And then came the lifesaving course, which was the most grueling of all. Swimming long distances, diving for bricks in ten feet of black water until I thought my lungs would burst, jumping in fully dressed and undressing in deep water, artifi-cial respiration. And of course, retrieving bodies in every con-ceivable situation, bodies of submerged victims, inert victims, panicked victims. But the course always stressed that we, as lifesavers, had to be in charge, controlling the dangerous situ-ations we confronted so that no situation would suddenly

turn and control us. And we learned also how to leave a hopeless situation rather than allow ourselves to be drowned by the
person we were trying to save. At the end of every day, all of
us were exhausted, but we were young and resilient, and by
the beginning of the second week, we were able to accomplish
feats of endurance under water and in long distance swimming that would have been impossible when we arrived.

It was there at the waterfront and in the dining hall that I
began to meet boys from other towns. We practiced saving
each other's lives every day, scouts from Laurinburg, Raeford,
Wagram, Red Springs. And in the evenings after dinner we
would tell jokes and visit back and forth between each other's
cabins.

The boys from Laurinburg were staying in the cabin next
to ours, and one evening, coming back from supper, I heard
shouting and cheering as though the boys next door were having an athletic contest, and I walked in to see what was going
on. The sun was still shining on that late summer afternoon,
and I remember that the upper part of the cabin above the
bunk beds was bathed with soft orange sunlight, but on the
floor below, the room was filled with shouting naked boys
cavorting like demons in some medieval painting. There was
a pile of money on the floor, and around it in a circle stood
six or eight boys fondling their genitals and in various stages
of erection. One of the older boys seemed to be directing the
whole thing, and he was standing on the sidelines with a stop-
watch egging the others on: "Okay, now. Ready?" The boys in
the circle all seemed to have achieved full erection. "On your
mark. Go!" And at the command, they began to masturbate
as fast and furiously as they possibly could. They were not yet
old enough to have learned that first come is not necessarily
best served, but in this case they were racing against the clock
for money. The room was suddenly filled with shouts and
cheers from the audience as people yelled support for the con-
tenders, and I soon realized that not only was there a winner's

pot on the floor, but that guys in the audience had placed bets with each other on their various champions. Maybe I had lived a life too innocent and isolated in the woods to know what really went on in the world, but never in my wildest and most depraved imagination could I have dreamed such a scene. I suppose there are few people in the world who have not at some time been so overcome by erotic excitement that they resorted to solitary relief. But in my own experience, it had always left me feeling lonely and ashamed—not because I'd been taught that it was wrong. Indeed, I had never heard anyone mention it at all. But the idea of doing it in public was totally inconceivable. And then while I was still wrestling with my shock, a great shout went up from the crowd. A tall, red headed kid named Hill was suddenly seized by a shudder. Blobs of semen shot half way across the circle to the accompaniment of *hurrahs* and simulated groans of ecstasy. "Atta boy, Hill! We knew you could do it! Way to go!" And then one at a time, the other boys in the circle began arriving at their own finish, spurting lines of bright fluid onto the floor.

I turned and pushed my way toward the exit with fragments of the Scout Creed flashing jaggedly through my mind. "A Scout is . . . brave, clean, and reverent? Morally straight?" The boy next to me seemed as disgusted as I was. "Remind me never to walk into that cabin barefooted," he said when we reached the door. And I could only look at him, nod, and walk away alone and nonplussed into the evening air.

Needless to say, the carnal caper in the Laurinburg cottage gave me a lot to think about. The boys from Laurinburg and Wagram swore more and said *shit* and *fuck* a lot more than most people I knew, but otherwise they just seemed like regular guys. They went to school and church, played football and baseball, and went to the same kind of scout meetings that I did. They stood once a week and gave the Scout salute and repeated the Scout Law and the Scout Oath just as I did at every meeting. "On my honor . . ." And I wondered if they paid any attention at all to the words they were saying. Did repeated creeds have any value? Or were they just noble sounding but meaningless formulae to make people feel good about themselves when they were, in fact, behaving atrociously? *Honor.* What was it, after all? How did one define it? Was there any relation at all between being brave, clean, reverent, and morally straight and a circle jerk conducted in a log cabin on the shores of Lake Singletary?

I didn't come up with any final answers, but the next day I went back to the waterfront and lifeguard training with renewed determination. My job was to do the best I could with whatever I was doing, no matter what else was going on, and I was glad to get back to it. But you can imagine my dismay when the instructor, totally by chance, paired me in practice with Hill, the red headed boy who had won the circle jerk, and we had to spend the whole morning rescuing each other in turn. That was democracy, after all. Everybody deserved to be saved. But afterward, I was sure to shower and soap down thoroughly when I got back to the cabin.

By that time, there were only two days to go before the end of camp and the Red Cross examiners would give us our final tests for lifesaving, but I had at least one more shock to confront before it was over. I remember walking back to the cabin one night with Hal, our senior patrol leader. He was a rising senior and had already passed his eighteenth birthday, and I remember that he was worried about being drafted before he finished high school. We talked about the war and how we all, whether we liked it or not, were involved with it one way or another, and we wondered how we would be planning our lives if there had been no war to consider. He was an intelligent guy, not especially athletic, but he had already achieved the rank of Eagle Scout. He had won his own lifesaving certificate years before, and I think that most of his active life—outside his studies and his playing trombone in the school band—was devoted to scouting. He was working as an assistant instructor on the waterfront that summer, and he had given me lots of pointers. "You've come a long way," he told me. "I've been watching you." And then, right in the middle of our conversation, I had to excuse myself, since the scoutmaster had found out I was a trumpet player and had asked me to play "Taps" for lights out. The whole camp was run on a kind of military model with "Reveille" sounding to get us up in the morning and "Taps" to send us to bed at night. An older boy named Paul—who was a truly fine bugler—had been playing all through the camp session, but for some reason, he was unable to play that day, and I was really flattered to be asked. "Go ahead," Hal said. "We'll talk when you get back."

"Taps" is such a hauntingly beautiful piece of music that every time I heard it or tried to play it, I got choked up. It somehow invoked the closing of every day that had ever ended, the end of every life that had ever been lived, the disappearance of every waking dream that had ever invaded the human mind. Drifting out across the darkened compound and beyond the trees, over the water and upward into the night sky, "Taps" awakened the ultimate sense of one's aloneness, arousing in the same instant the longing for one other soul with whom to bond while reminding us, with a sense of sorrow and compassion, that all bonds are temporary and that life is short.

Somehow, I managed to get my own feelings under control and just concentrate on the music that night, and when I finished and walked back to the cabin, I felt that I had acquitted myself pretty well. All the lights were out by then, except for low streetlights and lights in the latrine, but of course, boys were continuing everywhere to finish out late evening conversations or to read by flashlight. I came in and undressed (we all slept in our underwear at camp) and got ready for bed. I was then aware that Hal was standing behind me. "That was great," he said. "Not only have you come a long way with your swimming, but your playing has gotten really good."

"You think so?"

"Yeah, really. Come on over and let me finish what I was saying earlier."

It was darker on his side of the room where his bunk was at a slight distance from the other campers. Nobody was sleeping above him, so we sat on the lower bunk and continued to talk barely above whisper level. "You've really developed over the summer," he said.

"You think I can pass the Red Cross test?"

"Oh sure," he said. "No problem there. You'll breeze through. And if you're interested, after you pass, I was thinking about recommending you for the job of assistant instructor next year."

"That would be great," I said. "I'd like that."

"You know what to do and how to do it, and you've gotten really strong. I mean, you were always pretty strong, but look how you've developed it." He felt my shoulder muscles. "You didn't have that kind of muscle definition when you first got to camp. Or on your legs, either." He squeezed my thigh. "Hard as iron. Have you got a girlfriend?"

"Yeah . . . well, no," I said. "You see, I had one, but she moved away when her dad was transferred. And then . . ." I almost told him about Deanie, but for some reason, I held back. "There was another girl for a while, but I think she's in love with somebody else now."

"It's hard, isn't it?" he said. "I've had that happen. Leaves you feelin' mighty lonely." Hal patted my thigh again and fell silent for a moment, and then totally out of nowhere, he moved his hand over and laid it squarely on my crotch.

"Uh . . . what're you doing?" I said.

"Doesn't that feel nice?"

"Why are you doing that?"

He answered by taking my hand and trying to lay it on his crotch where I realized in an instant that he was erect and I jerked my hand away as though I had touched a wasp.

"I wish you wouldn't do that," I said.

"Don't you think it would be nice if two friends who like each other would lie back and make each other feel good before they go to sleep?" Hal asked.

He tried to put his arm around me, the way a man might embrace a girl. But by this time, I had skyrockets and alarm bells going off all through my brain. Understand that, at age thirteen in 1944, I had virtually no notion of homosexuality at all. It was an idea so strange that it simply had no reality for me. The closest approach I'd ever had to it was from Clarence waving his black prick at me in the back of the House of Flowers and saying, "Come here and hold this for me, white boy." Alfred had told me stories about "queer baiting" when he was in military school. He and some other boys would go on weekends into the parks and other public places where "queers" were known to hang out. They would send one of their youngest and prettiest boys as "queer bait" to sit on a park bench and look seductive, waiting to be approached by a queer, whereupon the other boys would leap out of the bushes and "beat the livin' shit out of the queer." His stories always appalled me, both from the standpoint of the boys and the standpoint of the queer. I couldn't understand either side. I often wondered what part Alfred had played in all this, what part it might have played in his leaving military school and in making him the person he was. But here in this case, Hal was five years older than I. I trusted him. He was my Senior Patrol Leader, my lifesaving instructor, and the guy who was going to recommend me for a job as assistant instructor the following year. He was an Eagle Scout, the young man who stood out front and led our entire scout troop in reciting the Scout Oath and the Scout Law every Thursday night. "On my honor . . . God and country . . . mentally awake and morally straight . . . brave, clean, and reverent . . ." And now he wanted me to play with his prick!

"What are you, a queer?" I asked.

"Well, you don't have to be nasty about it."

"You are, aren't you?" I asked. And by this time, I was on my feet and standing in the soft reflected light in front of him. "A damned, fuckin' queer!" By this time I'd absorbed all the scurrility in vogue with the Laurinburg boys next door, and I used it. "A fuckin', ass lickin' queer!" Words I'd never used before in my life. And I stormed back to my bunk on the opposite side of the building.

If the circle jerk next door had troubled me, this business with Hal *really* gave me something to think about. I simply had no place to put it. It didn't fit anything in my life and suddenly I felt unsafe in my bed. Would Hal try to follow up on what he'd started and come attempt to fondle me when I went to sleep? *Damn!* I thought. If the sonofabitch even touched me again, I would beat him to death! And then, as extra precaution, following the Scout Motto of being prepared, I reached under my bed to my knapsack and found my Boy Scout case knife, which I unsnapped from its sheath and slipped beneath my pillow. If the bastard came after me, he was gonna draw back a nub and no question about it!

But Hal never bothered me again. I don't even remember speaking to him after that night, and until this writing, I never told anyone about what had happened. I passed my lifesaving test and won my merit badge and my Red Cross certificate two days later, and I went home feeling pretty good about things. But, needless to say, Hal did not recommend me for the waterfront job the following year.

Chapter Fourteen

When I arrived back at home, I could see in a moment that my father had grown much stronger than when I left. He was able to walk more briskly and able to carry on a conversation for an extended period without stopping suddenly in mid-sentence as though his mind had shut down. He was still abstracted from time to time, drifting off into sudden silent realms where no one else could follow, but now as he prepared to return to duty in Miami, he seemed once more optimistic, almost his old self—but not quite.

He was anxious to have us come to Florida with him, and he made the whole prospect seem very nice. "A lot of vacation houses have been turned over to the military for use till the end of the war," he told us. "I'm sure I can get one of those." He told my mother to start looking for some reliable person to rent our house. And then he was gone, hooking a ride on an Air Force transport plane from Pope Field. I think the day of his departure was the last time I saw him truly resemble the man I had grown up loving. I watched him assemble his uniform. He put his wings and his Air Force insignia on his newly pressed summer khakis, picked up his suitcase, and walked with a bounce in his step to the car. He received and returned the salutes of other officers and enlisted men as he walked onto the base when we took him to meet his plane. "I'll see you soon," he said as he embraced us. And then my mother and I watched beside the chain-link fence as the twin engine C-46 taxied to the end of the runway and departed southward.

His call from Miami a few days later was almost ecstatic. "I've found the perfect place!" he said. "It's a villa on an island in the bay. It belongs to a man from New York who doesn't want to come down here while there's still so much submarine action off the coast, but I think it's perfectly safe. And beautiful! It has a marble entryway." He made it sound like paradise. "You'll have to go to school by boat," he told me, "but I don't think you'll mind that." And immediately my mother and I started packing things away and preparing to join him by September 1.

We never made it. In late August, he called again, and his voice when I answered the phone came from beyond the tomb. There was no small talk, no bright news, and no word, as was usual from him, of love or encouragement. Only, "Son, let me speak to your mother, please."

"Yessir. Just a minute."

And when she answered, I saw her face go pale. "But they can't do that," she said. And she was almost shouting, which for her was virtually impossible. "They can't just discard you like a piece of trash!"

But that is essentially what the Air Force had done. They had not been able to find a job for him in Miami, and they had concluded, after a final physical examination, that although he was certainly eligible to be released from hospital supervision, the condition of his heart, lungs, and eyes had made him unsuitable for continued military service. They had ordered him separated from active duty and returned to civilian life with no pay or allowances beyond the standard two months' severance pay and with what the doctors equated, even then, as a one hundred percent disability. However, I think that probably the severest blow of all was one that I did not discover until after his death years later when I was cleaning out his files and reading through his papers. I discovered then that the rating that he received on his final efficiency report, signed by a commanding officer who barely knew him and under whom he had never worked, was: *Unsatisfactory*. This, for a man who prided himself on doing things well, a man whose efficiency ratings over the years had been uniformly *Superior*, and who had been called by at least one commander, "the finest officer I know," must have come as the equivalent of Brutus' final thrust at Caesar.

When he arrived back at home, he was not in a coma, no, but clearly he was in a state of shock, hardly talking at all, wandering through the house and into the yard at all hours of the day and night, lost in a maelstrom of inner thoughts. I would see him sitting on the back step or under the tree behind the house with his mouth moving as though in violent debate, talking to himself or to someone beyond our sight or hearing with whom he had to try and square things. I know now in ways I could only imagine then that he was trying to make some sense out of his life. Feeling that he could neither support his family nor serve his country and now, with his heart and lung condition, could not even take up the plow and plant a garden as he had in 1935, he tried through phrase after phrase of turbulent silent rhetoric to justify himself, arguing perhaps with that last commander, or perhaps with his own father, against whose shadow of early easy brilliance I think he had struggled for most of his life. And of course, finally and most clearly, I think he was arguing against himself, the *real* last commander, trying to find something in his existence to prove that he was not really, after all, an inefficient piece of trash.

He began, almost ritually, to clean his guns and mine, oiling them and polishing them with affection. And once, this usually most careful and responsible of men, accidentally discharged his .45 pistol while trying to clean it on the front steps. My mother and I were in the kitchen when we heard the shot, and we rushed to the front to find him sitting there sheepishly like a naughty child. "It's nothing," he said. "The bullet went into the sand."

"Will you come in and put the guns away?" my mother asked. "Please." And he obeyed her. But when she was again alone with me in the kitchen, she looked directly into my eyes and said, "I am the most frightened woman in the world." And then she put her head against my chest, virtually forcing me to hug her. "I feel like all this is my fault," she said. ". . . that everything bad that has happened to us is my fault."

"Why on earth would you feel that?"

"Because I'm the one who persuaded him to get out of the Air Corps."

"What?"

"In 1932," she said, "he was offered a permanent commission in the regular air service and I asked him not to take it."

"But why?"

"Because all his flying frightened me . . . and I didn't like the people we had to associate with—didn't like their moral standards."

"And he gave up the career he loved?"

"It's all my fault," she said. "Because of me. Because he loved me. And now we're in all this mess."

I don't remember exactly what I thought about this information at the time, but I do remember feeling as appalled by her disclosure as I was by my father's accident with the pistol. I was appalled at her having ever asked him to give up his career, appalled at his ever having done it. And for love? But again, I was only a kid, and I said nothing.

For a time after the incident with the pistol, the shock of the *bang* seemed to awaken my father into greater awareness of the surrounding world. For a time, he began to talk more to us and to exchange ideas so that my mother even invited her friends, the MacPhersons, to come and visit us. But it was then that I saw a side of my father that he had never even insinuated before: his angry, raging bitterness. He and Mr. MacPherson were good friends, but if anything, they were too much alike—both children of the rural 19th century South, both with very little formal education, and both still harboring the attitudes and prejudices that had been engendered in them in childhood. Their favorite target of loathing was President Roosevelt and, of course, "his ugly wife Eleanor" who couldn't keep her nose out of "social issues that didn't concern her." Roosevelt wanted "to become the new Caesar," my father said. "Being elected so many times, he thinks he's now the dictator of the United States! And Eleanor wants to ride on his coattails in order to amalgamate and mongrelize the races!"

This was all very surprising to me since I knew that my father had voted for Roosevelt, at least for his first three terms, and had personally profited, as had we all, from Roosevelt's policies. He had always spoken highly of Roosevelt, had called him the "most forward looking man in America," but now came this 180-degree reversal of so much in my father's life.

I suppose that venting his rage with friends helped to relieve the pressures building in my father's soul, but my own friends also helped for a time. Without knowing anything of his pains, both Alfred and John came to see him when they heard he'd returned. And I remember Alfred especially, walking into the house, shouting in high good humor, and joking, "Where's the Major? I came to see the Major!" He found my father in the backyard and embraced him as though he might have been greeting his own father. The two of them seemed truly pleased to see each other, and my father sat down immediately and began to tell Alfred stories about Africa that he had never even told to me. The attraction between the two of them had always puzzled me, but I think now that I was seeing an example of the attraction that two pathological personalities can have for each other. They were two people who, like persons possessed of evil spirits in the Bible, recognized in their heart of hearts the kindred split, the radical dichotomy in the soul of another. They sensed that they were not alone, that they had a mate who also possessed the ability to be one thing one moment and its opposite the next in a way that leaves the outside world in total confusion.

For a time, my father seemed elated and flattered by the attention of these young friends. But soon afterward, he again withdrew to continue his dialogues with himself in the yard. And I began to feel with a daily increasing sense of horror that I myself was being drawn into his maelstrom and into the spiraling disintegration of the most important man in my life. Compared with the liberty that I had hoped for and expected to experience at his return, I felt now somehow trapped, emotionally paralyzed. I became consciously afraid that if I took my eyes off him, he would kill himself. But even watching him was no answer and was sometimes dangerous to the rest of us. When the three of us went anywhere, he would insist on driving, but then his mind would wander and the car would veer all over the road. When my mother would correct him, he would become angry and yell at her, even using profanity—a thing he'd never done before—for not thinking he knew "enough to drive a damn car."

"Where has he gone?" my mother asked me one night, speaking with tears in her eyes while he was outside taking one last stroll in the darkness before bedtime.

"Gone?" I asked. But I knew in an instant that she was not talking about his physical location, because that, indeed, was *my* question. Where had he gone? He was a man who had stood firm and maintained his integrity before the crooks on the city board of aldermen. He had flown that death defying aerobatic show before the stands with Amelia Earhart in attendance. He confronted his failures head-on through the Depression and when nothing else worked, he had scratched in the soil and brought forth food. He was the man who had loved me, taught me, nurtured me, and then gone off to war to help plan and conduct the greatest aerial armada in history.

"He's always been the sweetest and most gentle man in the world, and now I hardly know him," she said. "We have to do something to bring him back."

Years later, in a much more cynical mood, I said that I thought my father had died at age fifty-four, but had not been buried until age sixty-seven. But at thirteen, my cynical side had not yet developed, and I think that I understood her statement to be a personal directive assigning to me the mission of saving my father's life. Not that *she* gave me the assignment. She only voiced it. I *wanted* to save him, to bring him back. I needed him. And of course, I loved the man and would have done anything to see him restored.

One of the first things I did was to consult the minister of our Presbyterian Church, Dr. Walker Healy. He was an open and kind man, tall with a reassuring voice. He had a family of his own, and I knew that he enjoyed hunting and forest lore, apparently as much as I did, so I felt I could trust him. I went to the church one mid-week afternoon and found him in his study behind the sanctuary. For a long time during that first meeting, he just sat and listened to me very thoughtfully. Then he stood quietly and walked to the window before he said anything. "I know you're worried," he said finally, turning and sitting back against the window sill, "And I know you've taken on a very difficult job for yourself." And for the first time, I felt that someone who had some kind of understanding of the situation had heard me. "I'm not going to try to tell you what's wrong with your father," Dr. Healy said. "I can only tell you that going off to war is very hard on a man. Going through a sudden change of life is very hard on a man. And you describe him as a person who has lost all interest in living. So I'm going to suggest some things that might get him moving again." I remember only two of his suggestions, but those worked better than anything else we tried. "Get him to do something with you, even if it's only to play a game of checkers," Dr. Healy said. "Doing something helps focus the mind. Maybe you can plan a fishing trip and take him with you. But don't wait for him to suggest it, because he probably won't." And for the rest of that hour, Dr. Healy gave me hard, practical advice. Man to man. Not once did he treat me as a kid or belittle my fears. Not once did he retreat into religious platitudes. And then a few minutes later, after I had thanked him and was leaving, he stopped me at the door of his study. "Just remember one thing," he told me. "Nothing you do may work. And if it doesn't, I hope you won't feel that it's your fault. Do the best you can," he said, "that's all anyone can do. But the rest is up to God and your father, and neither one of them may ever explain why he won't cooperate with you." It was years later before I would truly appreciate the wisdom of Dr. Healy's words, but on that day, I felt ready to go home and go to work.

We had played checkers when I was much younger before the war. Actually, I felt it was a kid's game, but I was willing to try anything. I dug up the checkers and found the old card table that had been propped against the back wall of the extra bedroom that my mother used for storage. After dinner a couple of days later, I challenged him. "I bet I can beat you in a game of checkers," I said.

He looked at me with amusement. "You probably can," he said, "seeing that you'd be playing against a cripple."

This quiet acceptance of the possibility of defeat was not something I had expected at all, but I persisted, setting up the card table in the living room and laying out the checkers across the board. "Come on," I said. "I've almost forgotten how and I need you to teach me."

He gave an acquiescent sigh, as though the very thought of moving was the most difficult thing in the world, but finally he agreed. "All right," he said. "But don't expect much. Just one game." And we began.

I think now that by the time I was thirteen, I knew all the important things I would ever need to know. I just didn't know that I knew them. And of course, some things were so frightening and troubling that I could barely allow myself to know them at all. But I saw very clearly what was in front of me. And that night over the checkerboard, I began to see clearly just how radically my world had changed. When I had played checkers with my father at age eight or nine, I had felt that from time to time he held back and let me win, but now I saw clearly that our positions were almost totally reversed. He was the one who missed clear opportunities for moves and I was the one who held back until he found them or I pointed them out to him so that he could win. We ended up playing more than one game, and gradually it seemed that some of his powers of concentration returned. But I think that it was during those games that I discovered the paradox that, at least in some of life's situations, one can win far more by losing than by winning.

We continued to play checkers from time to time for the rest of that summer, but I didn't stop there. I planned fishing trips with Alfred and got Alfred to invite my father to join us. He resisted at first. It was too hot, there were too many bugs, or the riverbank was too overgrown this time of year. But Alfred was very persuasive, and as we assembled our fishing gear, my father finally acquiesced and the three of us walked all the way to the river. He had to stop frequently to catch his breath because his emphysema was clearly taking its toll of his energy, but going into the woods with us, he seemed to become more of his old self. Alfred and I dug fishing worms out of the riverbank for bait, and then we each chose a spot and began to concentrate on the business at hand.

But it was here during that fishing trip that I realized my father had never really stopped smoking, in spite of his heart problems, his emphysema, and his doctors' orders. No sooner had he sat down on the bank than he pulled a bent Camel cigarette out of a rumpled package in his pocket and lit up. At first, I didn't say anything. Who was I, after all, to tell my father what to do? And since I saw that it was the last cigarette in the pack, I thought there would be no more problem. But as soon as my father had finished that first cigarette, Alfred, ever helpful, pulled out his own package of Lucky Strikes and offered him another. "Here, Major, try one of these." And that's when I had to speak up.

"You know you're not supposed to smoke," I said. "You know what the doctor told you."

But it was Alfred who came to his defense. "Aw, leave him alone. The man's been off to war," he said. "He needs to have some fun." And this sympathetic logic, in spite of the facts of the situation, shut me up, at least for a while.

We each caught several fish on that trip and my father's mood seemed wonderfully improved afterward, even though he had to stop every fifty yards on the way back to catch his breath. But I began to see that my campaign for rehabilitating my father was going to be infinitely more complex than I had ever imagined.

The width of his mood swings was enormous. After one of our fishing trips, he would seem elated, almost hopeful, and then suddenly the cloud of futility and paralyzing despair would settle around him again and all of it would seem wasted. Finally, it was my mother who approached the issues head on. I remember that by this time, he had given up all pretense of not smoking, even around the house, and she confronted him late one afternoon as he sat again whispering to himself and smoking beneath the tree in the backyard. Dinner was ready and I think she had only walked out to call him in. But when she saw him smoking, she couldn't restrain herself. I had just washed my hands at the kitchen sink and was drying them with a towel at the back door when she delivered her challenge: "Are you trying to kill yourself?" And I think I stopped breathing altogether as I waited for his answer.

"You wouldn't lose anything if I did," I heard him say. "I'm worth a lot more dead than alive."

"You are so wrong," she said.

"At least then you'd have my life insurance."

"You have a son who needs his father."

"I'm nothing but a burden . . ."

"What kind of example are you setting for him?"

". . . a burden to myself and everybody else."

"You have a wife who loves you."

"Oh, darling, I feel so worthless!"

And suddenly she was embracing him, holding him now, I think, the way a mother might hold an injured child. "But you're *not* worthless! You're not worthless. And we're going to take some action to prove it, starting today."

I think that in a way, no matter how deep his despondency, she virtually shamed him into action, driving at least a little of the necessary iron into his soul. She had found his records and taken them to the offices of the Veterans' Administration and built a case showing that he had the equivalent of thirty years military service and had been released from the Air Force with a service related disability and without the compensation he was due. Getting it would require a long legal battle, and at first my father was totally hopeless about it. "They'll never reverse themselves," he said. "I saw what they did to General Billy Mitchell. They don't like to be wrong."

"But we have to try," my mother said. "You're entitled to retirement. The service is legally required to grant it. And besides that, we're almost out of money." And after dinner, she placed the pen and paper in front of him on the dining room table and sat beside him as he began to write the letters that would begin the legal process.

Now, of all the things I learned during that summer, I think one of the most important was a sense of perspective—although I certainly had no name for it at the time. It was the realization that no matter how burdensome, shocking, and painful my own world might seem to be, my friends were going through something equally shocking and maybe even more painful at the same time. I remember that one day Alfred came to my house just after lunch and he was acting a little strange, and then suddenly out of nowhere, he said, "I thought we were gonna have a dead nigger up at my house last night."

"What're you talking about?" I asked.

"I thought Daddy was gonna put some bullet holes in Jack."

"Really?"

"Yeah."

"Why?"

"He picked up the shotgun and chased Jack down through the woods," Alfred said. "Shot at him twice, but I don't think he hit him."

This was very surprising to me, since the relations between Alfred's parents and their employees had always seemed extremely cordial. They were almost like members of the same family. Jack, if you remember, was the chef in the motel dining room. And to the extent that he supervised everything that went on in the kitchen, nothing happened in the dining room without him. Both Jack and Phrobe had worked for Alfred's parents in Virginia and had come with them to North Carolina. Each of them had their own separate apartments at the back of the motel, and Alfred and I had visited them often.

...

"But why?" I said again. "What would make him shoot at Jack?"

"Jack got Phrobe pregnant."

"Oh."

"My dad was mad as hell. Jack talked back to him and told him it won't none of his damn business who he fucked. And that's when Daddy went for the shotgun. Called him every name in the book. I've never seen him so mad!"

Although, as it turned out, Jack had not been shot, he never again appeared at the Buckingham Court Motel. But the aftereffects of this incident were far-reaching for Alfred's family, and in a way, for me too. Even before that first day was out, they had decided to close the motel restaurant and remodel it as a home for themselves, thus releasing their own rooms for motel service. In addition, they had decided to send Alfred off again to private school. "We'd been talking about it for a while," Alfred told me. "But now it's definite. I'm going next month to Campbell College. It offers high school plus the first two years of college, and they'll let me accelerate so I can graduate earlier."

In a way, I was glad for him because I knew he was feeling edgy about always staying behind with the younger kids, but I knew I would miss him and I told him so.

"It won't be bad," he said. "I'll come home on weekends. And you can come up to see me—after I have a chance to check out the chicks." He put the best possible face on the whole situation. "At least I'll get away from all the bullshit at home," he said. "Be on my own for a change." But without either of us saying anymore about it, I could tell that he was probably even more troubled by these events than he had been by our winter automobile accident.

One of the long-range effects of the incident at Buckingham Court was to reveal itself before the end of the year when Phrobe had her baby, a beautiful black boy named Tom. And I think it's worth noting, considering that this was the American South in the middle of the 1940s, that Tom seems to have been a delight for everybody who had anything to do with him. When Alfred went off to school, his mother became so involved with Tom that I think she hardly missed Alfred at all. Whenever Phrobe was working around the motel, Alfred's mother took care of Tom. She fed him, she changed his diapers, and she bathed him. She took him to the doctor and made sure that Tom had the best medical attention possible. She took him shopping with her. And in the remaining years before I went off to college, I came to realize that other people in the community, including my own mother, were highly critical of her. "What do you suppose she's trying to prove, going everywhere with that black baby?" they would ask when they saw her driving by, puffing on her perennially present cigarette while Tom played in the backseat of her car. But Alfred's mother either had some private agenda of her own or she didn't care whether Tom was black or not. He was, after all, a beautiful little boy who lived on her property, and she treated him like a member of the family. And she was so totally impervious to public opinion that I think people eventually came to see her as just another one of the local eccentrics and left her alone. Later, I would see Alfred play with Tom during brief visits at holiday times, but I never heard him make any comment at all, either about Tom or his origin, and I never again heard him refer to the night of the big shoot-out at Buckingham Court.

But even before Alfred went off to school that year, our friend John came in for his share of additional trauma. I was up at Alfred's place one afternoon when John arrived, driving his father's car and obviously very upset about something. He had been to see Nadine, but hadn't found her at home, and there at Alfred's he seemed wound so tightly that he could hardly sit down. He wanted me to call Nadine later and make sure she knew he had been by. "Are you and Deanie having some kind of problem?" I asked him.

"No," he said. "No. The problem is my dad. He's drinking again and I don't know what to do." He told us how he had been searching all night, had even missed his date with Deanie, and then he'd finally located his father holed up in one of the local hotels. "He's really bad," he said. "He doesn't even know me and he's raving. I think he's got DTs. But I've got to do something because the hotel's going to have him arrested, and he sure doesn't belong in jail."

John's father was rather like E. A. Robinson's character of Richard Corey: charming, brilliant, and when he worked, extremely successful. Coming out of the Depression, he was the kind of man to make a lot of people wish that they "were in his place," until—on his various dark summer nights—instead of putting a bullet through his head like Richard Corey, he drank himself into stumbling imbecility and allowed the town to *tsk* and congratulate themselves for knowing all along that charm and financial success weren't all they were cracked up to be.

The three of us considered the various possibilities for helping John's father, and then John hit upon the scheme of calling a doctor who was one of his father's drinking companions. As I remember it, John told the nurse that this was a personal family call, and before long the doctor was on the line and John told him everything.

When the conversation was over, John hung up the phone and just sat there silently for a moment. I could see that he was having a hard time holding things together before he spoke. "He's going to send an ambulance," he said finally. "He's going to send an ambulance and take him to the hospital and hold him until he dries out. But I've got to meet the ambulance at the hotel."

"We'll go with you," Alfred said.

And I said, "Yeah, we're coming with you." And the three of us got into the car and drove into town.

The scene that followed was short, but it remains one of the most harrowing memories of my life. The hotel room was dark; the gaunt and half-clothed figure was almost unrecognizable in his raving and cursing. He was fleeing from the sight of us one moment and then charging us like the man possessed of demons at Gadara the next, waving his arms as though intending to crush us with his unworldly power before retreating into a darkened corner and cursing us again. Looking at it now, I doubt that the three of us alone would have been able to subdue him. But fortunately the ambulance crew was there, and they were able to hold him, strap him to a stretcher, and bring him down the stairs still raving and cursing through the lobby of the hotel while John, Alfred, and I looked on.

John saw him checked in and sedated at the hospital, and then we took John home with us. He stayed first a couple of days at my house and then a couple of days at Alfred's house before he felt up to going home again on his own. But I remember seeing his father about a month or six weeks later and finding him once again the totally charming and attractive man who had made so many people love him. He greeted and embraced me like family at the door of his office, inviting me in, and sitting down with John and me as though we were the only two people in the world that mattered. It was almost—though not quite—enough to make one begin to doubt that the intervening nightmare had ever actually occurred. However, I think I came through that summer with a kind of double vision that would remain with me all my life—a tendency to see all human beings as Janus-faced combinations of the angelic and the diabolic. And though I've never found a way not to get hurt by the diabolic when it asserts itself—whether in myself or in someone else—I have never again been surprised at finding it present.

Chapter Fifteen

My father succeeded in winning his pension. It took nearly all of the following year, and through all of that time, we were again living on borrowed money, hope, credit, and promises. But with my mother at his side providing the fuel and helping write the necessary letters, my father finally got the ear of North Carolina Senator Bob Reynolds who helped establish contact with a Washington lawyer named Wesley McDonald. McDonald took his suit to the Air Force, which then granted him what was due.

I, of course, overheard all the discussions concerning these letters—all of my mother's urging, all of her persuasion, and all her manipulation designed to goad my father into action. They were for his good, they were for her good, they were for *our* good, and I knew this. But somehow they enraged me. Somehow to me, at age thirteen, they seemed to make him less and less of a man. To me, he was a hero, and I wanted him to act the part and to be treated as the hero he was—free, independent, self-sufficient. She, on the other hand, treated him like a milksop. And her indulgences didn't stop when his pension was granted. They came to be a habit, a daily routine. She brought him breakfast in bed, she prepared his clothes, she brought him things to read, she prepared special foods, and she accompanied him to the doctor, the lawyer, wherever he had to go. And of course, she took over the family finances and paid all the bills. In short, she made it absolutely unnecessary for him ever again to have to think or act for himself. And, most appalling to me, he seemed to adore it. I had tried to manipulate him myself after his return. But I had done it because I wanted to see him become the man who had once made an audience gasp in fear and admiration as he rolled an airplane on its back barely twenty feet above the runway. He had done it not because it made money, but because it showed a man at his daring best. And I think the thing I wanted most in the world at that time was to see my father once again become his very daring best. On his own. Without any outside manipulations. Because it was the right thing to do. I prayed for it every night, and more and more often there went up a parallel accompanying prayer beside the first, which said, in essence, "God deliver me from ever being controlled and manipulated by a woman."

Of course, I know now that my mother could not possibly have won with me in that situation. She was facing hard reality and doing what she thought was necessary for survival, while I was demanding that the world conform to my ideal of how things ought to be and finding more and more often that the world just wouldn't cooperate. But it seems to me now that through that entire year, I watched helplessly as my father became gradually more introverted, inflexible, and childlike while my mother became more like a full-time nurse to him. I began to realize that my father was never again going to be the man he was before the war. The irony was that my mother's indulgence of my father had the effect of granting me much of the liberty and freedom that I had longed for during his absence. So at the same time I began to accept the fact that

I was totally powerless to influence things at home, I also began to take more seriously the teaching of my lifesaving instructor at Lake Singletary: "Never hesitate to swim away from a hopeless situation." And while I never fully stopped grieving for the father I had lost (and the man *he* had lost), I turned my face toward other things. As I entered high school, I tacitly resolved to mold for myself a life totally separate from the life of my parents.

Now, let me say at the outset that the main force behind this transformation, quite simply, was *girls*. As I have said, I had always thought girls were beautiful, but never in my life could I have imagined the beauty of the girls I found in senior high school in 1944. For the first few weeks I was dizzy. I was like a hummingbird lost in a flowering bower of bliss, unable to decide which way to turn because each blossom was more intriguing than the last. This is not to suggest that Ruth Ann and Nadine were not beautiful—and certainly, Nadine held a place in my heart that I wasn't ready to admit even to myself. Her beauty, knowledge, and marvelous capacity for language would remain unchallenged for years to come. But in junior high, Ruth Ann and Deanie were only two girls; in senior high, I could see two hundred comparably beautiful girls simply by walking down the hall at lunchtime, all of them in that wonderfully mysterious age between fourteen and nineteen, and each one sending out her own individual message on the winged aromas of fresh lipstick, clean hair, Life Buoy soap, and My Sin perfume.

Since Alfred had gone away to school and John was occupied each day with football practice, I had no one to discuss this with except Deanie, and I realized in an instant that talking to one girl about others was never going to work. But going to school became for me as exciting or maybe even more exciting than hunting or flying. And needless to say, the thought of unraveling the mysteries of the mostly "older women" I saw around me was infinitely more compelling than unraveling the mysterious value of x in Mrs. Zimmerman's algebra class or of discovering the logical relationship between the genitive, dative, and accusative cases in Miss Kate Broadfoot's Latin class. So although I—that is to say, my body—went to class regularly, no sooner would I place my backside in my chair than my mind would escape the room into a fantasy world of romantic adventure stories, using the girls I saw daily around me as my heroines.

Some of these stories I wrote down, but many I just dreamed as I went about my daily activities.

There was one girl in particular named Dot Drake who stimulated lots of stories, and along with Dot was her nearly inseparable friend Peggy, both of them about seventeen and seniors. Dot was tall and lissome, with chestnut-colored hair that hung glistening below her shoulders, and she was, without exception, the most graceful human being I had ever seen in my life. Every step of her foot, every movement of her hands with their crimson nails, every turning of her head, every raising of her arm as she straightened that cascade of hair, every shifting of her cobalt blue eyes produced a harmony that could not have been more profound or exciting if Balanchine himself had choreographed it. And her friend, Peggy, ran her a close second. Peggy was tall also, and her black hair hung nearly to her waist. But where Dot simply accepted her beauty as being part of who she was, Peggy used hers aggressively, self-consciously, powerfully, having found long before that she could turn her promising jet black eyes toward any male in sight and reduce him in an instant to a blob of quivering, acquiescent jelly.

Until this time, the most sophisticated picture of woman I had ever seen was the picture of Lauren Bacall gazing at Humphrey Bogart and lighting a cigarette in the movie *To Have and Have Not*, convincing me in an instant that smoking was *okay*. But where Lauren Bacall was only a celluloid image cast on a screen from Hollywood, Dot and Peggy were real. And on weekdays after school when these two walked into the Carolina Soda Shoppe, clutching their wallets as they slipped languidly into a booth and with slow calculation lit their Kool cigarettes, they appeared to me, at age thirteen, to be the most sophisticated women God had ever made.

I don't remember where I met them or how I came to know that the Carolina Soda Shoppe was the place to go after school, but certainly, on any weekday afternoon, the Soda Shoppe would be filled to bursting with thirsty teenagers striving to see and to be seen, while Dot and Peggy held court in one of the booths.

Why these girls would pay any attention to me at all I could not imagine. They were popular seniors who often dated older men, while I was a freshman and a country boy with no *entrée* into their social circle. But I was overjoyed whenever I found myself in their presence, and I think now that Dot was kind to me simply because that's the kind of person she was, whereas Peggy saw me as an amusing new target over which she could wield her powers. "Hon," she would say to me, gazing up from the depths of her black eyes and laying her hand warmly on my arm, "would you bring me a cherry coke from the counter?"

"Why yes," I would say, "I'll bring one for each of you." And I would scurry off happily, even feeling honored in the beginning to be in their service. I had already learned to carry some of my House of Flowers money with me for just such occasions, so I was covered in that way. But I soon realized that often when I returned from fetching the cokes or limeades they had requested, other older boys would have taken my place in the booth and I would be left standing, barely able to gather even the fringes of their conversation, while the girls quenched their thirst with the drinks I had bought.

I tried several ways to beat the odds in this situation. Often I would leave school quickly and hurry to the Soda

Shoppe ahead of everyone else in order to secure a booth to which I could invite Dot and Peggy when they arrived. Then I could enjoy their company locked in the corner while boys arriving later would be the ones to fetch and carry. On other days, to keep my ploys from being too transparent, I would be more direct and assertive, simply waiting until Dot left school and walking with her to the Soda Shoppe, where I would bid her a cool farewell and go home.

But it was from planning these kinds of tactics that I began to construct the romantic adventure stories that would so occupy my mind in class. And of course, I placed these stories in the context of the war. About a year earlier, the commanding general of the Ninth Infantry Division at Fort Bragg had been killed in an aircraft crash south of Fayetteville, and there was strong evidence that his airplane had been sabotaged. Not only that, but to add to the mystery, shortly after the general's death, a large cache of stolen army weapons and ammunition had been found hidden in the woods between Fort Bragg and my house, leading to the generally accepted conclusion that German secret agents were at work in the area. For me, this idea was not especially new. Although I had been preoccupied with the domestic aftereffects of the war for several months, the war itself continued to be daily with us. And it was not all fought in far-off lands. While major battles were raging in Europe, as General Patton pursued the Nazis toward Belgium, and in the Pacific, as General MacArthur maneuvered to retake the Philippines, German submarines were daily sinking U.S. ships within sight of the North Carolina coast in a trough of sea, which came to be dubbed "Submarine Alley." Several cells of German agents had been intercepted along the coast as they tried to deploy radio and navigation equipment for better targeting. And closer to home, my own aunt, Norma, at her house near Charlotte, had rented her extra bedroom to "a lovely man" who had opened a photography shop in the town of Belmont. And you can imagine her dismay when, two weeks later, her house was staked out by FBI agents who arrested her lovely roomer and charged him with espionage. Those who lived through this era can remember the posters hanging in every post office, courthouse, and barber shop depicting Uncle Sam standing before a background of sinking ships or dead soldiers, reminding us with all his national gravity that "Loose Talk Kills" or "Loose Lips Sink Ships."

So it was not a great stretch for me to place Dot and Peggy in a scenario involving spies, sabotage, and national security, starring myself as the hero. And it seems to me that Miss Kate Broadfoot's Latin class was an especially fecund ground in which to spin these yarns. Needless to say, in all of them, Dot would be cast in the role of the beautiful heroine, innocent, honest, and pure in every way, while Peggy, in her desire for power and her flirtation with "evil sensuality," became my Mata Hari, the instrument of Axis forces, doing all she could to destroy with her wiles the wisdom of men and the forces of freedom and democracy. If I had been writing an opera, Dot would have been the light soprano and Peggy the dark contralto. The climax of these stories would always be a fire, a battle, or a flood during which, at great risk to life and limb, I would succeed in saving Dot and winning her everlasting love while the evil Peggy perished in the flame or drowned in the flood. And of course, I never stinted at depicting myself as sterling through and through so that after I had single-handedly defeated the Nazis and the inflamed Dot had offered herself to me so shamelessly, I would decline with honor. "No," I would tell her kindly, "I am going off to war." And I would be in the midst of walking out alone into the sunset just as Miss Kate interrupted my closing reverie to inquire whether a particular Latin noun was in the nominative, genitive, or accusative case.

As you can see, I came to enjoy the life of my imagination much more than the daily life around me—that is to say, until

Friday night when the teenage club would have a dance, sometimes in the school gym, sometimes at the YMCA, and sometimes in the auditorium at the infamous Honeycut Development where I had first confronted the deeper wiles of female sexuality.

These events were amazing. They were always well attended and well chaperoned by both teachers and parent volunteers, and they were completely free of any teenage misbehavior that I can ever remember. It was an age when drinking and drugs simply were not part of teenage social life, and consequently, many of the problems that would later plague youthful gatherings just did not exist for us. I knew only one boy in all my high school years that had a reputation for drinking, and he never attended these social gatherings. Our problems were primarily social ones: how to dress properly for social occasions (boys in jackets and ties, girls in pretty dresses), how to meet new people, how to dance the jitterbug, the fox trot, the Westchester, or the Charleston to the appropriate music, and how to carry on an interesting conversation with someone of the opposite sex. It was an age also when overt sexual relations between unmarried people were totally out of the question. It happened, of course, but fear of pregnancy was a major deterrent for both sexes, and anyone—especially a girl—suspected of going all the way was likely to be severely ostracized by other girls and treated with considerable disrespect by many of the boys. However, as a result of these prohibitions, the dance floor became the most socially acceptable alternative to sex, a rhythmic and melodic way to get as close as possible to the real thing without getting anybody into trouble.

It was here on the dance floor that I truly learned the heretofore occult language of ballroom dancing from Dot and Peggy, who were two of the more sensual dancers I've ever met. Although it had been rumored around the school that Dot was seriously dating a much older man named Hugh

Gilmore and had in fact been seen parking with him in his Packard automobile late at night, she frequently came alone to these weekend dances. Some people came with dates, but it was not a requirement, and both boys and girls attended alone or in groups, which certainly, for us younger ones, allowed plenty of opportunity to circulate freely. But dancing with Dot or Peggy was like dancing with a beautifully shaped liquid form. Dot would simply mold herself to my body, withholding and defending nothing from cheek to toe, exquisitely sensitive to my every movement as though glued to my front. Ultimately, I would lose all sense of who was leading. We would move to the music as though of a single mind, gliding across the floor to recordings by Tommy Dorsey, Frank Sinatra, Gordon Jenkins, or maybe, once a month, to the music of a local band hired especially for the occasion. Mind you, I was the rankest beginner, but Dot, so flexible and graceful, could give me the illusion of being virtually a pro as I floated with her through the crowd.

Ironically, my first date to these weekend events turned out to be Nadine. Or rather I should say, it was a half-date. John was busy playing football, and frequently on Fridays, he would ask me to bring Deanie to the game and to the dance where he would meet us and later take us home in his father's car.

They continued to include me in most of their activities, even their most intimate moments of passionate kissing, and I continued to be the trusted friend who knew and saw everything, yet said nothing. But it was about this time that John experienced a series of major crises in his life that ultimately would affect all of us. First, playing his style of kill or be killed football, he injured his knee at mid-season and spent most of that fall on crutches as the mere observer of the game he loved so much. The three of us still went places together, but certainly, he was handicapped when we got to the dance floor, and I did most of the dancing with Deanie. In short, I became the one who publicly held her in my arms on the dance floor, while he was the one who privately held her in his arms in the car on the way home. Driving was difficult for him with his injured knee, and often I would drive while he and Deanie would try to inhale each other through their kisses in the back seat. My relaxed demeanor about all this must have changed at some point, because I remember that one night when John was spending the night at my house after we had taken Deanie home, he went further than ever to speak of his love for her. He spoke fervently, almost worshipfully, as though she were the only thing in this world that really made his life worth living. I had parked the car in the driveway and we were still sitting there beside the camellia bush talking in the fresh October air when he turned to me and said, "You're in love with her yourself, aren't you?"

For a moment—which seemed like an hour—I was speechless. I had long ago accepted their relationship. I was reconciled to being no more than the jester in their court of love, a kind of secretary of the interior to their emotional lives, and I did not presume to have access to something that was clearly beyond my reach. In short, I had denied my own feelings to the point that I no longer even knew what they were. Having them now expressed to me by someone else shocked me. "Why no," I said. "Of course not."

"Yes you are."

"The two of you belong together," I said. "You're beautiful together. You're my closest friends. I wouldn't for anything . . ."

"It's all right," John said.

"Besides, I'm interested in Dot now," I told him. Of course, I knew in my secret heart that Dot was in actuality a kind of faraway confection whom I could never even hope to get really close to, but she served in that moment as part of my waffling smoke screen.

"It's all right," John said again, totally ignoring me. "I guess that if you love a beautiful woman, you've got to know that other people will love her, too. But I wanted you to know that I knew."

I don't believe we ever mentioned it again. We went into the house that night with John hobbling on his crutches, acting as though the exchange in the car had never occurred, and for the rest of that fall the three of us continued our triangular friendship as before. But John had in that moment introduced me to myself in a brand new way, slicing through my denials and rationalizations to reawaken the throbbing of my pain, love, desire, frustration, and even my anger at always being the one left standing just outside the door. And yet, with Alfred gone, these two had become the dearest people in my life. I supported them and honored their choices, and I would have done nothing to rupture our friendship.

Several days later when I came to breakfast early, before my father had wakened, I found my mother sitting at the table holding the newspaper with a very grave look on her face. "What's the matter?" I asked.

For a moment she just looked at me. "I didn't want to tell you," she said finally, "but now I think you ought to know."

"Know what?"

"It's so awful!"

She pushed the newspaper toward me and pointed to an article in the lower left corner of the front page, which was captioned, as I remember it: "Woman Arrested on Morals Charge." And it took only an instant for me to understand why my mother had pointed it out. The lead began with the name of John's mother, identifying her as ". . . a socially prominent woman in the City of Fayetteville" and stating that she had been arrested Wednesday night in a room at the Prince Charles Hotel and charged with being a "woman of bad reputation." At the time of her arrest, the article continued, she was in the company of an army officer from Fort Bragg. Both parties were charged with illicit cohabitation, fornication, and adultery.

"Poor John," my mother said. "Poor, poor John!"

I know that for a long time I remained totally silent as my mind began to wrestle with the words in the newspaper. I knew most of those terms from having learned the Ten Commandments and from the Bible stories we had studied in Sunday school—adultery, cohabitation, fornication—but their precise meaning and application was lost in that great forbidden cloud that generally surrounded the subject of sex, and none of them were words I wanted to discuss with my mother. Applying them to a real, familiar human being was almost inconceivable. "It's really bad, isn't it?" I asked at last.

And my mother said, "Yes, it's about as bad as anything could possibly be. In fact, it would have been better if she had died before anything like this could have happened to her children. Be especially nice to John when you see him."

But John was not in school that day or for the rest of the week, and I remember being glad that he wasn't there because I knew instinctively that nothing I could do or say would be right. I felt paralyzed at the thought of seeing him, completely devoid of words. Not to offer support to my friend in time of crisis seemed heartless and cruel, but even to speak of what had happened with his mother was unthinkable.

As it turned out, time relieved the stress somewhat, and when John returned to school the following week, he was behaving normally, and the event with his mother became another one of those things that we stored away, never to be mentioned.

The arrest of John's mother and her army officer may seem shocking to us in light of the more relaxed attitudes toward sexual freedom that prevail at the end of the century. She was, after all, a divorced woman spending the night with the man of her choice, but laws prohibiting fornication and adultery were, and still are, preserved in the legal codes of the majority of the states of the United States, and in the 1940s and '50s they were stringently enforced—especially in the Bible Belt of the South. Years later, as a reporter in Lumberton, North Carolina, I would routinely cover the police station to report the previous night's arrests, and day after day I would read the list of morals charges phrased according to the official legal formula: "It is hereby charged that Sally Jones and Hilton Smith, with forethought and malicious intent, did cohabit, fornicate, and commit adultery in violation of the statutes of the State of North Carolina . . . ," charges lodged against young people parked in country lanes, against people in the back halls of churches, in hotel rooms, in the homes of friends, in their own homes when a spouse was absent. The phrasing may sound quaint and amusing, but I'm sure that often it crashed with the destruction of a tidal wave across many beleaguered families struggling for survival. I never learned the final disposition of the charges against John's mother, but immediately after her arrest, she moved out of the city and out of the state, leaving John and his younger brother completely under the protection of their alcoholic father.

John dealt with the situation as best he could, even heroically, I thought. Knowing fully that everybody in town knew the scandalous reputations of his parents, he in his mild mannered yet resolute way, quietly challenged the world each morning. He continued in school, and he continued seeing Deanie and me and his friends from the football team, never complaining, never sinking into self pity, and even maintaining a sense of humor until, at the end of November, one additional blow fell that would change all our lives forever: Deanie's father was transferred to Fort Hood, Texas, and Deanie, of course, would have to go with her family.

To tell immediately which one of us was more distraught at the news of Deanie's departure would be difficult. She had become so much a part of my thinking that I felt sure the whole fabric of my life was going to unravel the instant she left town. But I'm sure now that for John the pain was much greater. Her family's moving preparations took hardly a week, and on the last day, I went with him to her house to say good-bye. I remember that we joked with each other about such things as the "big bangs" I liked to get from my homemade shotgun shells, and she promised to write to me, and then I hugged her and walked home so the two of them could share the final minutes alone before her family drove away. The thought of her going made me feel like I had suddenly been condemned to a starvation diet of bread and water, but when John arrived at my house a short time later, I pretty quickly saw things with a different perspective. It was a winter day and leaves had already fallen from the trees, but it was warm, and I met John in the yard. He was struggling, but nothing he did could keep the tears from streaming down his cheeks. "Now," he said, "now I have no one left in this town—no one but you and Alfred and maybe your parents. But I don't think I can live here anymore."

I think my only response was to nod, because it was another of those situations in which there was absolutely nothing one could say. But when John drove away, I knew that he was determined to leave the City of Fayetteville forever.

He wasted no time. The following week he told me that his father, who had been sober and working for several weeks, had agreed to send him to a private school in Florida. "I want to begin a new life," he said, ". . . go where no one knows me."

"When are you going?" I asked.

"Right after Christmas," he told me. "In January."

"Oh," I said. And I realized clearly then, for the first time that I, too, was about to begin a new life.

Alfred came home for Christmas vacation and the three of us got together often as we always had, but the very air around us seemed charged with the process of rapid change. John was preoccupied with his plans for going off to school in January, and Alfred clearly had become a different person from the effects of the school he had been attending since September. In that single semester, he had developed a new jargon, a new attitude. He had made new friends with a number of veterans who had been released early from military service and returned to rebuild their civilian lives, impatient now with the polite restraints imposed by civilian instructors at a Baptist school. Alfred told us of late night trips to Raleigh, Greensboro, and Winston-Salem, of all night beer parties, of brawls in bars, and visits with certain exotic women in the company of his older friends. Both John and I heard these stories with a sense of dismay, but I don't remember that we ever said anything critical. Alfred was older than we were, after all, and his stories were exciting, but given the recent events in Fayetteville and our continued sense of mourning after the departure of Nadine, they made me, at least, feel depressed and confused rather than entertained.

I think the climax of all these changes came for me that year when I went hunting with Alfred about two days before Christmas. For several seasons, on December 23rd, we had developed a kind of annual ritual of taking a long hunt across the winter fields of Stubbs' farm, tramping over the empty cotton stalks and the yellowing pea fields and the remaining husks lying in the cornfields, not far from Teeny's old house, after the fodder had been cut. Normally, it was a good place to find doves and quail and rabbits, but on that day as we proceeded slowly along under a gray winter sky, we found nothing at all, and I remember that as we came to the final field before reaching the highway, Alfred looked at me and said, "If we don't kill something pretty soon, I'm gonna have to kill you."

It was a typical Alfred *non sequitur,* and I paid no attention to it as I kept on walking, saying something innocuous like, "Yeah, things are pretty quiet."

And then Alfred raised his voice a little and said, "Wait a minute. I don't think you heard me."

"What?" I asked.

He stopped and when I looked over at him standing maybe ten feet away, I found myself looking right down the muzzle of his Iver Johnson 12-gauge single barrel shotgun. I'll never forget the sound of the click as he cocked the hammer. "I said I'm gonna have to kill you," he said. And in that instant, my blood pressure and heartbeat rocketed up about a thousand percent.

"Alfred," I said, "I'd appreciate it if you wouldn't point that gun at me."

"You don't think I'll kill you, do you?" he asked.

I stood frozen in place, knowing better than to move even one centimeter. "Alfred . . ." I was looking right into his dark eyes, but I didn't see anything that I recognized. They were opaque, leaden, unblinking, the eyes of a total stranger. I had fired his shotgun. I knew that it had a hair trigger, and I knew that I had to be very careful.

"You don't think I'll do it," he said louder.

"Alfred . . . please . . ."

"You don't, do you?"

I reached down for an answer. I knew what he was like when confronted by a challenge. I knew what he was like at the slightest suggestion of bad faith. I knew that there was as much logic involved in this standoff as there had been on that morning two years before when he had hurled the knife into the doorpost beside my head. And I also knew that this time, if he pulled that trigger, he wouldn't miss.

"Goddamn it!" he shouted then. "Give me an answer. You don't think I'll kill you, do you?"

And as calmly as I could possibly speak, I said, "Yes, Alfred, I think you'll kill me if you want to. But I hope you won't, because I think I'm your best friend and I think you'd miss me." And then I turned and walked away half expecting to get a wad of birdshot in the back of my head.

He lingered behind and then a moment later caught up beside me with the hammer lowered, and we walked on homeward together in silence.

I would dream often about that incident in the cornfield, and for years, in moments of repose, I would find myself suddenly reliving the scene with the same quickened pulse, hearing the same click of the hammer and looking again down the barrel of the gun to find a total stranger where my friend had stood.

Yet, Alfred and I continued to be friends. We even exchanged Christmas presents. I visited in his house and he visited in mine. And the incident in the field became another one of the many topics we would never mention. But I never hunted with Alfred again, and I knew beyond question that our friendship had changed forever.

Chapter Sixteen

The year ended in a whirlwind of both agony and joy for the entire United States. Ever since the dark days of the initial Normandy invasion in June, the Allied armies had experienced a series of unprecedented successes. Paris had fallen in August, and the Germans had continued their retreat into Belgium, leading many of us at home to feel that the Allies, and especially the United States, could experience only victory. Then in December of 1944, the picture changed suddenly at the Battle of Ardennes when the reconstituted Panzer divisions of Field Marshall Karl von Runstedt made one last effort to stop the over-extended U.S. advance in what became known as the Battle of the Bulge. Nightly, we listened to the news on the radio as the major fighting focused on Bastogne where the 101st Airborne Division under General Anthony McAuliffe was entirely cut off, deprived of air support by bad weather, and surrounded by superior German forces making it appear that much of the U.S. Army was about to be annihilated. Our national sense of horror at this impending disaster continued until late in the month when we heard of

General McAuliffe's one word response to German General Kokott's request for his surrender: "Nuts!" And from that day on, the tide of battle seemed to change. The weather improved, the air force was able to re-enter the conflict, and by December 29, the Battle of the Bulge was ended with the Germans once again retreating toward Trier.

I remember that we celebrated the new year with joy and prayers of thanksgiving for the American victory. But I remember thinking also that our victory—with its seventy-seven thousand casualties—came like every other good thing, at enormous price.

I began 1945 with probably the greatest feeling of isolation and aloneness of my life. Not only had John, Alfred, and Nadine gone away, but also when I returned to school, I learned that even Dot had eloped and married Hugh Gilmore over the Christmas holidays. And then, to cap it all, my parents received my first term report card.

Now, admittedly, I had never considered grades important at all. I had spent the fall dreaming and pondering the complexities of human relationships and the depths of human suffering, but in my classes I had done little more than inhale the musty odor of the assigned books. My mother was gently dismayed, and in her even-tempered way urged me to do better from now on. But my father came out of his invalid state with a fury. What did I think I was doing? Was I just throwing my life away? How dare I fail to make the most of my opportunities! It was the only time in my life that I remember his considerable capacity for rage being so focused on me.

Suddenly, we were organized. Like a military base. And to me it seemed like a surprise frontal assault. From the beginning of that school year, I had to bring my daily assignments for him to review before I turned them in. And then afterward, I had to bring all my graded papers home for him to examine. There would be no more social life, no more dances, and no more movies—no nothing outside of home and school until those grades improved.

Of course, initially, I felt more isolated and estranged from the world than ever. Although I had seen my father infuriated at other people, I myself had always been spared. I had always received his unquestioned love and support, and now his righteous rage at me was extremely painful. He was implacable. I had already progressed further in school than he ever had, but that of course, was the root of his fury. "A man without an education is a lost soul in the modern world," he told me, and he would just be damned if he was going to stand aside (Unspoken: the way his father had done.) and let my basic laziness or anything else keep me from getting the education I needed . . . because he loved me, even if he had to punish me to prove it.

In truth I knew he was right. I couldn't find a single justifiable argument against his basic logic. And yet, in my childish way, I had to resist his harshness. I would dawdle. My mind would wander. I would somehow fail to see how the same basic math principle or grammatical construction applied in two different situations. He might not have had much formal education, but he had studied the math necessary for flying. He had taken correspondence courses. He had read widely. And he could spot an awkward sentence or a piece of sloppy arithmetic half way across the room. "Damn it!" he would say. "When are you going to learn to pay attention?" He could tolerate one mistake, but for me to make the same mistake twice was to ignite his entire arsenal of unexpended, red-faced rage. "Passive resistance!" he would shout. "I've seen it from soldiers who didn't want to do their jobs. It's your worst characteristic and I will not tolerate it!"

How I hated those exchanges! I think that down deep, I actually wanted to please him and live up to his expectations, but for some perverse reason, in the face of his pressure, I just couldn't acquiesce with any grace at all. And it would be many years before I would be able to see that I was, in fact, ironically getting exactly what I had prayed for during all those months of my father's most severe reclusive state. He had found something other than his own corrosive sense of disappointment and shame to be interested in, and it was *me*. He wanted to perfect me. And I, in my flawed human state, was resisting that possibility.

My mother, of course, was deeply disturbed by our confrontations. As was true of many Southern women, she had adopted the familiar term *Daddy* when speaking to my father, although he never reciprocated as some men did and called her *Mother* or *Mommy*. "Daddy," she would say, stroking his shoulders in her attempt to calm him during our sessions, "you're so hard on him."

"Hard on him! He needs somebody to be hard on him."

"But he's trying, and you're getting so upset. It's not good for you."

In the beginning, he would try to calm down at her request, but one night, I remember he had had enough. "So, I suppose you think all he needs is for you to hold his hand and make excuses for him," my father said. "Is that what your plan is—to go through life with him and hold his hand and baby him? You're always defending him and making excuses for him." Of course, in the middle of all this, I wanted to disappear right through the floor. I hated his being angry with me, but to see the two of them in conflict over me was an unspeakable horror. "Well let me tell you something," my father continued, "there *aren't* any excuses! Out there in the world there aren't any excuses. You either do the job you're supposed to do or you don't do it, and nobody gives a damn why you failed. They just find somebody else who *will* do the job. Now, let him be a man and learn how the job is done."

There was so much truth, so much anger, so much bitterness, resentment, self-criticism, self-loathing, regret, *and* hope entangled in those few sentences that I felt I had been overcome by a tidal wave. It would take me half a century to unravel it all, but the immediate effect was that I did begin to pay attention.

Certainly, he was right about my mother's tendency to make excuses for me, because surely she had always sought to exempt me from the rules that applied to everybody else. It wasn't so much what she said, but that her attitude seemed to convey the idea that I was somehow superior or "special" and should be allowed to advance through life without having to put up with the tribulations of the common herd. Her attitude embarrassed me, but since I was often its beneficiary, I found it hard to resist.

Her favorite excuse was health. I was too sickly, too sensitive, or too delicate to have to work and be judged by the world's harsh standards. When my father was away, she had made excuses to my teachers. She knew many of them, and I always had the feeling that they really wanted to help "Lottie's son." And once that very summer, when I had worked briefly with other school kids at a peach packing plant, she had accompanied me and embarrassed me by explaining to the manager that I had a delicate skin and should not be required to pick peaches from the trees in the orchard where I would be exposed to so much heat and peach fuzz. The manager had been very kind and given me a job in the shelter of the plant itself until one day, when I was helping load peaches into the back of a car, I jumped off the four foot loading dock with a full bushel basket of peaches in my hands and landed firmly without either falling or rupturing myself. The manager saw me do it, and I can hear his shout to this day, "God Almighty, Boy! Are you tryin' to kill yourself? I thought you were supposed to be sickly." He laughed uproariously and told the story to everybody at the plant and even told my father when he came to pick me up at the end of the day. "Didn't even fall over!" he said. "A jump with that much weight could kill a man. What do ya call him at home? Hercules? Tell his mamma he ain't so delicate as she thinks he is."

So although I bridled under his discipline, I knew my father was right about some things, and I began to apply myself so that my "probation" could be lifted.

But strangely, several days after this shouting match about my mother's tendency to coddle me, I was led to see that there was a lot more behind my father's anger than I was equipped to understand. My mother came into my bedroom one night and I could see in an instant from the nervous way she moved back and forth around the room that she was very upset. She was dressed for bed in her nightgown and heavy chenille bathrobe, but the skin around her eyes was taught and drawn, and she was far from being ready to sleep. "Your father is so angry," she said. "I just don't know what to do, and you're the only one I can turn to."

"What's the matter?" I asked.

And she sat on the bed beside me. "He says I don't love him anymore . . . that I love you more than I love him. He says I spend so much energy on you that I have nothing left for him."

In all the annals of speechlessness, I think this moment was for me closest to the Biblical experience of being "struck dumb." I remember that my ears were extremely hot, but for a long time I was totally unable to speak as my mother sat there and looked at me. Just why she would tell me such a thing or what she expected me to do about it, I cannot imagine, but clearly, she seemed to expect me to do something. And just as clearly, I knew that I was going to stay completely out of it. "It's silly," she went on finally when she realized I wasn't going to say anything. "Of course I don't love you more than I love him. I love you both very much. He is my husband. You are my son. I love you both with all my heart. He just doesn't . . . doesn't seem to understand."

I didn't understand either. Certainly, it seemed to me that she did almost everything for him, and although I didn't approve of the way she coddled him, I had been mightily relieved when he had returned and diverted her attention from me. Still, I didn't say anything, and finally she rose and departed, leaving me feeling horribly inadequate for failing to say or do whatever she needed. I think all I did was nod as she left the room. But I did not sleep easily that night. And by the next morning, I woke resolved to be meticulous about my school work and to meet my father's demand for high quality performance, feeling then that it was the only thing that would reduce the level of conflict within the family.

The result was that by spring, I was successful in bringing up my grades and regaining my father's approval. He actually complemented me and seemed relieved to lift my restrictions. And the conflicts that had existed, like everything else important in those days, were never mentioned again. But I realize now that in spite of my enforced isolation over those few months, I did not wither away socially or personally. At school, I developed new friendships with people like Rudolph Singleton and Jack Crosswell, whom I would later hunt with and double date with, and I met Martha Lazenby whom I would invite often to the movies the following summer. But I remember the period now primarily as a musical and epistolary period. After I had completed my school assignments, I worked more on my piano playing and trumpet playing, and I sang a lot, all of which my father approved. Strangely, for a Southern man of his generation, he found nothing odd about men who were musical, and it wasn't until much later that I learned about the bias many Southern men had toward any man in the arts. Before World War II, a male artist, especially a singer, was often seen as a "sissy," not quite male, someone to be ridiculed for being delicate or sensitive or for trying to create something pretty—all feminine qualities. Unless, of course, the artist was someone like Caruso, with a voice so powerful that he could virtually lift the roof off a building, or a poet like Kipling, who wrote about soldiers, or a novelist like Jack London or Zane Gray, who wrote adventure stories about men against the wilderness, or perhaps a humorist like Mark Twain who could make people laugh. The visual arts hardly entered the equation at all, since most Southern men were so rarely exposed to them except in the form of china painting practiced by skilled young ladies on Sunday afternoons or as commemorative statues honoring the founders of the nation or the fallen heroes of the Confederate Army. My father one day confessed to me that he had loved to sing as a child, but that he had been so ridiculed by other boys that he resolved never to sing again. "After that," he told me, "the only place I would ever sing was in the cockpit of an airplane where nobody could hear me." So he encouraged my music as long as it didn't interfere with my other studies.

But strange as it may seem, in addition to the sustaining power of music, I was also sustained through this period by my absent friends. They all wrote to me, Nadine especially, writing detailed letters about her new home and her activities on her high school newspaper. Although I would never see her again, ours was a correspondence that continued well into our college years. I think now that I was the brother she never had and she was the sister I never had. She wrote to me about John and John wrote to me about her, and then gradually she began to write to me about other boys she had met in Texas. By the time John returned from school for the summer vacation, their love affair was a thing of the past. John had met a girl named Louise—who looked very much like Nadine and whom he would eventually marry. And Nadine had met a boy named Pat, another football player, whom she would marry. But through all this, my correspondence with Nadine continued unabated.

I think it was during this early correspondence that I began to learn truly about the creative power of the written word. Alfred wrote me occasional little bits of information or jokes, but John, Nadine, and I exchanged our thoughts. And the need to shape them and organize them coherently in writing helped us to find out what our thoughts actually were. I remember that John was distraught after injuring his knee again during spring football practice, effectively destroying forever his hope of winning a football scholarship to take him through college. But Nadine was excitedly traveling hundreds of miles across the Texas plains to cover football games or musical events for her school newspaper. "Distance doesn't mean the same thing out here that it does back east," she told me. "We just get in a car and go as fast as we can." But she was anxious to escape the limitations of high school and family. She went to school in the summers and graduated early. And three years later, as I was entering my senior year in high school, she was entering the school of journalism at the University of Texas where she married Pat, her football player, even before the first semester was ended. She sent me pictures of Pat and herself, and then—before the year was out—she sent me pictures of herself and their baby. Her letters were not so frequent after the baby was born, but we did continue to write until, when I myself was a sophomore in college, I received the last letter I would ever get from her. It was a long, discursive, introspective, and even poetic letter written on a portable typewriter from the deck of a ship in the middle of the Pacific Ocean. She had left Texas forever. Her marriage had ended and she was enroute to visit her parents who had retired to Hawaii after the war. She was gazing into the swirling waters of the Pacific and wondering which way her life would go. But she included no return address.

Chapter Seventeen

If my generation was later to be identified as the "Silent Generation," I think our silence was the result of the stunning magnitude of events that were taking place around us during our formative years—events that would change the world, but events in which we were too young to participate. Surely, when I think back to my own life during that spring and summer of 1945, I feel presumptuous in mentioning myself at all. Of what possible importance was I when compared to the surrender of Nazi Germany, the opening of Buchenwald, the death of President Roosevelt, of Hitler, of Mussolini, the bloody Pacific battle of Okinawa with its hundreds of thousands dead, the resignation of Winston Churchill, the dropping of the first atomic bomb, and the surrender of Japan? All in six months' time. We watched, we waited, we gained our importance vicariously from our association with those who had participated, and except for our shouts of joy at their victory, we kept our hands over our mouths. Compared with those who had transformed the world, what earthly thing did we have to offer? What great causes had been left for us to deal with? Admittedly, it was the narrow and limited vision of youth, but nonetheless, it existed in the air around us as we pursued our studies, our music, and our friendships. Had we but known it, three other events of that year would point the way and give us plenty of causes and plenty of bloody burdens to be concerned about. One was the partitioning of Korea into two nations, North and South. Another was the rise of Ho Chi Minh to the Presidency of Vietnam. And the third, which may ultimately prove to have the farthest reaching implications of all, so far as the quality of life in the United States is concerned, was the signing of Jackie Robinson as the first American black man to play in the previously all white world of big league baseball with the Brooklyn Dodgers.

In 1945, though the forces of the United States had crossed broad oceans and broached successfully the borders of enemy nations, the frontier of race relations in the United States had hardly even been approached, much less crossed, especially in the South. It was a problem so close to us and so familiar to us that even the victims of injustice themselves could hardly see the many inequities that existed on every side. I had lived all my life in a world of maximum segregation, and although I had always seen black people, even played with them and visited in their homes when I was a child, I lived essentially in a white world, and the entire structure of the community was designed to keep it that way. We are able to admit now that all sections of the United States practiced (and often still do practice) segregation in some form, but in the South, law prescribed segregation. There were white and colored drinking fountains, white and colored public toilets—if there were public toilets at all. There were white and colored entrances to movie theaters. Black people were required by law to sit in the rear of all busses and to occupy separate cars in all passenger trains. I remember the signs saying, "No Coloreds Served" behind the cash registers of many restaurants and the sign, "Colored Only" over the backseat of the busses I rode daily to school. There were segregated churches, segregated libraries, segregated dining rooms. A black person looking for a meal away from home had either to enter the back door of a white restaurant and buy food, which he could eat outside, or find his way into the Negro section of town, "Little Harlem" in Fayetteville, in order to obtain service. If hotels were stringent in segregating the sexes, they were fierce in their policies of segregating the races; they simply denied black people service of any kind. And of course, there were segregated schools. Now, I remembered my sadness on being separated from my friend Teeny at age six when he had been taken off to the colored school while I was taken to the white school, but even given that memory, this segregated world was the one I had been born into and the only one I knew, and it seemed to me as a child perfectly normal. To my parents, who had been born during the period of Civil War Reconstruction, the laws of segregation carried the power of the Ten Commandments.

Of course, segregation itself was a major cause of injustice. White people, even those of good will, were insulated behind the protective walls of home, automobile, and church. Most of them avoided public transportation and drove their cars at a comfortable distance along the more scenic routes away from the unpainted houses and unpaved streets of the sections that in any Southern city could be identified as "nigger town." They didn't often see the black man being told to go to the back door or experience directly the humiliation of the black woman being ordered by the bus driver to relinquish her seat and make room for white passengers. They didn't see the black child being turned away from the public library or visit the deteriorating classrooms in the colored schools, and they found comfort dealing with the mostly smiling and cooperative aspects of black workers whose smiles were presented as often as not for the sake of political and economic survival. And since the police department was totally white, black people knew that to create a public scene about anything was to get into a whole lot of trouble. But it was during this time at the end of the war in 1945, when the world was reeling from the shock of Nazi racial atrocities, that a number of people began to agitate for greater racial justice and equity here at home.

Among the most vocal advocates was Eleanor Roosevelt, whose support of desegregation and greater access to public facilities for all people made her an anathema in the South. I remember my parents' reaction to her: "She just doesn't know what she's talking about!" my mother said. "She's never lived in the South. She doesn't know these people. Yet she thinks she can sit up there in Washington and tell us how to live!" My father's solution to the Eleanor problem was more primitive, simply to "wring her neck" the way you would the neck of a chicken for Sunday dinner.

And of course, another object of Southern scorn was the National Association for the Advancement of Colored People, which was becoming more and more of a national force. Their arguments were based simply on these kinds of questions: if black men were worthy to fight and die for American freedom and democracy, why were they not worthy to receive service in a public restaurant or to travel unrestricted on public transportation? And if *separate* was really *equal* in the public schools, why were black veterans with high school diplomas and GI Bill entitlement not worthy to enter equally into the major state universities? And if black people were worthy to be taxed for public service, why did black residential areas remain without paved streets, public water, sewerage service, and without police protection?

To address and correct any of these inequities would be to dismantle completely a way of life and to unravel a fabric of attitudes, assumptions, and beliefs that had existed literally for centuries. It was hard for even the most articulate segregationist to form a reasoned and humane response to these questions. And where reason will not suffice, fiery emotions are brought fully into play.

I mention all this primarily as background because I, as a teenage boy, understood little of the history and inequity of racial politics. I just felt the emotion around me. I had, after all, been raised on the glories of "our Southern Heritage." Both of my great grandfathers had been surgeons in the Confederate Army. One of my relatives had served on General Stonewall Jackson's personal staff. Another, an ex-Episcopal priest, had served as Robert E. Lee's commander of artillery and had nicknamed his artillery battalions Matthew, Mark, Luke, and John after the four gospel writers. I had always been taught that "the Civil War was not about slavery; it was about *states' rights,*" and I had grown up playing in battle trenches that had been dug to defend the "Southern Nation" from invaders who were out to destroy *states' rights.* Nothing in my school history courses challenged these views in any way. Everyone seemed to agree that the Civil War had not been about slavery and that the modern South in no way set out to subjugate Negroes. The South had numbers of outstanding Negroes, I was told—and here someone like Booker T. Washington was usually named—and Southerners were proud of their accomplishments. Yet, when the issues of segregation confronted my parents or those of their generation, they could become apoplectic with rage in one moment and in the next disavow any animosity or prejudice against Negroes. They only wanted to preserve the "Southern way of life," they said. And I was nonplussed at the vehemence of my parents and their friends whenever Mrs. Roosevelt, the NAACP, or school desegregation were mentioned. Just why the people of their generation so furiously advocated "keeping the Negroes in the their place" I couldn't quite understand. The only unpleasant black person I had ever met was Clarence, with his aggressive penis and his switchblade. But all

the others had been absolutely wonderful to me, and I could-
n't see the problem. So I listened.

I remember my own budding consciousness of the reality
of these issues in terms of "little" events. I was coming home
from school on a crowded city bus one afternoon when a
black man got on and paid his fare. Of course, he was expected to go to the back of the bus, but for some reason the white
people standing in the aisle did not move out of his way until
the bull necked bus driver, in a fit of frustration, locked the
brakes, stood up, and with hands on his hips, addressed the
entire busload of passengers, "Okay, folks, let him pass! Let
him get by. He may be black, but it's not gonna rub off on ya."
Everybody laughed at this, and I could hear the repeated
phrase echoing around the bus, "It's not gonna rub off on ya.
Let him get by." The man continued to the back and I lost
sight of him, but for some reason—while I saw the humor in
the idea of it "rubbing off on you"—I felt the event as an act
of ultimate cruelty, and I was left with a troubling and lingering question, "Why did they have to do it that way?"

Mind you, I was not doctrinaire or revolutionary in any
way. I just tended to see events in terms of their effect on one
person at a time. I had previously been totally unconscious of
the law's having anything to do with me at all. When no black
people were on board, my school friends and I had often sat
in the "Colored Only" seats at the back of the bus and joked
with each other about turning dark if we sat there too long. If
the only vacant seat was beside a black person, I had often sat
there and nobody had ever said anything. But as the subject of
access to public accommodation was discussed more frequently on the radio and in the newspapers, I grew more conscious of the rules. I remember hearing a light skinned man
with a New York accent talking to a group of black men
behind a truck at my bus stop one afternoon. "How long are
you going to wait?" the man asked his audience. "How long
are you going to let them push you to the back? How long are

you going to let them keep you out of schools and out of jobs? Now I'm a clean-cut guy from New York, and I tell you, we don't wait for anybody to give us anything. You've got to take what you want. Get it for yourselves!" My bus came, and I didn't hear the rest of the man's talk, but I told my parents about it at dinner. My father's reaction was very deliberate and considered, "If they keep on, they're going to create a race riot around here just as they did in New York and Detroit," he said. "You can't go around stirring people up and expect nothing to happen." And it was then that I was told *never* for any reason to allow a Negro to sit beside me on a bus. "If you give in to the little things," I was told, "they'll take over something else and it'll never stop. A line has to be drawn somewhere."

I didn't have to deal with these issues anymore for a while because school ended, and in all the celebration about the end of the war that summer, our minds were totally changed to other things. I went off to another church conference at Red Springs, and as seems to have happened so often in my life, I became so preoccupied with the girls I met there that everything else dropped for a time into total insignificance. But my experience at the conference was different this time because for the first time, I learned that I myself had the power to engineer something. And my major instrument was music.

One afternoon, early in that weeklong conference, I sat down and began to play on the piano in the hallway outside the dining room. I was hardly a virtuoso, but I had memorized several pieces of both popular and classical music, and for a time I played away in total unself-consciousness until I realized suddenly that I was surrounded by young people, most of them girls. I know that my pianistic ability was and always has been very limited, but I played with enthusiasm, and it wasn't long before a red haired girl named Zelma Grantham sat down on the bench beside me and began to sing in a very nice soprano voice, and soon others began to sing along with the song I was playing. It was a heady moment, I tell you. Being the center of favorable attention has rarely caused anybody much sadness, and by the time the dinner bell rang that day, I realized I was onto something important. "I've got some music in my room," Zelma told me. "I'll bring it tomorrow and we can have a wonderful time."

"Great," I said. "I'll look forward to it." But by the end of dinner that night and as the week went on, I realized that my whole status in life had changed. I was no longer just one of the group. People I had never seen before knew my name and apparently wanted to be around me. So the next day I went back to the piano. Zelma came with her sheet music, and we played and sang together and the girls standing around "oohed" and "ahhed" and said it was "so romantic, just like in the movies." I had to fight for control to keep myself from quivering like an excited puppy out of sheer delight.

As I say, it wasn't my virtuoso skill that intrigued people. I think it was the mere fact of a boy making music at all that somehow set me apart. And I don't think anybody ever realized how glad I was that Zelma had brought her sheet music along. My repertoire was limited, after all, and I soon would have had to repeat myself, but when Zelma began to play, I realized she could play better than I, and I gladly relinquished my position and sang along happily beside her to the apparent delight of those around us.

Now clearly, Zelma and I had formed a fast friendship, but as the week went on, I encountered a major dilemma when I volunteered to write for the single edition newspaper that was to cover events of the conference. For it was on the staff of this newspaper that I met yet another red-haired girl named Mary Johnson Stevens. She had green eyes, the cutest freckles I ever saw, a good figure, and a wonderful way with words and verse. I thought she was spectacular. She was three years older than I, but she didn't seem to care. Our field was word interplay, and it offered an endless land to be cultivated. But the result of this delightful experience was that for the first time in my life, I felt that nothing I did was entirely right. If I joined Zelma to make music in the afternoon, I felt that I was being unfaithful to Mary Johnson and the world of words, and if I worked with Mary Johnson on the newspaper in the morning, I felt that I was being unfaithful to Zelma and the world of music.

I didn't have to resolve this conflict then, because the conference ended and we all returned to our homes. But the happy upshot of it all was that I gained two more epistolary companions. Both of those girls wrote to me and I wrote to them. And then before the summer was out, I traveled on the Carolina Trailways bus to visit each of them at their homes in the nearby towns of Lumberton and Fairmont. But it was on one of these bus trips that the troubled issue of race relations was resolved, at least in my mind, forever.

The incident occurred one afternoon in late August, about two weeks after the Japanese surrender, as I was on my way to visit Zelma in the little tobacco town of Fairmont about forty-five miles from Fayetteville. I remember that it was hot. There was no air conditioning on Trailways busses in those days, and all the windows were open as we pulled out of the crowded station, with its sun baked smells of exhaust fumes and oily asphalt, and headed south. It was a time when most busses traveled on an "on call" basis. If you couldn't get to the station, all you had to do was stand beside the highway and wave the bus down, and I remember that an elderly black man a few miles out of Fayetteville hailed our bus. We were fairly crowded, but I was still sitting alone beside the window about three quarters of the way back when the man got on and came down the aisle. He was tall, with white hair and a dark mocha complexion, and I remember thinking as he came toward me that he carried himself with enormous dignity. He approached slowly, searching for a seat in the back as we began to move, but seeing that the only available seat in the entire bus was beside me, he stopped and with the utmost politeness said, "May I sit beside you, sir?"

It's amazing what can pass through a person's mind in an instant. I was flattered by his address and impressed by his manner, and my unvarnished child's response would have been to say, "Yes, of course." But in that same instant, I was overwhelmed by everything I had recently heard about segregation and the need to keep the races apart in public places, phrases like, "This is the South and we don't do it that way here," or "We have to defend our Southern way of life," and of course, my father's unambiguous command, "Don't you ever allow a Negro to sit beside you on a bus." The effect of this cauldron of conflict must have been imprinted on my face in the moment that it took me to respond, but the man waited, and finally I blurted, coming down on the side of law, tradition, and parental admonition, "No. I don't think it would be right."

He looked surprised, but even so, he smiled at me ever so slightly as though he knew exactly what had been going through my mind, and then he said, "Oh, well thank you, sir." And he turned and moved on to stand in the back of the bus.

I didn't move or look back at him, but my heart was pounding. *I did it,* I thought. *I did what I was supposed to do.* I had stood by the law. The law is there for a purpose, I had been taught. You have to obey it. And I had done it. I had defended "our way of life." I had obeyed my parents. *Yes. You did the right thing,* I told myself. *Yes. There was nothing else you could do.* And I went on, looking out of the window and justifying myself in this way until we pulled into Lumberton and stopped at the station, which was across the street from the dusty yard of a large tobacco warehouse.

I had planned not to look at the departing passengers as they came down the aisle, but somehow I couldn't help doing it, and I turned toward them just as the tall man came abreast of my seat—which was still half empty. For a second our eyes met, and there was again the slight suggestion of a smile on his face as he spoke in that voice of absolute stately dignity, "Thank you, sir," he said again. "Thank you very much," and continued ramrod straight down the aisle and out the door.

Neither the flooding Nile nor the rampaging Mississippi could have shocked me more than the flood of emotion that washed across me a moment later as I watched the man walk around the bus, still straight and dignified as he crossed the street toward that tobacco warehouse. His white hair and mustache reminded me of Uncle Sandy, the man who owned the mule and who had helped my father to plow and plant our garden during those bitter years of the Depression, tall Uncle Sandy for whom I as a child had always felt such admiration, and suddenly I wanted to get out of the bus and run after this man. I wanted to say, "I'm sorry!" I wanted to invite him back onto the bus to sit beside me so I could tell him that I knew I had done something wrong, that I had meant nothing against him at all, that I had only done it because—and here I ran into the seemingly unscalable face of a cliff—because the law said I should do it, because my parents said I should do it.

Of course, by this time, the bus driver had closed the door and we were pulling away from the station to resume our trip toward Fairmont. But now I was, quite literally, feeling like shit. I felt like the most worthless human being on the planet. I hadn't felt so bad since the day my mother had accused me of infidelity for spending so much of my time with "that little Catholic hussy from up the way" while she was all alone after my father had gone overseas. But this time there was a difference. My mother's accusations had made me feel bad because I had failed to do my duty, had failed to meet her expectations and the expectations of the world; this time, I felt bad because I *had* done my duty. I *had* met my parents' expectations and the expectations of the world by obeying the law. And I *still* felt worthless.

I knew instinctively that, even in my effort to do the right thing, I had violated or proved unfaithful to something valuable, some rule or some law or some principle, but at fourteen, I still had no vocabulary for it, no clear frame of reference in which to place it, no available abstract phrases such as "civil rights" or "human dignity" or "racial arrogance." I did have a firm idea of *respect*, however, an idea that had been drilled into me from earliest childhood—respect for one's parents, respect for elders, respect for one's neighbors. In Sunday school it had been taught to me in the phrase, "Love thy neighbor as thyself," and as we rolled along beside the browning late summer cornfields and cotton fields and tobacco fields of southern North Carolina, I concluded that the problem was one of *respect*, that in obeying my parents and the law, I had failed to show the tall black man proper respect. And yet, strange as it might seem, it had been my father, the vehement segregationist, who had taught me respect for black people in the first place. I had never forgotten the day when, at age five, beside the mule in our garden, I had addressed "Uncle" Sandy merely as *Sandy*, and my father had pulled me up short. "You call him 'Uncle' Sandy," he had told me firmly. "He's not kin to us, but it's a term of respect, and you must show him respect at all times." It had been my father's attitude of showing equal respect for *all* people—his evenhandedness—that had been the basis of his popularity as a young man. It had been one of his most lovable qualities. And yet, in this situation, his allegiance was elsewhere, and in obeying him, I had violated the very thing he had always taught me, and I felt that something valuable had gone out of the world.

That day my mind nearly strangled itself in the tangled knot of these paradoxes. I hardly remember my visit at Zelma's house at all. I think we talked and played the piano and maybe sang a song or two, and then I caught the late afternoon bus for the trip back to Fayetteville. But returning home, I was not the same boy who had left a few brief hours earlier, for I believe that it was on that return trip that I became, for all practical purposes, an outlaw. Not a *criminal*, but an *outlaw*, at least in my thinking. For there was no conclusion I could reach except that my parents were *wrong*, the law was *wrong*, and that any attitude or law that denied people respect was *wrong*. There wasn't much I could do about it; I was only fourteen. But I realized with sudden crystal clarity that parental guidance and legal guidance could be very poor systems for finding one's direction through life.

My parents were not bad people; they were, in fact, good people and would later reveal that goodness to me in astounding ways. They loved me and I loved and respected them, was dependent on them, but they were wrong. And I think that it was on that day that I began to seek consciously a system outside of tradition or law that could serve as a guide through my own life. And I resolved that I would never again knowingly allow myself to be used as an instrument of disrespect or injustice.

Chapter Eighteen

I would discover many new facets and complexities of Southern race relations over the following year. Indeed, with my newly awakened consciousness, they began to present themselves to me almost daily. But although, at fourteen, I had no power to do anything and no person with whom I felt comfortable even discussing these issues, I felt optimistic in a way. The South was not really an evil place, and the sins of the modern South, I felt, were more likely to be the product of blindness, habit, and laziness rather than of intentional injustice. If *I* was able to see and detect the inequities around me, I thought, then other white people of good will must be able to see them too, and eventually things would have to change. It may have been an attitude much like "waiting for Godot," but I was young and I had yet to learn just how much hard work and suffering are required to bring about any social change. So I think I simply resolved within my own mind to speak out in support of justice and legal equality whenever I had the opportunity, and although I felt rather like an undercover agent operating in enemy territory, I went on living my life as best I could in the world that I knew.

With the end of the war, the attitude around the country became more and more one of celebration. There were parties, dances, and weddings. Nightclubs and roadhouses where people could eat, drink, and dance became popular gathering places all round Fayetteville, Fort Bragg, and Pinehurst. In addition to the Main Post Officers' Club and the Sergeants' Club at Fort Bragg, every regiment had its own non-coms' club and officers' mess, and each of these places had its own program of after duty entertainment. And early in the fall, after a gala dance at Breece's Landing featuring Tommy Dorsey and his orchestra, several of us from the high school band decided that we, too, should form an orchestra and provide the live music at some of these places.

I think that most of us in the marching band had started playing because we were attracted to one of the stellar performers of the day. For me, it was Harry James on the trumpet. For others, it was Tommy Dorsey on trombone, Jimmy Dorsey on saxophone, Artie Shaw on clarinet, Gene Krupa on drums. The marching band was fun, but who wanted to play marches all the time? And since none of us had ever really heard these instruments in a classical setting, popular dance music was the place where *real* musical life began and ended.

At first, when I suggested organizing the orchestra, I got enthusiastic response from other players, but when most of them were confronted by the need for regular rehearsal and for pooling our money to buy music, the number began to melt away like ice cream in July until we had only eight people who were willing to stay with the project. Weeks Parker, a clarinet player, was enthusiastic and indeed had already bought a number of stock dance band arrangements that we could use immediately. So we began with Peck Jones and Bryan Watson on saxophone, Bobby Ward on trombone, Richard Bracey on piano, Nub Smith on bass violin, Neil Reichle on drums, and of course Weeks and me on clarinet and trumpet. Later we would add an electric guitar, but we

started with just the eight of us and held our first rehearsal in
early fall.

It was excruciating!

Shocking!

Either an eye opener or a killer, depending on one's per-
sonality.

None of us had ever played with a group smaller than a
marching band, and now for the first time in a small ensem-
ble, we discovered there was no place to hide. We could detect
every faulty attack, every note imperfectly tuned, every rhythmical lapse, every missed cue. Those professional guys had
made it sound so easy! They were like fine silk and spun glass;
we were like a shattered mirror. I thought we were going to
disband out of sheer, horrified disappointment. "What the
hell makes us think we can play dance music?" Peck Jones
asked. "This is crazy!" And it took a lot of persuading and
telephoning late into the night for me to convince them all to
return for a second try. But return they did, and gradually we
improved.

Stock arrangements were expensive and sometimes more
difficult than we could master at that stage, so Richard Bracey
and I began to buy the sheet music of the popular songs and
write our own arrangements. We didn't know much about
harmony, but we began to learn fast in the rehearsal sessions
on Saturday morning that we held in Bracey's living room.

Now, I had a vision about the orchestra, and I believed
that with hard work, we could really make something good
out of it. But it was not the only thing I was doing that fall. I
was also working on *The Bulldog*, our school newspaper, I was
on the debating team, and for a while, I was even a member
of the junior varsity football team. But the transforming event
of my high school career that fall occurred one afternoon after
school when I thought I was totally alone in the school hallway. The empty space was very resonant, and as I arranged
some books in my locker, I burst into song, delighted to hear

the echo of my own voice. It wasn't long, however, before I realized I was not alone, and I turned to find Miss Edith Cherry, the school music teacher, standing behind me. "Who are you?" she asked.

I told her.

"Why aren't you in my choir?" she asked.

"Well, I guess I just never thought of it," I said.

"Well, I want you," she said. "And I want you to sing that song as a solo on the program we're giving in chapel next week."

"You do?"

"Yes. You sound great. Come by tomorrow and we'll rehearse. I'll play for you."

"Okay," I said. And I went home walking on clouds.

It was a series of firsts for me. My rehearsal with Miss Cherry the next afternoon was the first time I had ever actually had anyone accompany me on the piano, and that was in itself an eye opener. But the following week, when I walked to center stage for the first time in my life and found myself standing alone in the spotlight before an audience of nearly a thousand people who were waiting for me to sing, I was stunned almost to paralysis. Over the week I had planned for it, dreamed about it, prepared myself in every way I knew, but *nothing* could have possibly prepared me for the shock of the real thing, and suddenly, quite literally, my knees began to quiver. I remember standing there, tightening the muscles in my legs, fighting to hold the damn things in place. But my knees had minds of their own. They were like Jell-O in an earthquake. I wasn't at all sure I could keep them from buckling under me. And as if that weren't enough, although I had been to the bathroom at least five times in the half hour before we went on stage, I now suddenly had to pee to the point of bursting. I stood there at center stage, shaking in that interminable silent moment before anything happens and thinking, *If I collapse on the floor and wet my pants in front of a thou-*

sand people, I'll never be able to walk down the streets of Fayetteville again. And then, Miss Cherry began to play the introduction to my song.

The song was "There's No You," a tune that was very popular on the radio and on jukeboxes of the time, and I had played it and sung it often by myself. I had also rehearsed it thoroughly with Miss Cherry. But on that stage, the introduction drifting toward me through the clouds of my brain, sounded about as familiar as a Chinese opera accompanied on nose flutes, and as the moment approached for me to sing, I had not the slightest inkling of what the words were. My mind was a blank slate, as though I had been returned to infancy and never before heard a word of English. Since the auditorium was so large, Miss Cherry had been good enough to provide me with a microphone, and in that state of total absentia, with my body completely disconnected from my mind which was still unable to recall even the first syllable of the song, I leaned toward the mike and opened my mouth.

It wasn't until I heard the song coming back to me from the speakers of the public address system that I realized something was actually happening, and my first thought was that someone had turned on a phonograph player. There was actually a lag of several seconds before I realized that, in fact, *I* was making the sound. *I* was singing those words, which were filling the room. They were actually coming out of that opening, which was my mouth. And I thought it sounded great! It came like a splash of cold water, waking me from my torpor. I heard the voice moving forward, the words perfectly clear, spinning out the tune, elongating the syllables the way Deanie had once pointed out in Frank's singing, and suddenly, I was overwhelmingly happy. I was enjoying what I was doing! And a few minutes later when the song ended and the audience exploded with applause, I was swept upward on a wave of delight that took me about as close to heaven as I ever expect to be on this side of the grave.

Again, in that shocking year of change, I was not the same boy I had been a few brief minutes before. So many things were changed in me as a result of singing that one song, that even a half-century later, it's difficult to enumerate them. There would be one or two other transformational moments in my life, in army flight school, for instance, when I thought my plane was going to crash, or even later, when confronting the broken bones of my injured child. But I think now that they all have had something in common with that first moment on stage and with that other all defining moment at age four when I nearly drowned—that feeling of being in over one's head, of being emotionally, intellectually, and physically exhausted, of being frightened beyond the capacity of language to express, and then of taking *one* additional action and having everything suddenly click into place. The source of the strength to take that additional action remains for me a mystery, coming as it has from somewhere far beyond the depths of my conscious being. But it has always left me walking the earth with a sense of wonderment and gratitude.

And that was my initial feeling after the performance that day. I was happy, yes, extremely happy. But I was also in a state of awe. In a way, I felt that *I* had not actually sung the song, but that I had been taken over by some superior force, which had simply used me as an instrument, and I felt hypocritical accepting congratulations for something I myself had not really done. This, of course, was something I couldn't possibly have expressed at the time, even to myself, so when people said I had done a good job, I just said, "Thank you." And gradually I came back into the real world and realized for the second time that year that I was no longer anonymous. Every teacher and student in that entire school seemed to know me. The girls twittered and the boys—even some of the toughest ones on the football team—seemed to acknowledge that I had done all right. And when I went back to rehearse with our dance band, it was already concluded that I was going to be the vocalist as well as being the trumpet player. This would eventually have the effect of producing a power struggle within the band, but that was still in the future.

Chapter Nineteen

The result of all this affirmation was that I reached the mid-fall of 1945 in a state of near bliss. I felt that all things were possible. In spite of the loss of my closest friends the previous year, I was now making new friends, and I felt totally unlimited; I felt that I could do or be anything at all. I could be a musician, a writer, a singer, a doctor, a composer; I could help conserve the forests. I had no doubt that some day I would marry one of the pretty girls who found my singing pleasant and that we would have beautiful and brilliant children and that when the time came for me to die, I would still live forever in my children and in my magnificent accomplishments.

And I set out to prove it by becoming involved in almost everything available. I continued with our dance band, of course, but now I added Miss Cherry's chorus and continued with the marching band and worked on the school newspaper. I joined the debating team. For a time, I even played fullback on the junior varsity football team. And my teachers, once they got to know me, let me get away with murder—except for Mrs. Newberry, the geometry teacher. I had to work for her, but I didn't mind because I liked the logic of geometry and because, after her class, I would go to chorus rehearsal and sit near Doris Jackson, the lovely little soprano in Miss Cherry's choir, who had fainted beside me one day in rehearsal and who had felt so wonderful in my arms when I picked her up and carried her to the infirmary. Added to all this was the fact that I had now obtained my learner's permit and was *legally* learning to drive. And then there was Lilly.

Since my father had succeeded in getting his pension the previous year, my parents had managed to pay off most of their debts, and starting in the spring, my mother had hired a white haired black woman named Lilly McDaniel to help with the house work. I liked Lilly. I always thought of her as elderly because of her white hair, but I realize now that she was not much older than my mother who was fifty-five at the time. Lilly was patient and good-spirited, and when she worked alone, either in the kitchen or while ironing clothes on the back porch, she sang some of the most eerily beautiful spirituals I've ever heard. They couldn't be called "blues" exactly. They were deeper than any blues I know, more anchored to the spiritual backbone of the whole human race and the struggle to keep the faith when confronted by catastrophe. Her songs were highly rhythmical but all in minor or modal keys and melodies that left questions hanging in the air even when the words themselves were positive. Often I would stand in the next room or sit in the yard out of sight when she ironed clothes on the back porch so I could listen to her songs without disturbing her concentration.

Lilly only came to work about three days a week, walking in the morning from her house about two miles away. But in the evenings my mother would drive her home, and that's when I could go along and get my "legal" supervised driving experience on the highway as I prepared for my upcoming driver's license exam. I would drive sedately down the road with

my mother beside me and turn in at Jones Street, the unpaved
dead-end lane beside Mount Zion Baptist Church, a rickety
wooden structure propped upright by six external wooden
braces to compensate for its eroding foundation, and we
would bounce over the rutted street to Lilly's unpainted clap-
board house. I remember that in winter it would often be
dark, and we would wait in front until Lilly got inside and lit
her kerosene lamp before we drove away.

But it was Lilly's presence in our lives that brought on the
first of the many fruitless ethical battles I had with my parents. I remember that it occurred at a time right after the
NAACP had presented a much-publicized manifesto on the
evils of racial segregation and the need to integrate the public
schools. And predictably, both my parents were incensed at
the idea, which had been widely discussed in the local newspaper and on the radio. "It's the most ridiculous thing I ever
heard!" my mother said one evening at the supper table. "Can
you imagine yourself going to school with a whole room full
of black children?"

I think that at first I only grunted. The three of us, my
mother, my father, and I, were sitting at the table in the dining room, but I knew that Lilly was in the kitchen within easy
hearing distance barely ten feet away, and I just wanted my
mother to stop talking. But she wouldn't.

"These people from up north are so glib, telling us how to
live," my mother went on. "The school rooms smell bad
enough as it is. You can imagine how they could smell if they
were full of Negroes."

"Mother . . ." I said, but I could hardly find my voice. I
had never heard her go on this way. I wanted to disappear, and
my heart was pounding like the anvil chorus. I didn't want
Lilly to have to hear this sort of thing, and yet I knew that if
I tried to stop it, Lilly would have to hear even more. But my
mother kept on at full conversational voice as though I had
never tried to interrupt her.

"Negroes just don't learn the same way we do," she said. "Of course, they can be sweet and good with simple jobs, but they're just not as smart as white people."

And with that, I couldn't stand it any more. "Have you considered who's in the kitchen?" I asked. I know I must have hissed across the table because I spoke through clenched teeth trying to keep the volume down.

"What?" my mother asked, with total innocence. "You mean Lilly?"

"Yes, I mean Lilly?"

"Oh, don't worry about Lilly. She doesn't understand what I'm talking about."

"What?"

"She doesn't listen to these conversations."

"Do you think she's deaf?"

By this time I was almost shouting, and my father was looking at me with total surprise. I doubt that he had ever before seen me speak in anger, and he wasted no time calling me to account. "Just a minute!" he said. "I will not have you speaking disrespectfully to your mother."

"I'm not speaking disrespectfully to my mother," I said. "I just want her to have some consideration for . . ."

"If you say one more word, I'll send you from the table," he said.

And by now, my mother also was looking at me with shock and a slight hurt expression in her eyes. "I never heard you speak to me in that tone of voice," she said. "I hardly know what to say." She glanced woundedly around the table. "But it looks like dinner's over and it's time to take Lilly home."

It was a scene that would be replayed first in my thoughts and then in my dreams and then in fact re-enacted again and again across that dining room table. And only another "only child" can understand fully the emotional cost of challenging my parents. But challenge them I did—and with very little effect. My mother later came to me in my room and told me that my words had "hurt her deeply," and I tried to explain why I thought her own words had been nothing but acts of egregious cruelty. And yet, she professed not to understand. "I only spoke the truth," she said. "Is that so bad?" But at fourteen, I lacked the analytical ability to take the argument further, and as I grew older, I would come to see that *nothing* I did or said would change my parents, no matter what my abilities. My words had challenged not only them, but also their entire belief system, the fabric of their existence, which they were not in the least likely to question. And over time, I came to feel with great discomfort that the only way any real social or political change could ever occur was for the older generation to die and for a newer, more enlightened generation to take their place.

And then, even before that fall was over, I came home from school one afternoon to encounter a scene which I will offer to help explain why Southerners—at least the ones of my generation who had eyes and any degree of social conscience—all tended to grow up slightly crazy. It was a time when Lilly had not appeared for work in over a week. My mother at first thought she was sick, and we went to Lilly's house to find out, but no one was at home, and I just concluded—although I didn't say so—that Lilly had gotten fed up and found kinder employment elsewhere. So you can imagine my surprise on this day when I walked into the house and found Lilly sitting at the dining room table with my mother holding her hand. I could tell in an instant that the situation was very grave. Lilly's skin was ash gray in color and she was fighting unsuccessfully to hold back her tears, and my mother looked up at me and said, "Son, something terrible has happened. Lilly's daughter has been killed."

"Oh," I said. "I'm so sorry." And as I touched Lilly's shoulder, my mother slipped her hand free and poured Lilly a cup of tea from the pot on the table.

"It's so awful!" Lilly said. "So awful. And the man still walkin' 'round the street."

"Are you sure he's the one who did it?" my mother asked.

"Oh yes, Lord! I know he done it," Lilly said. "I tried to make her stop seein' that man. Bootlegger. Gambler. Sells whisky to everybody in the neighborhood. Think nobody can touch him. But she wouldn't pay no mind to me. Oh, Jesus! She had to see her man. Had to have one more drink. Bunch of chil'ren found her body at the end of the street—down there behind the water pump. Look like he choked her. Beat her."

"What about the police?"

"Pshaw . . . police don't care what happen to black folks."

"Oh, Lilly . . ."

"I seen that man in front of my house. I told him, 'God is gonna punish you for what you done.' An' he followed me up the steps to my door and said, 'Listen to me, old woman. You say one word to anybody an' you gonna be dead as Bessie.'"

"He's got to be arrested."

"How they gonna arrest him? Ain't nobody gonna say nothin'. He'd kill you quick as look at you."

"*We're* going to have him arrested," my mother said.

"Oh no! Bless Jesus!! If he find out I told . . . no. He'd kill you, too!'

"That's why we have to have him arrested," my mother said. "Because, Lilly, none of us will ever have another peaceful night as long as he prowls the neighborhood." And she looked at me and said, "Your father is not well enough, and I don't want him to be involved with this, so I want you to go with us to see Sheriff McGeachy."

"Oh Lord, I can't see no sheriff!" Lilly said. "I never talked to no sheriff . . ."

"I'll do most of the talking," my mother said. And she went to tell my father what we were doing.

As I remember, he did not object or offer to accompany us, but he did the one characteristic thing that he would repeat many times during my teenage years—he handed me his .45-calibre pistol as I went out the door. "Keep this under the seat of the car," he said. "If you have any problems, don't hesitate to use it." And we drove off to see the sheriff in Fayetteville's gray stone court building just south of the Market House.

Sheriff McGeachy was a member of our church, and he had been sheriff for about thirty years. We hardly knew him personally, but his niece, Ann Byrd McArthur, was in my class at school and we did know his family, so he greeted us cordially when my mother led the way into his office. A fleshy faced man in a brown business suit and rimless glasses, he shook my hand and invited my mother to sit down, but it was my mother who invited Lilly to sit in the chair beside her as she began in a very straightforward way to outline the things Lilly had told her about Bessie's death and how the bootlegger, named Hercules, had killed her. Sheriff McGeachy listened very attentively to these allegations and asked Lilly some questions, and then he kind of steepled his fingers in front of his face and said, "I don't think there's much we can do about this."

"Why?" my mother asked.

"Because nobody in that community will testify," the sheriff said. "I know you've both heard the phrase, 'I don' know nothin' 'bout it.' Well that's all the answer we get down there."

"Lilly knows something."

"That's true. But we need more. I don't want to move against this man 'til we're sure we can put him away."

"He threatened her," my mother said. And then she stood. "He threatened her and she works for me. That's almost the same as threatening me. This man Hercules is more than just a threat on Jones Street, Sheriff. He's a threat to everybody in the community, and as one of your constituents, I want to know that you have done everything possible to protect my family and to make this community safe."

"Yes Ma'am," the sheriff said. "I understand what you mean." He stood, smiled, and was as cordial to us going out as he was when we came in. "I'll do what I can," he said.

I wish I could tell this as an exciting detective story in which I was personally involved with the apprehension of Hercules, but such just was not the case. I thought about Hercules a lot, however, and I always made sure the .45 was in the car when I drove Lilly home, and once I actually saw Hercules in the headlights when I turned around at the end of Jones Street, which upset Lilly so much that I tucked the pistol into my belt and walked with her to the door of her house before I drove away. But finally it was the sheriff and the police who acted. Sheriff McGeachy called my mother one afternoon about two weeks later to tell her that Hercules had been arrested on a liquor charge. "He sold un-tax paid whiskey to a police officer," the sheriff said. "We'll continue to check on the possibility of a murder charge, but this is quicker and safer, and I think we can send him away for a good long time."

So the case of Bessie's death was effectively closed. But the true mystery, the inexplicable thing to me, is the relationship that continued between my mother and Lilly. I know the psychological theories about benign despotism, dominance, power, *noblesse oblige*, self-congratulation, expiation of guilt, and just plain cruelty. But I also know from long observation that over the years, at one level, their friendship became deeper. I think the two women would have done anything possible to help each other in time of trouble. Yet on the surface, things continued the same. My mother never stopped saying insulting and painful things about Negroes, voicing them with parrot-like frequency in Lilly's hearing, yet Lilly continued to work for her, as though words meant nothing, for nearly twenty-five years. When my father died, Lilly was with my mother to commiserate and help. And then, when my mother later moved away to a nursing home in Richmond, Virginia, at age eighty, the two of them continued to exchange Christmas presents and to write long affectionate letters to each other until Lilly died at nearly ninety. This mystery, and the dichotomy of mind that it reveals, is to me now far more fascinating than the question of whether or not Hercules was ever overtly punished for his part in the death of Bessie McDaniel.

Chapter Twenty

If Alexander Pope is actually right about human happiness depending on our hope and on our ignorance of the future, then surely I possessed enough of these essential ingredients in December of 1945 to guarantee my eternal bliss. And although it was short lived, the period following my fifteenth birthday was one of the happiest and brightest periods of my entire life. It was a time when everything seemed to be going exactly right. The good guys had won the war and Germany and Japan had been defeated, justice had prevailed and Hercules was in jail, my articles were appearing in the school newspaper, people were asking me to sing for all sorts of public gatherings, and to top it off, our dance band had landed its first public engagement to play for a dance at the Main Post Officers' Club at Fort Bragg on New Year's Eve—an event that would be followed by literally hundreds of engagements over the next three years. I could imagine an unlimited and successful future evolving for me in everything I touched. And I remember thinking, speaking my thoughts aloud as I looked into the bathroom mirror one morning toward the end of the year: "I want to be this age forever."

My euphoria began on my birthday, when with my father by my side, I went to the Highway Patrol Headquarters to be tested for my driver's license. Of all our early rites of passage, receiving the driver's license probably marks the most visible external break between childhood and youth. Circumcision, baptism, the first haircut, the first firearm, menstruation, shaving, the first kiss, confirmation, bah mitzvah all leave us forever changed, but receiving the car keys and the driving permit bestows a measure of freedom greater than all the others and makes us instantly a part of a larger world directed totally by our own discretion. I was nervous on that day and the patrolman who examined me was totally unsmiling, but I passed with ease, and I remember my joy at my father's smile of congratulation afterward as he handed me the keys and slipped into the passenger seat beside me with the order to take him home.

Needless to say, I was intoxicated by my new sense of freedom, and within an hour after receiving my license and returning my father to the house, I went for my first legal solo drive, going directly to the Carolina Soda Shoppe where I parked in front, just as I had seen the older guys do, and sauntered casually inside to order a coke at the counter. Hardly anybody there missed the fact that I had driven on my own. "Gee, I didn't know you had your license."

"Yeah, yeah," I said, leaning back against the counter, trying my best with my five-foot-ten-and-a-half-inch frame to be as cool and unassuming as Gary Cooper himself might have been after riding in off the prairie. "Just got it, in fact."

"Really?"

"Yeah."

"Was the test hard?"

"Well, I passed it," I said, still cool. "Couldn't have been too hard, I guess."

And then a few feet away beside the glass front door, Emory Williams, the school clown, began to laugh and jump around like an excited chimpanzee, pointing first outside at the car and then at me and giving a great *whoop* of delight. "Wonderful!" he said. "Gets his license and his first traffic ticket within twenty minutes!" And the whole room exploded in laughter as I reached the front door just in time to see a policeman slip a summons under the windshield wiper and walk away. "Guess you didn't see the *No Parking* sign," Emory said. I grinned, did my best to join in with the laughter, and then walked rather stiffly to the car in an effort not to reveal the depth of my embarrassment.

But all was not lost, and I think I learned two important lessons that day. First, about posturing—don't. And second, about consciousness—be observant in all things and read the fine print. The summons did indeed charge me with illegally parking in a *No Parking* zone, but as I read the details of the ticket, I realized that the officer had written down the wrong date. I went directly to City Hall to settle the matter, and I pointed out the date discrepancy to the clerk. "It has tomorrow's date on it," I said.

The woman looked crestfallen. "Gimme that," she said. "I don't know what I have to do to make these officers get their paper work right." She tore the ticket in half and put it on the side of her desk. "I'll take care of it," she said. "But you be careful from now on."

"Yes ma'am," I said. And I walked out restored fully to my state of bliss.

But I was just barely beginning to experience the freedom afforded by my driver's license. You see, Doris Jackson, the pretty little soprano from Miss Cherry's choir, had continued to faint periodically in my presence throughout the fall. Now I do not in any way intend to belittle the seriousness of these fainting spells. Nobobdy seemed to know what caused them. But they occurred so often around me that people—even the teachers—began to think of me as the resident expert on Doris and to call on me in a time of emergency. I have carried

Doris from rehearsal rooms, classrooms, the gymnasium, upstairs, downstairs, even from a bus to her hotel room once when we were on a concert tour, and I learned that by rubbing the back of her neck or washing her face with a warm cloth she could be brought around fairly quickly.

In any case, this sort of thing has an amazing effect on a young man. It makes him feel important; it makes him feel needed. It makes him feel that he is, in fact, living up to the chivalric ideal of helping maidens in distress. And when the distressed maiden is both pretty and talented, it makes him feel profoundly responsible for her whole life—along with a number of other profound emotions, which certainly I at fifteen could hardly even begin to enumerate.

I remember depositing Doris on the day bed in the nurse's office one afternoon and stroking her very lovely brow while I waited for the nurse to arrive. The nurse took a long time that day, and I remember stroking Doris's eyelids, her cheek, her temples, the back of her neck, seeing her in a way I had never seen anyone before and stunned nearly to speechlessness by the delicate molding of her features. I have seen Picasso's drawings called "Sleep Watchers," and I recognize so readily that mood of protective awe in the eye of the watcher as he gazes upon the vulnerable tenderness of the sleeper. So was I at that moment in awe of Doris as I continued my ministrations, feeling totally responsible and totally protective of the mysterious beauty of the girl beneath my hands until a few brief minutes later when Doris opened her eyes with a flutter and gazed up at me from wherever she had been. She was never confused, always instantly aware of everything around her on awakening from one of these seizures, and she looked up at me from the considerable depth of her eyes and said, "You're very good to me, you know that?" And she raised up, put her arms around my neck, and kissed me.

It was a stunning experience, something I had not even begun to anticipate, and I could only smile and hunt awkwardly for words, which I was totally unable to find before the nurse came in and relieved me. "Let me know if I can help in any way," I told the nurse. And then I remembered that on that day my parents had allowed me to drive the car to school—a thing I very rarely did—and I told Doris that I would give her a ride home afterward.

It was a first. It was a beginning. I had felt a kind of child-like love and passion for both Ruth Ann and Deanie, but the maze of emotions I felt toward Doris was simply overwhelming. I think that in helping her and in being concerned for her health, I had invested myself in her life in a way I had never done for anyone other than for my parents when they were ill. And the fact that Doris was sexy as well as being pretty, talented, and intelligent, of course, did nothing to impede my investment. So not only did I drive her home that afternoon, but as I walked her to the door, I invited her to go with me to the Christmas dance the following week. When she accepted, I remember being distantly aware that once again during that turbulent year, my life had undergone an abrupt and radical change.

My date with Doris for the Christmas dance, of course, marked the first time I ever drove the family car on a date. But there were other firsts as well. I wore my father's tuxedo—the first time in a tux for me and the first time the suit had been worn by anyone in about twenty years. My mother had to let out the hem of the trousers to accommodate my much longer legs. And then, following my mother's social guidance, I ordered my first corsage, an arrangement of cymbidiums, which I had come to love when I worked at the House of Flowers. And last, just before I left the house to pick up Doris, my father called me quietly aside and, behind the closed door of the bedroom, gave me the first and only advice he ever gave me about my relationships with women. I was already about seven inches taller than he, but something about his demeanor that night made our size difference completely negligible.

"Remember," he told me, "when a man takes a woman out, he assumes total responsibility for her welfare during the time she is with him. And it's his duty to return her to her home in the same condition she was in when he took her out."

"Yessir," I said. "I know that."

"In addition," he told me, "the world can be a very dangerous place and women can be vulnerable. It's your job to defend your date against all dangers—even to put your life on the line for her, if necessary." And to this end, he reached into the drawer of the bedside table and once again handed me the .45-calibre pistol. "Keep this in the car," he said. "But never hesitate to do what is necessary to defend the life and welfare of the woman you're with." Then he threw his arms around me and kissed my cheek. "God bless you," he said. "Have a good time and be home by eleven-thirty."

It was a spectacular evening. There were so many first time events falling together at once that I could hardly contain all the explosive excitement suddenly bursting inside me, but I remember the evening mainly in terms of isolated images and sounds. First, of course, there was Doris as she appeared beneath the stairs of her parents' house in her gold and red off-the-shoulder evening gown and wearing the corsage I had sent her. I remember catching a glimpse of the two of us reflected in the mirror of the hall tree and actually thinking that we were the most beautiful people I had ever seen in my life. And, of course, I met her parents and was surprised to realize that they spoke what I would call a backcountry Southern dialect. I report this simply as fact. They were a respected family. Mr. Jackson was superintendent of buildings and grounds for the entire city school system, and he seemed to approve of me, but the effect of all this was to make me admire Doris even more. She was a Southern girl in a Southern town, but she spoke perfectly grammatical sentences totally without any trace of Southern dialect whatsoever, as though she had decided to create herself completely on her own terms, and it was a quality I admired a lot.

The dance itself was a confectioner's dream—bolts of red crepe festooned from the ceiling, candles, the aroma of spiced tea combined with the smell of perfume and lipstick and Mennen skin bracer and meatballs and cheese and green and red punch along with the sounds of the twelve piece band, hired from out of town for the occasion. Doris and I danced well together, and I found out during the breaks that word had gotten around that our band had been hired to play at the officer's club on New Year's Eve, and everybody said that maybe next year we could play for the Christmas dance, and then later in the evening people urged me to sing a song (I think it was "All the Things You Are")—which I did with the big band backing me. And who can blame me for wanting to remain fifteen forever and for the dance never to end?

It did end, however, and I drove Doris sedately home through the quiet streets of Fayetteville. But I remember that as we stopped for a traffic light, she looked over and said something that was shocking in its directness because it made me see myself in a totally new way. "You know, I think every girl in town is envious of you," she said.

"Envious of me?"

"Yes," she said. "You have the longest eyelashes I ever saw. Especially in this light. We all want them for ourselves."

I laughed, but it was enough to keep me totally quiet until I stopped in front of Doris' house a few short minutes later, and then there was no need for words because we simply took one look at each other in the soft reflected street light and quite literally crashed into each other's arms with such force that I actually saw stars. Talk about intoxication! I think I had denied my desire to do this sort of thing ever since Ruth Ann had left town, and the sudden collision with Doris was like the proverbial voyage over Niagara in a barrel. Not only that. Doris was a much more skilled kisser. She was able to teach me things in a few seconds that the younger Ruth Ann had never been prepared to do. It was a heady few minutes, and I certainly would have been willing to stretch it into infinity, except that I felt duty bound to meet my parents' curfew and return home on time. So we broke the clinch and I walked Doris to her door where we kissed in lingering passion for another five minutes or so before I floated back to the car where I had the presence of mind to wipe the lipstick off my face as I sped toward home to meet my parents who, I knew, would be waiting up for me.

And now, I think that this is the place to end this portion of my story. For although I wasn't aware of it at the time, I think that by age fifteen, I had been given all the things I would need to know in order to conduct the rest of my life. The job before me would be one of discovering and interpreting the full meaning of what I knew and of learning how to apply it. I don't mean that I stopped learning. Far from it. I would subsequently experience a series of new and life changing revelations. For instance, when I got to college I heard a Bach chorale from inside out, as performed by a perfectly tuned choir, and it changed my way of hearing forever. I learned about dramatic structure, and it changed my way of seeing life forever. I read the opening of *A Farewell to Arms* and it changed my idea of language forever. I would go on to experience the wonder of solo flight, the awe of the Grand Canyon, the sunset over the Aegean off the coast of Sounion, the mystery of holding my child in my arms. And last of all, I think that I finally learned the difference between loving a woman from inside out as opposed to loving her from outside in—a thing that few men can ever really learn before they have lived a certain number of years and met the quota of disasters necessary to satisfy the needs of their own individual learning curves. But the foundation that made it possible for me to experience all these things—with the possible exception of the last—was laid by the time I was fifteen.

And now, looking back at that turbulent transitional year of 1945, I think the thing that stayed with me and served me longest was my father's final exhortation as I prepared to go out on that first date with Doris. He of course, had no illusions about remaining fifteen forever, and he knew a great deal about frustrated hopes and vanished dreams. It was the first time he had referred to me as a *man*, and I realized with blinding clarity that he no longer thought of me as a boy at all. His words amounted to bringing things full circle, to healing the rifts and the doubts and the disappointments that had come between us. For they told me that—in spite of his sickness, his weakness, and his prejudice—that all the qualities I had always loved in him were still alive and that he meant for me to observe them: a man tells the truth, a man respects all people, a man values learning, a man takes full responsibility for his actions, a man will not hesitate to put his life on the line to protect the people and principles that he values. And only now do I fully realize that it takes nearly a lifetime of hard work and discipline to become truly a *man*.

My last coherent conversation with my father took place just after the end of the Korean War, by telephone from Gary Army Air Field in Texas on the day I completed my first solo flight as a student in the army flight training program. He had already been admitted into the Veterans' Hospital for what would become his final illness, and his nurse had to wheel him down the hall to the telephone while I waited in the booth at the officers' club. When he answered, I could hear his wheezing, his breath so slight that he could hardly complete a phrase. "Dad, I did it!" I told him. "I soloed today—three take-offs and three landings, in the rain, no less." He congratulated me and sounded very pleased in spite of his wheezing. And then I said, without even thinking about it, "At last, I'm as good a man as you."

And he said, "Oh, Son, if you're not a better man than I am, I'd be greatly disappointed."

"That'll be hard to do," I said. "I remember everything you ever taught me."

And then he began to cough. "God bless you, boy," he said. "God bless you. Be careful. I love you. Remember that. I love you." And then in the midst of his coughing, the nurse came on the line to tell me he couldn't talk anymore. Three days later, he fell into the coma from which he never recovered.

A month after his funeral, I was sleeping in my bunk at Camp Gary at 2 A.M. during a blinding Texas rainstorm when a plane flying low over the field awakened me. The plane circled round and round so low over the housetops that I thought it was going to crash into the tower. It was frightening to me because the plane seemed to be in trouble and the field was closed at that hour. The nearest lighted field was up at Austin or down in San Antonio, and I worried about that lone pilot in the Texas night until after about the eighth pass, he leveled off and headed south. That was when the truth hit me, as it had not done even during his funeral service: "Your father is dead." And for the first time, I wept for him.

I inquired the next day, but no one else at the base was even aware of the plane that had circled in the night, and there were no notices of missing aircraft. I began to wonder if I had dreamed it. But then I knew I couldn't have dreamed it. My tears had been too real, my thoughts too clear. And I began to feel that maybe I was the only one who had heard it, the only one who could have heard it, that maybe I'd received a special visitation. Of course, my rational side scoffed at this idea, but my more mystical side persisted. And while my rational side was busy learning to place its faith in instruments and betting my life on the invisible power of low frequency radio orientations, VORs, NDBs, and ground controlled radar approaches, my more mystical side continued to feel that maybe the spiritual world could broadcast communications just as powerful as those radio waves which guide our planes to their destinations and that possibly—just possibly—in the spirit world, my father had finally won back his wings and on that night had flown through the Texas rain to give me one last salute before departing permanently to his final duty station, to that wonderful place where old pilots can fly as much as they want to and where there is no bad weather and where there are never, ever, any forced landings.